VALENSHEK LEGACY #1

TATE JAMES

Tate James

Heist: Valenshek Legacy #1

First published in 2022
James, Tate
Heist: Valenshek Legacy #1

Cover design: Emily Wittig
Editing: Heather Long (content) and Dolly Jackson (line).

"What's your dedication going to be for Heist?"

"It's a mystery..."

smirk

If you know, you know.

HEIST

VALENSHEK LEGACY #1

TATE JAMES

one

JOHN

Contrary to popular belief, thieves—the good ones, anyway—were not often in life or death situations. If a person knew what they were doing, if they were even a half decent cat burglar, they got in and out with their prize and never encountered another person. If they were a really *good* thief, they could get in and out with their prize while hundreds of people were around, and never raise even a sniff of suspicion.

So when a bullet ripped the leather of my jacket sleeve as I sped away from the luxury Hamptons house, I was so shocked I nearly crashed my motorcycle. Then again, considering who I'd just lifted a priceless diamond bracelet from—one of two iconic bracelets that Marie Antoinette had owned—it really wasn't so surprising that I'd nearly been caught.

A sleek black Bentley chased me down the otherwise silent street, and another shot whistled past me close enough that I could practically smell the gunpowder, and I swallowed hard. She was just playing with me now.

"Not today, Carol," I muttered under my breath, taking a sharp turn at high speed and ripping up someone's immaculate lawn as I cut down the side of their house. Oops. So much for not leaving a trace.

That boat had already sailed. Now I needed to make sure it didn't sink.

Thank fuck her car couldn't follow me this way. A couple more shots rang out through the night as my bike took air off someone's patio and hit the soft sand of the beach. But then I was free and clear, flying down the dark, firm sand and thanking my decision to take a dirt bike as my getaway vehicle.

I was experienced enough not to count my chickens before they hatched, though. Especially not after stealing from a woman as powerful and cunning as Carol Atwood. One didn't reach her position within the ruling council of the Mercenary Guild with just luck and charm. So I meticulously followed my plans to cover my tracks, changing vehicles and clothing multiple times until I finally gave myself a moment to breathe several hours later.

Times Square was the easiest place in the world to turn invisible, in my professional opinion, and since it was so close to the Hamptons that was where I ended up. Despite the hour being well past midnight, the streets were still busy, and I blended seamlessly into the tourists as I pulled on my *I heart NYC* t-shirt and strode into an all-night diner.

Stealing priceless jewels made me hungry, so I ordered enough food to feed a small army before settling in and pulling out my phone. The corner of my mouth tilted up when I saw the single missed call on my message bank.

Slipping my hand into my secure pocket, I verified that my prize was still in my possession before listening to the voice message.

"John, you're lucky I didn't splatter your brains all over my neighbor's lawn," the woman's voice said with an edge of amusement. "Thanks for the excitement. I feel twenty-three again. You owe me a diamond bracelet, though, you little shit."

I chuckled silently as the message ended, then deleted it from my phone. Carol was right, I *had* been lucky. Luck was literally the only thing that could have saved my skin with her on the other end of a gun, because acquaintance or not, she didn't pull punches. Or bullets.

My food arrived while I people watched the various patrons coming and going from the diner, and I took my time to eat. Big greasy burger, fries, soda. Delicious. When I was done, I paid my bill, tipped generously but not enough to stick in the waitress's mind, then popped into the restroom where I'd stashed a different jacket and hat three days earlier, in a loose ceiling panel.

With my appearance slightly altered for the dozenth time since leaving the Hamptons, I made my way to the drop point in Grand Central Station.

The Game had been running for a long time. Long enough that the technology had developed and stakes had been raised to protect not only the players, but also the committee who set the tasks, judged each round, and enforced the rules.

My wits were on high alert as I approached the lockers, using my key to access number 85. This locker was *not* a locker. It was a game piece. Unlock it, place the stolen item in the drawer, close it up again. Give it thirty seconds for the internal computer to verify the authenticity of the piece while the hidden camera verified my identity as the Game player assigned *that* task. If the details all matched, I'd get a green light and the results would be passed to the committee for review on whether my time and *social impact* qualified me for the next round. In this case, the *final* round.

If the light turned red…well, I'd already be dead so it wouldn't matter.

Not that it'd ever happened. The light only turned red if someone either turned in a forgery or they'd stolen someone else's item. Essentially, if they'd cheated. If there was one thing that thieves all hated, it was cheats.

I may have been an unscrupulous thief and had little to no regard for anyone other than myself, but I never cheated. I was too fucking good for that. Even so, there was a moment of tense worry while the "locker" decided my fate.

The light turned green, and I let out a long sigh of relief. This particular test was over. Now I just had to *wait* and see what the final stage of the Game would entail.

I hated waiting.

But I hated losing even more, so I unlocked the box once more and retrieved the diamond bracelet from the drawer. The Game was about the art of stealing, but the committee held no interest in keeping the stolen items. They were ours to do with as we saw fit, and most players already had buyers lined up and ready to pay big dollars.

Since I'd lifted this particular item from an acquaintance—we wouldn't take it as far as *friends*—I wasn't dumb enough to try and flog it on the black market. Carol would skin me alive next time our paths crossed.

My hotel for the night was a big chain five-star property. Not for the luxury, but for the security. Sleep deprivation did shitty things to judgment and focus, so when I rested I needed to be safe. Within reason. A huge part of that was remaining damn near invisible, which was no small feat considering my size.

I'd worked *hard* in my life to perfect the art of blending with backgrounds, of not standing out to anyone, despite being six foot five and built like a Marine. There was a shitload of psychology involved, and I'd worked with some of the best masters of deception, but the effort was worth it.

The staff at reception barely gave me a second glance as I collected my key, and that was just how I liked it. Unremarkable, totally forgettable.

I slept like I always did, in a deep, dreamless rest, waking up feeling refreshed. It was an acquired skill.

Breakfast was delivered by room service, and I ate it absentmindedly while staring at my phone and waiting for it to light up with my next task. The last task, and the hardest one. This wasn't my first rodeo, in fact it was the fifth Game I'd participated in. I'd won the last four, and I would be winning this one, too. There was no room for mistakes, *especially* not now.

Frustrated at the delay on the committee's end, I got dressed and left my room.

The elevator was empty as I made my way down to the lobby, but my lips creased into a smile when the doors slid open. A beautiful platinum blonde woman stood waiting for me, the toe of her designer shoe tapping on the marble floor and her blue eyes hard.

"Carol, what a lovely surprise," I greeted her, stepping out of the elevator like she *hadn't* nearly made me flinch. "Are you here to see me?" It was second nature to slip into an American accent while speaking to her.

Her tongue clicked, the creases around her eyes deepening as she extended her hand palm up.

I sighed and rolled my eyes but pulled the bracelet from my pocket and handed it over. I didn't need it anymore, and it was one of those items that Carol owned because she liked to *wear* it. That was how I lifted it in the first place, during one of her dinner parties.

"How'd you know I'd be here?" I asked, tilting my head to the side with curiosity.

She gave a huff of laughter. "John, *please*. Don't ask

questions you already know the answers to. My people are everywhere."

Good point. I envied their reach some days, but not enough that I'd ever sell my soul and work for them. I liked being the master of my own fate.

"Steal from me again, John, I'll taxidermy your tight ass and mount you on my wall, Game or not. Are we clear?" Carol's eyes narrowed, her elegant appearance nothing but a smoke screen for the accomplished assassin lurking beneath her skin. Retired or not, Carol was still a force to be reckoned with.

"Crystal clear," I agreed with a toothy grin. "How's—"

"None of your business," she cut me off before I could inquire about her youngest child. "He's too young."

I shrugged one shoulder. "I started younger than him. Children have quick fingers and often go unnoticed."

Her answering smile was brittle. "You didn't have a choice, John. Koen does." She checked her watch and gave a curse. "If you'll excuse me, I'm late for a meeting with my *other* problem child."

Amusement rolled through me as she stalked away across the hotel lobby. Carol had five children, but only two gave her wrinkles. They were my two favorite Atwoods.

Not five minutes after Carol disappeared, while I was helping myself to a Rolex straight off a man's wrist while he waited for valet, my phone buzzed. Excited, I pocketed the thirty thousand dollar watch and checked my messages.

"Finally," I muttered aloud, wandering away from my mark as I read through the instructions for my final task in the Game.

I already had a rough idea of what would be involved, from both my past wins *and* from life experience. My grandfather—Christophe Valenshek—had been one of the early winners of the Game. Since he'd gotten older he had transitioned onto the committee, dedicating all his time to crafting challenges for the new generation of world-class criminals. It'd been his passion, and he'd turned a simple competition between peers into a worldwide event. Now, it was like the Olympics for shady underworld figures, and while *some* rounds leaned more toward the assassination and espionage arena, most of the tasks favored career thieves.

This was the first Game to run since my grandfather died, but I had been confident they'd honor his legacy by sticking to his already mapped out Game levels. Not that he'd *ever* given me clues—Chris hated cheats just like I did—but I was observant.

"Van Gogh's *Poppy Flowers*," I murmured, reading the task again. The committee didn't go making things easy. They provided the item details—its name, a photo, and its last official known location—a deadline that I needed to complete the task within, and my drop point. That was it.

That was all I needed, though. They couldn't make things *too* easy or they'd never pick a winner.

Luckily, all my years upon years of watching black market art auctions was paying off, because I knew who currently owned *Poppy Flowers* and roughly where he might be keeping it. Of course, *knowing* where to find it was only a fraction of the challenge. This one was really going to test my skills just to lay eyes on the piece, and this time I wasn't the only thief on the job.

It was the last task of the Game, so three of us would *all* be hunting the same prize. The deadline for this was irrelevant; whoever got it first would win. It'd better be me.

two

TRIS

TWO MONTHS LATER

I was late. I *despised* being late. But I'd had a half-decent Tinder date last night and slept through my alarm, so here I was. Late to my favorite class of the week, one that I'd taken over teaching when the professor, Dr. Bailey, had been hospitalized a few weeks earlier.

Everyone thought he would pull through, but he only seemed to be deteriorating, and it was just a matter of time before the university found a replacement. Until they did, I was making the most of my increased responsibility.

Or, I had been until last night's date had bought me my seventh mango daiquiri and I decided he was actually pretty hot after all. I vaguely remembered the sex being pretty great, too. Or, shit, it'd want to have been utterly mind blowing since it'd made me late this morning.

My brain was still buzzed enough that I needed a refresher of what I planned to teach today, so I scrolled through my notes on my phone at lightning speed while hurrying down the corridor of my elite school. How the hell I'd landed my position as Dr. Bailey's teaching assistant, I had no clue, because it was a chance of a lifetime and definitely not one I intended to fuck up.

My focus was so engrossed with revising my teaching notes, I almost ran straight into a man standing in the middle of the fucking hallway.

"Shit," I gasped, "sorry, didn't see you there."

He gave a small laugh. "I get that a lot."

Something about the depth of his voice—and that hint of an accent-—made me pause and glance up. And up. And *up*.

"Somehow, I doubt that," I muttered. The guy was enormous. How *had* I not seen him? He looked like some kind of Greek god who just landed on earth. Confused and totally off balance, I glanced around to see why he was just standing there. In the fucking way.

Then my brows hitched when I realized he was looking at a painting hung outside the administration office. It was framed in an awful, heavy gold thing that did the picture itself *zero* justice, but it matched the rest of the ostentatious old-man decor of the university, so whatever.

"Uh..." I indicated the painting. "Were you admiring the student art?"

His brow lifted slightly and he turned his face back to the painting. It was a big one, taking up a third of the wall space, and was done in Neoclassical style depicting a woman reclining on a chaise sofa while reading a leather-bound book.

"Admiring?" he repeated. His face was interesting, his nose slightly bent like it'd been broken and healed wrong, but his mouth...holy shit, those lips. "I don't think I'd say *admiring*. I was actually wondering how on earth this was chosen for display at Boles University. It's awful."

My lips parted in shock while my mind quickly placed the accent as British. "It's *awful*?" I peered at the award plaques mounted beside the golden frame. Somehow that word seemed so much more insulting in his accent. "Respectfully, sir, are you fucking blind? This is exquisite, and clearly I'm not the only one who thinks so." I pointed out the awards, because maybe he *was* visually impaired and I was just being rude for no reason.

He just shrugged one of those massive shoulders. "There's no accounting for taste on those panels. This painting is a clear mockery of classical art with a myriad of hidden elements designed to disrespect the viewer and the poor fools who awarded those accolades."

My lips twitched with amusement but also outrage. Yes, the image had some *very* subtle areas of defiance, but it was only more impressive for those features. In my opinion.

I clicked my tongue, sliding my phone back into my bag as I gave the rude man a prim look. "You're delusional. And severely lacking in taste yourself, sir."

He fucking *rolled his eyes* at me. What the hell? This man had to be pushing forty and he was rolling his eyes like a child. It sparked my temper something wicked.

"No, I believe you are. The woman in this image is reading erotica for starters." He pointed to the open book where the words *dripping cunt* were written so tiny and faint you almost needed a magnifying glass to make them out. "The way she holds the book is flipping the viewer off, her dress is so sheer across the chest you can see the outline of her nipple where the light strikes her side, and for God's sake there's a vibrator peeking out from under her dress." He pointed out the rather modern detail near the base of the painting, and I held back my smirk.

"So, you have problems with a female-focused, sexually empowering painting, is that it?" I retorted, wrinkling my nose. "How very misogynistic of you. No wonder you lack artistic taste."

He gave me a sharp look then flicked his eyes between the painting and me a couple of times. The woman in the image had raven black hair cascading over the arm of the chaise, and rosebud lips that he was clearly just connecting as familiar. *There it is. The penny just dropped, huh?*

"Ah, I see. Artist's *muse* are you?" He said it like he was calling me a bad name.

I tucked my bag up higher on my shoulder and straightened my glasses. "Actually no." I turned to face him directly, tipping my head back to meet his eyes. "Artist."

His eyes widened briefly, then he winced. "Shit."

My smile was brittle. "Can I help you find someone? You seem lost."

He ran a hand over that military style haircut, having the grace to look embarrassed. "Actually, yes. I was looking for Dr. Bailey's teaching assistant, Tristian Ives? I was told he would be running the eight-thirty undergrad lecture for Survey of Renaissance through Modern Art."

Irritation rippled through me. "Oh, *he* is. Just head

down the corridor that way, take your first left, follow the corridor all the way to the end, then take the door to the right of the big bronze statue." I gave him directions well away from the class in question.

His smile was cool. "Thank you. And, uh, my apologies." He gestured to the painting. "But it's still awful."

He walked away before I could bite back, but it didn't matter anyway. I was *really* late now. Spinning on my heel, I hurried into the lecture hall where some hundred and fifty first-year students were chatting and socializing.

"Sorry I'm late!" I said, projecting my voice like I'd learned to do in ten years of drama classes. "I'm here now, though, so please find your seats and quiet down."

This class was generally a pretty good one, with students who were actually interested in learning. One of the girls in the front row raised her hand and asked after Dr. Bailey's health.

For a few moments, I took the time to explain what I knew of his condition. He'd been admitted to the hospital a few weeks earlier with what seemed like a minor stroke. His condition had deteriorated since then, though, so no one knew whether he'd recover.

Luckily for me, I'd helped him put together his lesson plans at the start of the academic year, so I was well-versed on all the content he'd planned to teach. With any luck, he would recover and return to class soon. My job was to make sure his students didn't all fail the course in the meantime.

The door to the class creaked open as I was returning to the podium to take a look at my notes and start the lecture. Glancing over, I found my rude friend from the corridor had worked out that I'd directed him to a janitor's closet and must have gotten directions from someone else.

"Alright, I apologize for the late start today," I addressed the class. "Most of you already know me, but for those who don't—" I leveled a cool glare at Mr. Marine "—my name is Tristian Ives, and I'm Dr. Bailey's TA. You can all call me Tris. Let's get started."

For the rest of the class I ignored the huge man folded into one of the tight seats of the back row, but he didn't make it easy. He hadn't brought any notebook or laptop. He just seemed content to sit there and listen, his fingers interlaced on the desktop like he was interviewing me for something.

It was disconcerting, to say the least. That, combined with my residual hangover, meant my enthusiasm was dampened somewhat. But still, I made it through the lecture and breathed a sigh of relief when the three-hour seminar ended and I dismissed my students.

"I think we got off to a bad start," the big man suggested, approaching my lectern with his hands tucked in his pockets.

I arched a brow while packing my laptop away. "Oh, you think?"

His smile was tight, like he was containing the urge to be an asshole. Again. "Tris, was it? I'm John." He extended one of those *enormous* hands for me to shake, and I eyed it with suspicion. Then, because it was getting awkward, I extended my own hand.

"John," I repeated, letting him shake my hand briefly before I pulled away. "Can I ask why you were looking for my class, John? I assume you didn't just come here to trash my *award-winning* painting. Perhaps you'd like to offer criticism of my teaching, too? Oh wait, I forgot the part where you assumed I was a man, too. God forbid a *woman* hold a TA position in an elite university like Boles." I gave a mock gasp, pressing my hand to my chest as though scandalized.

Yeah, I was prickly when I was hungover. Okay, fine. All the time.

He tilted his head to the side, his gaze shrewd. "Tristian *is* usually a male name, and you have absolutely no online presence whatsoever, so could you blame me for making an assumption?"

"You know what they say about *assuming*, John," I

replied, slinging my bag strap over my head and freeing my long hair with a sweep of my hand. I didn't have the time to stand around chit chatting with a bad-mannered man, no matter how sexy he was. "You looked me up online? Creep. Should I be calling for campus security right now?"

He gave a low chuckle, and it did delicious things to my pussy. Dammit, maybe I needed to booty call that guy from Tinder on my way to work. Come to think of it, though, if this asshole could get me hot and bothered that easily, the sex must have sucked last night.

So there. He was wrong. I *did* have an online presence, I just wasn't dumb enough to run my profiles under my real name.

"You think pretty highly of yourself, don't you Tris?" His question was sharper than teasing, and it made me pull up short.

I whirled around to glare at the big, handsome prick. "Yes, John. I do. It's called confidence and self-respect. If that's a problem for you, absolutely *no one* is making you continue this conversation. In fact, I'm actively trying to *leave*."

He blew out an exasperated breath. "This is…I don't usually come across so bad on first meetings," he admitted with a frown. "This is out of character for me. I'm usually very charming, Tristian."

I rolled my eyes back at him. "Now who thinks highly of themselves?"

His full lips ticked up. "Point taken. Can we start over? Maybe go for a coffee? You look like you could use one."

My laugh was edged with disbelief. "Smooth, John. Hot tip, if you're asking a girl out maybe *don't* imply she looks like crap." Even if I did have eye bags big enough for international travel.

He winced but persisted. "Fair point. Dinner instead?"

This guy was unbelievable. "Thanks, but no thanks. I'm seeing someone." I checked my watch and huffed with frustration. "And now I'm running late for work, so please do me a favor and stop following me."

I picked up my pace as I hurried across the campus grounds, but he kept up easily with those long legs. It was almost insulting how many steps I took to every one of his.

"Work?" he asked. "Isn't that here?"

I clicked my tongue with irritation. "No, *this* is for my doctorate and barely covers tuition and gas, genius. I also need to pay life bills, so right now I need to get to my real job before my boss decides there are hundreds of other talented artists floating around Whispering Willows, and hires one of them instead. Goodbye."

John finally took my hint when I reached the parking lot and unlocked my car with the remote fob. "Well, maybe I'll see you around, Tristian."

"Hopefully not, *John*," I shot back, then climbed into my car and slammed the door shut. He gave a little mocking wave as I reversed out of the parking lot, and I extended my middle finger in response. Childish, yes, but he fucking started it.

Ugh, what a way to start my week.

three

JOHN

Well…that went badly.

I stood there like a fucking Muppet, staring after Tristian's crappy Toyota Corolla as she disappeared down the street away from Boles. It'd been a *long* time since I'd been so significantly off my game, and it left me flabbergasted.

"What the fuck just happened?" I muttered under my breath.

"Looks like Tris handed you your ass," someone said from beside me, and I was startled to find a twenty-ish guy in a Boles sport jacket standing there with a smirk on his face. "Don't take it personally, old timer. She's a cold bitch on the best of days." The kid clapped me on the shoulder like we somehow had common ground, then headed off to his car while chuckling to himself.

What the shit? I dusted off my shoulder where he'd touched me and stalked back toward the art wing of the university. Fucking kid had probably been shot down by Tris plenty of times himself and thought that made us equals. Even if he did call me *old timer*. Jesus, I was thirty-six, not eighty.

Either way, I was off to a *rough* start and desperately needed to make up for lost time. It'd taken me two months to get this far, mostly chasing a false lead in Dr Bailey, and then hitting dead end after dead end while researching the elusive Tristian Ives. Or *trying* to. I wasn't lying when I said she had no online presence, it was like she didn't exist.

The only lead I had was that Dr. Bailey had let slip that he suspected his teaching assistant was involved with a known crime family. Lucky for me, that family happened to be the ones who'd last purchased Van Gogh's *Poppy Flowers* at a black-market auction.

Tristian Ives was my way in, I was sure of it. But I'd just totally fumbled that first meeting, first by insulting her painting then by assuming she was a he, and she *really* seemed like the kind of girl who made up her mind on someone in the first ten seconds.

My only defense for my total fuck up of a first impression was that she'd caught me totally off guard. She was *gorgeous,* and when I'd been expecting to find a brown-nosing *male* doctoral student, it knocked my whole game plan.

I'd orchestrated things to get close to Tristian within the university setting, but now that I'd met her, my plans were already changing in my head. This could potentially be easier than I'd first thought, if she could get over our rocky start.

With that renewed sense of hope, I made my way back to the administration office and greeted the elderly secretary with a charming smile. She sent me straight through to the dean's office, and I strode in with a confident set to my shoulders.

"Ah, Dr. Smith," the dean greeted me, rising from his desk, "or do you prefer Professor?"

I shook the man's hand with a quick pump. "Just John, please."

"New age, got it," the dean enthused, then indicated for me to sit. "You'll fit in well here with that younger approach. Did you manage to catch Tristian's class just now?"

I folded myself into the hard wooden chair and casually hooked my ankle over my knee. "I did, indeed."

"She's impressive, isn't she? I never said this, but Stephan falling ill is probably the best thing to happen to his students. Tristian has a much more effective way of getting through to them." The dean shuffled some papers, then folded his fingers together on the desk in front of him. "But of course, now they have you. Are you looking forward to starting tomorrow?"

"I am," I confirmed, "but if it's okay I'd quite like to take this week just to audit Dr. Bailey's classes. Just sit in the back and observe the students to get an idea of the general structure. That sort of thing."

The dean's brows rose, but he nodded hesitantly. "Uh, yes, sure. If that's what you think best."

"I do," I confirmed with a confident smile.

"Well, like I said on the phone, we at Boles are eternally grateful that you could take this position on such short notice. Whatever we can do to make this work for you, consider it done." He sat back in his chair, like he was happy that his part was done. "Marla has your ID card and office keys ready, and I understand you've been assigned a cottage on campus for accommodation?"

I inclined my head. "Yes, much appreciated. I think I'll check it out now, then head into town to get the lay of the land. This is my first time in Whispering Willows, so it'll be nice to take a look around."

Rising from my chair once more, I shook the dean's hand and went to see his secretary to get all my keys and cards. As of today, I was the new professor of art history at Boles University, and I'd take on the undergraduate studies courses. More importantly, I'd be filling in as the adviser for Dr. Bailey's graduate students.

As I said to the dean, I took my time getting situated in my new accommodation for the afternoon. Mostly revising and reviewing my notes on *Poppy Flowers*. I'd lied about this being my first time in Whispering Willows, but my stupid ass had been tailing a false lead the whole time. How utterly frustrating.

Faced with the prospect of needing to actually cook dinner for myself—since I'd opted to take the free on-campus staff accommodation rather than a hotel—I decided to cut my losses for the day and head into town.

Whispering Willows wasn't a huge city. It had been built around Boles University, which started out as a very exclusive college for the children of wealthy families. Mostly ones who made their money in somewhat less reputable industries than the legacies of Stanford or Harvard. What had started as a small community for staff and supporting businesses had grown into a full town. Complete with controlling crime families—like all prosperous towns.

I'd laid fairly low for the past few weeks, not wanting to take any unnecessary notice, but this time I was shifting into a position that required notice. I was a professor at Boles, and I needed to seduce my new TA. So I headed toward a bar I hadn't yet visited but had already marked out as the most popular student drinking spot.

Maybe I could casually pick up some more information on my new target. Sure seemed like she'd gained a bit of a reputation, if the jock earlier was to be believed.

I took a seat right at the bar, ordering myself a plate of hot wings and loaded fries to go with my beer. Thieves who claimed they didn't drink so it didn't impair their skills were just shit at their jobs. A real professional could lift a diamond necklace right off a princess's neck while three sheets to the wind, and get away totally unscathed.

"You're new here, aren't you?" the pretty bartender asked as she delivered my food to me.

I nodded. "Yes, just today. I'm John."

She smiled, giving a small eyelash flutter that she probably didn't even notice she was doing. "Nice to meet you, John. I'm Krista." She pointed to the name tag on her very low cut shirt. "What brings you to Whispering Willows? Sounds like you're not from these parts."

Given that I was using my "real" identity for this cover story, I'd reverted to my "real" accent over the general American one I often used while state-side. Of course, nothing about me was truly real, it was just the name and accent that I found most comfortable, so I'd adopted them for my day-to-day life. I sure as shit couldn't put *Hermes*—my underworld codename—on my passport, could I?

Someone tried to get her attention from further down the bar, but she ignored them as she waited for my response. I glanced down toward the impatient customer, then cleared my throat as I looked back to the flirty bartender.

"Uh, I'm here for work," I told her truthfully.

"Oh yeah? What kinda work?" she asked, even as the customer called out again.

I arched a brow. "I think someone wants a drink."

She blinked at me a moment, then blushed and took the hint that I wasn't interested, quickly disappearing back along the bar to serve more patrons. I probably could have pumped her for some information, but I just wasn't in the mood for empty flirting. I wanted to eat my wings, drink my beer, and ruminate on how I acted like a total moron this morning with Tristian. Tris. She said to call her *Tris*.

The androgynous name strangely suited her somewhat aggressive nature.

I winced as I replayed that whole conversation about her painting again. How I'd assumed she was the artist's muse like some sort of painting groupie. What was wrong with me? I knew better than to make sweeping generalizations like that. I also knew better than to let my mouth run away with itself, and yet I couldn't seem to shut the fuck up under her unimpressed gaze.

As if summoned by my thoughts, a familiar raven-haired beauty stepped through the door of the bar, accompanied by some boring looking guy in a sweater-vest. Was this the boyfriend? Shit, I thought it was actually going to be a *challenge* to seduce her, but if that was the kind of guy she was dating...

"Can I get you something else?" Krista the bartender was back.

I shook my head. "No. Thanks." I barely even glanced at her, my eyes locked on the prickly woman across the room. She was too far away for me to eavesdrop, and that just wouldn't do at all.

Patience was my middle name as I polished off my food, waiting as Tris and her *date* got situated in a booth near the little stage where a band was setting up. For someone with a reputation at Boles for being a "cold bitch" she seemed perfectly comfortable laughing and flirting with the sweater-vest-wearing loser. It only confirmed my suspicion she'd shot the jock down and his ego was bruised.

When she was distracted, I relocated myself to the booth directly behind hers. It was occupied by a couple of frat boys, but they quickly evacuated when I gave them a death glare and short command to *fuck off*.

Sometimes my size came in handy, where it was usually a hurdle to overcome in my line of work. What I would give to be a foot shorter and half the width I currently held. The tight spaces I'd be able to access… ventilation shafts, wall cavities, garbage chutes. Some thieves had no idea how easy they had it.

For the next hour, I listened to Tristian's date tell her all about his day at the Whispering Willows country club. He wasn't there as a guest; he apparently worked there as a golf pro, which was fancy speak for the instructor. He spent all day teaching rich pricks how to improve their putting, and thought that was great material for a date conversation.

It droned on so long even I started feeling sleepy, and I nearly laughed out loud when I heard Tris cover a yawn with a fake cough.

When he got up to use the bathroom, I couldn't help myself. I turned around in my seat and leaned over until my chin nearly rested on her shoulder. "I dunno about you, but I think he's hoping for a hole in one tonight."

To her credit, she didn't flinch. "Crass humor should be beneath a gentleman scholar like you, John," she replied in a cool voice. "Or did you not proclaim my artwork as *awful* and *insulting* this morning for a few subtle suggestive elements?" She turned her head just enough to arch a brow at me.

Fuck. She was close enough to kiss…I wonder how she'd react?

"Are you stalking me, John? First you admit to internet research and now you're creeping on my date. This is getting uncomfortable."

Okay…she had a point. It didn't look *great*, but surely I could spin it somehow. Or maybe just leave it mysterious? Yes, she seemed like the kind of woman who'd be driven mad with a lack of information, so maybe I'd opt for silence over bullshit explanations.

"Mere coincidence," I murmured, settling on a middle ground. "I'm glad for it, though, I learned so much this evening. Like the fact that your boyfriend loves to listen to himself talk so much he wouldn't *actually* notice if you fell asleep. Does he talk while he fucks you, too?"

Her jaw tensed and her cheeks turned the prettiest shade of pink, but she tipped a graceful smile toward Captain Sweater-Vest as he made his way back from the bathrooms. "I have no clue," she admitted quietly, for my ears only. "But I'm sure I'll find out." She rose out of her seat, tossing that silky hair over her shoulder and lightly smacking me in the face with it.

I shifted backward on reflex as the heady scent of her

shampoo filled my senses. When I looked back over, she had her arms looped around Golf-Dick's neck and her lips sealed against his. He kissed her back with the enthusiasm of a hungry bulldog, and I rolled my eyes. Apparently Tris wasn't over our little clash just yet.

She must have suggested to her date that he was going to get lucky because he tossed money onto the table and all but dragged her out of the bar. I watched them go, and a shot of smug satisfaction rippled through me when she glanced over her shoulder.

I waved, she flipped me the bird. Cute. That was becoming *our thing*.

When they were gone, I pushed up out of my own seat, intending to head back to my cottage. I paused as I passed the table Tris had been at, though, glancing down at the money Tiny Dick had dropped. Then I frowned, doing the math on what they'd ordered. It was enough to cover the bill, but nothing more.

"Cheap prick," I muttered, adding some notes from my own wallet before continuing out of the bar. As much as I'd like to pretend this was just another job, far from my first and not even the hardest one I'd pulled off...something felt different.

She made it different.

four

TRIS

The sex was beyond terrible. When John joked about my date—Chad—trying for a hole in one, I didn't think he meant one *minute*. Goddamn. His attempts to get me off were almost laughably bad, too, as he frantically rubbed my left labia. Eventually I took the easy way out, faking it, then bailing out as fast as humanly possible. Thank *fuck* we weren't at my house where I needed to kick him out.

"How was your date?"

The question nearly made me jump out of my skin as I tried to unlock my door well before midnight. I whispered a curse and spun on my heel to glare at my neighbor, Nelson.

"It's not even eleven o'clock and I'm home alone. How do you think it went?" I retorted.

The old guy chuckled, rubbing a hand over his white-whiskered chin. "That's what you get for using that phone app shit. No one is on there to find a relationship, Ivy-girl, only hook ups."

I rolled my eyes. "Last I checked, I also didn't want a relationship. Stay out of it, you old badger. None of your business."

He chuckled. "Fair enough. Come over, I need your thoughts on a project I'm working on."

I wrinkled my nose. "Give me ten minutes to shower and change."

Nelson grimaced. "Spare me the details, kid. Come over when you're sanitized, I'll open some wine."

I snorted a laugh at his phrasing, then let myself into my own apartment. I loved my home. The whole building used to be an old warehouse for something or other, but Nelson and his partner Hank bought the property years ago to convert into trendy open-plan units.

This top floor was just them and me, just the way we all liked it. Nelson was the closest thing I had to family, so I loved seeing him every day. Even if he was a sarcastic ass about my love life.

After showering, I changed into pajamas and wrapped up in a dressing gown before letting myself into Nelson's apartment without knocking.

"Honey, I'm home," I called out, making my way over to the kitchen island where a full decanter of red wine sat waiting beside some crystal wine glasses.

"Ivy, how was your date?" Nelson's partner Hank asked, coming through from their art studio with his arms open for a hug.

I gave a dry laugh as he squeezed me, then accepted a glass of wine when I poured it. "It was forgettable," I admitted. "Nelson said you're working on something new?"

"Yes!" Hank's grin spread wide, and his eyes sparkled with excitement. "Come see."

We poured an extra glass of wine for Nelson, then Hank ushered me through to their art studio, which was separated from the living area with an industrial-style roller door.

"Ooh, we're working with jewelry this week?" I enthused, seeing the equipment and supplies out on their work benches. "You know I love sparkly things."

Nelson stood up from his chair and gestured me closer. "That we do. What do you think of this?"

I moved around to take his place, peering down at the piece he was working on. Then I looked at his reference image, printed out and stuck on the tabletop beside his workstation.

"Hmm." I placed my wine down, grabbing their

jewelers' loupe to take a closer look at the ring. "It's good," I told them, putting it back down.

Nelson narrowed his eyes. "Good?" he repeated. Hank groaned and ran his hands over his head, leaving his silver hair sticking up all over the place.

I arched a brow at Nelson. "Yeah. Good. Nice."

"Nice." He spat the word like it was the worst insult in the world.

"Christ, Ivy, just tell him what's wrong with it," Hank pleaded. "I don't have the energy for this before bed."

I bit back the desire to laugh, instead keeping my expression cool and calm. "There's nothing *wrong* with it. It's a good attempt."

Hank threw his hands in the air and Nelson's jaw nearly hit the floor.

"A good *attempt*?" my mentor screeched.

"Now you've fucking done it," Hank muttered. "Have I mentioned I hate you?"

Nelson was already storming out of his studio in a rage, muttering curses and gesturing wildly about the *green around the gills, no-talent child* giving him criticisms.

I grinned at Hank, but he just scowled back at me.

"Fix it," he told me in a firm voice, pointing a scarlet fingernail in the direction Nelson had just gone. "You broke it, you fix it. Until you do, no wine." He snatched up my glass before I could reach for it, and I gave a pout.

"You're no fun," I grumbled, giving a dramatic eye roll. "Nelson!" I called out, knowing full well he could hear me. "Your claws on the left side are thicker than the right. Even them out and it's flawless."

There was a moment's pause, then Nelson came stomping back into the studio with his glasses in hand. Tossing an indignant look my way—that almost made me crack up laughing—he pushed me aside and perched his glasses on his nose. Then he picked up the ring and loupe to check my observation.

"No, they're not," he snapped. "You're wrong, they're perfect."

Hank sighed heavily, holding out his hand for the ring and loupe. He took his time checking them, then even fetched out a pair of delicate calipers to measure each claw holding the central pear cut diamond. No one spoke while he checked it, and I stole my wine back from where he'd put it down.

Yum. Hawkes Bay Syrah.

"So?" Nelson prompted when Hank set the ring back down on the table.

His partner winced. "She's right."

Nelson let out a long, irritated sigh, then gave me a narrow-eyed look of respect. "You're good, Ivy. That damn ring has been bugging me all week. I knew something wasn't right but couldn't put my finger on *what.*"

I grinned, satisfied that I'd been right. It was a test, of course; it always was with Nelson. "Always happy to be of service."

"So, tell us about this failed date tonight," Hank prompted, waving me back into the living room with him.

I yawned, taking one of the big comfy armchairs and tucking my feet up under me. "Nothing to tell, he was a self-involved ass who came in one minute or less."

Nelson made a gagging sound, and I shared a grin with Hank. Nelson and I weren't related, but he liked to act like my dad some days. The last thing he wanted to hear was the finer details of my crappy one-night stand.

"A better story would be to tell you about the insufferable *bastard* I met at Boles this morning," I offered instead, speaking before I could use my better judgment to shut up.

Hank's brows rose in interest. "Oh? Do tell."

"What'd he do to earn that violent look in your eye, Ives?" Nelson asked, already bristling in my defense. Fuck I loved him.

I drew a deep breath, blowing it out slowly then gulping my wine. "Alright. Let's start from how he called my *Literary Woman* an *awful* and *insulting* piece of art."

Nelson chuckled. "Well, it was always intended to be insulting, in fairness. He's dead wrong about it being *awful.* No accounting for taste, though. Was he handsome?"

Breathtakingly so, yes. "What? I wasn't flirting with him, did you miss the part where he insulted me to my face?"

Hank and Nelson exchanged a smirk. "Uh huh, okay not flirting," Hank agreed, sarcastic as fuck. "So what happened next?"

"What's his name, this insufferable bastard? Or shall we just call him IB?" Nelson gave me a teasing smile and I glared at the two of them.

"Were you two drinking before I got here?"

Hank snorted a laugh, taking another sip of wine. I'd take that as a yes.

Rolling my eyes, I answered Nelson. "John. His name is John."

"Sounds fake," Nelson muttered.

"Definitely fake," Hank agreed.

It was *really* hard to remain annoyed and not smile at their antics. The both of them were pushing seventy on a good day—neither one would admit to being a day over fifty though—and they bantered like schoolgirls.

"Well, fake or not, *John* then went on to assume I was the *artist's muse,* then said he was looking for Tristian

Ives." I pursed my lips, pausing for dramatic effect. "Because John heard *he*—Tristian the man—would be covering Dr. Bailey's class."

Nelson smirked, he always called me *Ivy* because he said *Tris* wasn't pretty like I was.

"Oh, how was it taking over the lecture?" Hank asked, getting thoroughly distracted.

Nelson whacked him lightly with the back of his hand. "Hush, I want to hear more about fake-name-John. Why was he looking for you, Ivy?"

I scowled. "Focus, old man. He thought I was a guy."

Nelson just shrugged. "Easy mistake to make with a name like Tristian. What happened next?"

I'd need another glass of wine at the rate I was gulping it. "Well, he sat in the back of the class and listened like a creep, then followed me out to my car to try and ask me out on a date or something—"

"Oh, I knew this was gonna get good," Hank whispered, and Nelson nodded his agreement.

"—which resulted in him implying I looked like crap, I told him where to shove his bad manners and left him standing there in the parking lot."

Both men blinked at me.

"That's it?" Hank asked, tipping his head to the side in disappointment.

I frowned. "I was late for work at RBD's."

Nelson sipped his wine, squinting at me. "What *else* happened, Ives?"

I rolled my eyes. He was like a damn bloodhound. As briefly as possible, I told them about how John had shown up on my date at the bar, and how he'd taunted me about my boring, self-centered date.

"And he was right," Nelson mused. "How does that make you feel?"

"Oh shut up," I snapped. "It was an easy guess considering Chad barely stopped for a breath in an hour of chatter about putting and drivers."

Hank was frowning, though. "But you still slept with him? Chad?"

I shrugged. "I have *needs,* too." Or, maybe the technical term was *high sex drive and no stable relationship*.

"I don't need to hear about your needs, kid," Nelson told me in a gruff voice, going all paternal again. "We heard quite enough of that last night when you brought that British boy home."

I wrinkled my nose. "He was British? I don't remember that." One last gulp finished my wine. "Anyway, I need sleep. Let me know when you think you've fixed that ring, and I'll take another look."

Nelson waved me off, still irritated that I'd spotted his flaw no doubt. I rinsed out my glass in their sink, kissed their prickly cheeks goodnight, and then returned to my own apartment.

Why the fuck I'd thought it was a good idea to tell the two of them about John, I had no idea. Maybe I'd just needed to decompress with someone older and wiser than myself? Not that they'd given me any useful advice on how to deal with the big, sexy bastard. But it'd shifted a small amount of tension out of my mind, summarizing it all out loud.

Maybe now I could push his imperfect face out of my mind and forget we ever met. Chances were, he was only passing through and I'd never see him again. Right?

five

JOHN

The woman was infuriatingly stubborn. Maybe under other circumstances, I'd appreciate her strength of character but not when I was on a fucking deadline. Every day that ticked over, I was questioning myself. Maybe I'd gone about this all wrong. Maybe I should've been trying to weasel my way into the Grimaldi family directly, like my competition would undoubtedly be doing.

It wasn't like I hadn't been *trying*, either. I'd been turning the charm level up to blinding and genuinely groveling to try and get Tristian Ives to give me even the time of day, but she was unshakable.

After a full week of sitting in on her lectures, and finding convenient excuses to run into her around campus, I was running fast out of patience. And time.

Somehow she eluded me all weekend, despite the fact I'd tailed her back to her apartment—so I knew where she lived—but come Monday morning I was *irritated.*

So it was for that reason that I decided to take a more forceful approach.

"Fucking hell," Tristian muttered when I stepped out in front of her before she made it into the lecture hall. "You *again*? Haven't you taken the hint by now, John?"

I smiled and watched as her gaze ducked ever so briefly down to my mouth. Tristian Ives wasn't half as disinterested as she liked to act, because that wasn't the first time I'd caught her looking at me with...*heat.*

"What hint is that, Tristian? I'm just here for my favorite class. Again." I tucked my hands into my pockets, nodding for her to walk ahead of me into the theater.

She scowled, suspicion all over her face, but continued through the door anyway. I shadowed her all the way over to the lectern rather than taking my usual seat at the back of the room.

"What?" she snapped, whirling on me.

I just smiled and placed my hands on her slim hips to move her out of my way.

"John, what the fuck—" she hissed, but I turned my smile on the class.

"Good morning, class," I greeted the room,

projecting my voice without the need of a microphone. "Thank you for tolerating me this past week as I audited all of Dr. Bailey's classes. I am Professor John Smith, and I'm here at Boles to replace Dr. Bailey indefinitely." I turned my Cheshire Cat grin on Tristian, who looked like she was about to throw up. "Tristian has been doing an excellent job covering Bailey's absence, and I very much look forward to working together. Shall we begin?" I extended my hand to one of the empty seats in the front row, inviting her to sit that sexy ass down.

The moment it took her to shake off the shock was way too enjoyable for me. It didn't last nearly long enough, then her shocked gaze hardened with fury as she took a seat with the rest of the class.

She sat there, spine rigid and jaw tight, like she was just going to glare daggers at me for the whole three-hour lecture. Joke was on her, I *actually* knew what I was doing in this role. That was why I had an edge over my competition for *Poppy Flowers* and why I'd chased this route at accessing it, because my day job—between stealing shit to satisfy my addiction—was at Aalto University in Finland, teaching Art History.

When I'd expressed my desire to *substitute* for Dr. Bailey here at Boles, my own employer had been happy to give me a six-month sabbatical. More than enough time, in theory.

I hadn't accounted for Tristian Ives being such a tough nut to crack, though. Nor had I accounted for my intel on Dr. Bailey being inaccurate enough to waste my time for a month.

Across the next three hours, I made sure to make *my* TA understand that I wasn't just a creeper who wanted to get into her pants. I mean, I sure as fuck wouldn't say no, and ultimately that would make my plan work so much easier, but that wasn't my number one objective. Right now, as far as she was concerned—while I called on her to answer a question for the dozenth time—I was simply here to teach.

As the class drew to a close, Tristian looked like she was preparing to run. That simply wouldn't do, at all. I needed to gloat and really rub it in that she was now stuck with me.

"Miss Ives," I practically purred, offering her a lopsided grin, "stay behind."

She pursed her lips and folded her legs, staying in her seat as the rest of the students filed out of the lecture hall. I was content to wait it out, so I just leaned against the lectern with my eyes locked on hers as several hundred students casually wandered past, in no hurry to get anywhere.

Her dark lashes framed her ice-blue eyes like prickles, and I had no doubt she'd plotted my death a thousand different ways since I stole her class out from under her. Maybe it spoke to my emotional damage, but that thought turned me on.

After the last student left, a heavy silence fell across the empty space. Tristian stared at me, waiting. I *liked* being the center of her attention, so I just stared back. I was in no hurry to be anywhere, but based on her schedule last week, I was pretty sure she was.

Sure enough, her patience ran out long before mine.

"You probably could have mentioned this sooner, *Professor Smith,*" she snapped, her tone clipped. It was like she couldn't decide if she should be embarrassed or furious and had settled on both. It was cute.

I inclined my head, tucking my hands into my pockets. Her gaze darted down ever so quickly, but I caught it. She totally just checked out my bulge.

"Yes, I could have," I agreed. "But where's the fun in that?"

Her dark lashes narrowed around her eyes, turning them to slits of fury. "I didn't realize we were having fun."

I smirked. "Sure you did. So, do you have plans this evening?"

Her perfect lips parted in disbelief. "You're still asking me out? That *has* to be against the rules. You're a professor, and—"

I gave a fake gasp. "I am? Oh wait, I knew that. It's why I just taught this class." My smile was pure sarcasm. "Unless I'm mistaken, Tristian, I believe I am also your student advisor in Dr. Bailey's absence. So, let's try that again. Do you have plans this evening?"

Her teeth ground together so hard I could hear it. "Actually, I do." She inhaled sharply, then pulled a notebook from her bag. Quickly, she scribbled down some information then ripped out the page. Standing up, she looped her bag over her shoulder and held out the paper to me. "These are the times Dr. Bailey and I used to meet in an advisory capacity."

I took the paper from her, noting the neat, flowing cursive of her handwriting. Pretty and old-fashioned. I half expected to find them all at boring times, during the day, but they were all late nights or painfully early mornings.

"I see," I murmured. "I can work with this."

"Good," she huffed. "We can meet in the campus library, and—"

I laughed, cutting her off. "No. You want to do academic work before the sun is even up? You can damn well come to me." I took the pen out of her hand and scribbled my address and phone number on the bottom of the page, then tore it off to hand back. "I'll expect a phone call if you can't make it on time, Tristian."

Her answering smile was tight and cold. "Of course."

She started stalking out the door, and I took a moment to check out her ass in the charcoal gray pants she was wearing. I liked how she dressed for classes, like some kind of sexy secretary.

"What are they?" I called after her, not wanting to let her leave just yet.

She paused, spinning to face me. "What are what?"

I tipped my head to the side. "Your plans tonight. Another hot date with Golf-Pro Greg?"

Her lips creased in a smile before she could catch it. "His name was Chad, not Greg."

I grinned wider. "Seriously?"

Tristian rolled her eyes and turned to leave once more. "None of your business, Professor Smith. Enjoy your afternoon."

The door slammed hard after her, and I gave it to the count of thirty before I followed. She was in a hurry to get to her *other job,* and I was almost certain that had to be working for the Grimaldi family. Over the past few months, my information network had learned that several paintings the Grimaldis had procured were in need of restoration.

Everything had pointed to Dr. Bailey as the logical choice within Whispering Willows, since he had experience working as an Art Conservator within several museums in his past. But now I was thinking Tristian had more in common with her old advisor than she let on.

If she was the one employed to restore paintings within the Grimaldi collection, then she was the *very* best tool to use for access. She could plausibly remove the painting from wherever it was kept to clean or maintain, she could remove it from its frame, she could even swap it out for a forgery…if I had one. My usual forger had gone dark over a year earlier, and I didn't trust anyone else to attempt a Van Gogh replica. Especially on my time frame.

No, my best bet was to use pretty little Tristian Ives for access, then snatch and run.

Simple.

This job could burn my most authentic cover identity, no doubt about it. But if any job was worth reinventing myself *again*, then it was this one.

I followed her at a distance across campus, keeping her in my peripheral vision as she unlocked her Corolla and climbed inside. She didn't look around to check if anyone was following, because why would she?

My own car—a new purchase over the weekend—was closer to the exit of the parking lot. I waited patiently in my driver's seat as she drove out of the Boles campus, and then I followed at a distance.

I'd tried this a couple of times in the last week, but I'd been too conscious of my Corvette being recognized, so I had always lost her on the far side of town. Hence my new Ford Focus, blending in with every other idiot in town.

This time I had no concerns following her the whole way through town, and I stayed on her tail right up until she turned off into a private driveway some twenty minutes or so from campus. I kept driving but committed the location to memory. I'd revisit here another time, because I'd put money on it that the grand estate she was now driving up to was a Grimaldi property.

It was nice to have things swing my way again. For a moment there, I'd been worried.

"Back on track," I murmured to myself as I circled back into Whispering Willows. I had hours to kill yet before I needed to stalk Tristian on her date, and I couldn't think of anything I'd rather do than break into the dean's office and steal the antique silver trinket box off his bookshelf.

Simple pleasures.

six

TRIS

John fucking Smith. Nelson and Hank were right, it totally sounded like a fake name. I'd spent way too long—while I was meant to be working—looking him up online. Apparently, he wasn't making it up. Professor John Smith, on loan from Aalto University in Finland, held a PhD in Medieval Russian to Early Modern Art with a focus on the Romanov Dynastic Period. Among other things. But *that* just so happened to be the exact area of focus for my own doctorate.

It should have been a good thing. Right? He should be the *best* advisor imaginable. And he would be...if I didn't want to punch him right in the crooked nose every fucking time I saw him. Smug fuck. Maybe if he quit constantly *flirting* I could approach him from a professional, academic level.

Somehow, I suspected I'd have an easier time asking the sun to turn blue.

I didn't have a one-on-one session with him until mid-week, thank fuck for that, but I would have to see him during Art History on Tuesday. It was an afternoon class, so I usually worked the morning at RBD's, where I was employed to clean and restore some priceless artwork.

Priceless…and very stolen.

I justified it to myself by reasoning that my employer, Luther Grimaldi, hadn't stolen the paintings himself. He'd paid good money for each and every piece at auction, and who knew how many times those pieces had changed hands prior to his acquisition of them. I'd looked up the Picasso I was currently working on and discovered it had been missing since 1986 and was now worth somewhere in the ballpark of $5 million. Mr. Grimaldi had only owned it for a year, so the original thieves were long gone.

Besides, no artist in their right mind would pass up the opportunity to work with paintings like this, no matter *where* they came from.

Because of that, I was *extremely* cautious not to fuck it up. And I didn't just mean the work itself—I was easily talented and experienced enough to do what was required—but there was more involved than that. Mr. Grimaldi was a *particular* man. Moody.

I never wanted to be on the receiving end of his bad favor, so I made sure I was *never* late for my scheduled work times. I kept my damn head down, never spoke out of turn, and did everything possible to avoid running into any of the other employees. Most days, I came and went without seeing a single person, and that was how I liked it.

Tuesday wasn't one of those days. Even before I opened the service entrance door I could hear the rumble of voices further inside the house. I paused a moment with my key in the first lock, then heaved a small sigh and turned it. I couldn't just hide outside all day, so I might as well hurry the hell up and get to my studio where I would be left alone.

Security at RBD's was intense but to be expected. It took me a few minutes to get inside the manor and lock the doors behind myself, and then I held my breath as I attempted to tip-toe my way down the hallways to get to the gallery and my workshop within.

My path took me right past the marble-floored ballroom, though. In my eighteen months working at RBD's, the only thing I'd ever seen the ballroom used for was...well...it definitely wasn't dancing.

"Good morning, Tristian!" Mr. Grimaldi called out in a cheery, heavily accented voice as I tried to scurry past unnoticed.

Groaning inwardly, I paused and turned on a smile. "Good morning, sir."

My employer was right in the middle of beating the stuffing out of a blood-covered man who hung by his wrists from the ceiling, and he went straight back to it after greeting me. Which was fine—Mr. Grimaldi was a scary motherfucker but always extremely kind to me—except for the fact that he'd now drawn attention to my arrival.

Which was why I had all of three seconds to get into the gallery before—

"Tris, hey, wait up."

That voice made my shoulders instantly tighten, and I fought the urge to ignore him entirely and keep walking. But, considering the violent scene I'd just passed, I valued my own safety too much to piss the Grimaldis off.

So I steeled my spine and pasted my smile on as I turned around once more.

"Hi, Dex," I greeted the handsome guy who'd stopped me. "Busy morning?" I nodded back toward the ballroom where pained moans and sobs could be heard.

He gave me a roguish smile and shrugged one shoulder. "Business, you know?"

I absolutely did not. I went *out of my way* to keep my nose out of the Grimaldi business. "Sure," I murmured weakly. "Uh, I'm kind of late. I should…" I indicated the direction of the gallery in a broad fucking hint that I'd like to *leave*.

Dex never took the hint, though. Either he didn't get it, or he deliberately ignored it, but the result was the same. "Late? You work for me, Tris, you're fine." His laugh was easy and arrogant. He gave me the creeps.

I wet my lips, unable to hold my tongue. "No, I work for your *father*, Dex. And he's paying me to work certain hours. So." I took a step backwards, softening my rejection with a smile. "I'll see you around." Unfortunately.

"Yeah, definitely. The old man wants me here for a few weeks to take care of some shit, so I thought maybe we could get a drink sometime?" He took a step forward, reaching out like he was going to place a hand on my hip.

I smoothly shifted just out of casual reach as I shook my head. "Business and pleasure shouldn't mix, Dex. It was nice to see you, though." Lies. The idea of his being here for *a few weeks* made me want to scream.

He didn't like to be told no. He never had. "Come on, Tris, don't play hard—"

"Dexter!" Mr. Grimaldi bellowed. "Leave Tristian alone. She has important work to do!"

I tried not to look relieved. "We should probably *both* get back to work, huh?"

The flash of anger that crossed Dexter Grimaldi's face sent a shiver of pure terror through me, but he gave me a tight smile and sighed. "I'll come find you later, Tris."

It wasn't a question, it was a statement. So I gave a vague nod and practically *ran* the rest of the way to Mr. Grimaldi's gallery and my workspace within. It took another series of security protocols to get into the gallery in the basement of RBD's, and I breathed a long sigh of relief when the doors auto-locked behind me.

Silence pressed around me like a warm hug, and I left the ick of Dexter Grimaldi outside. This was an art-lover's haven, and working with such greatness was well worth being occasionally hit on by a mafia heir.

I slipped out of my shoes right there at the door—hating the hollow sound of my heels on the floor—and took my time to go around to each and every painting on display. Mr. Grimaldi was the only other person to ever come down here, and I suspected he hadn't granted access to anyone else. He saw me doing this routine one morning when I'd arrived for work, and I'd told him I was just paying my respects to the masters.

It wasn't totally a lie. But I also liked to check them for any signs of tampering. If someone else in RBD's employ decided to attempt a swap for a fake—to make a quick buck or million on the black market—then I would catch the blame first. So, to save my own skin, I made it a habit to check *all* the pieces for authenticity at the start of every single work day.

Once I was satisfied that no one had touched anything, I let myself into my workshop with yet another biometric lock and got to work.

It was easy to lose time while working at RBD's. I played music through noise-canceling headphones while I worked, even though the gallery was fairly well soundproofed already. It took no time at all to settle into my groove, pulling on some gloves and a mask then removing my current project from the locked safe within the workbench. It was a cleaning project, removing literally centuries of dirt, grime, nicotine, and fuck knew what else. All with a swab smaller than a cotton-bud.

When my watch vibrated against my wrist some hours later, I gave a small sigh of regret. Without my alarm, I'd easily lose track of time, and today more than any day I needed to make sure I wasn't late to class. I refused to let John think he'd shaken me with his little power play the day before.

I packed away my supplies, locked up the painting once more, and pulled off the old sweater I'd been wearing over my "school clothes" to keep them clean. I didn't have enough time to go home and change between RBD's and Boles, but since I was only cleaning and not painting today, I'd gone for the sweatshirt cover-up.

Underneath I wore a wine-red pleated skirt, sheer stockings, and a white silk blouse that showed more than a hint of cleavage thanks to my killer push-up bra. No, I wasn't trying to *seduce* my professor, but I didn't hate the way he looked at me.

My watch vibrated again, reminding me to hurry the hell up or I'd be late. I quickly locked up my workshop, tossing my bag over my shoulder and looping my huge paint-covered sweatshirt through the strap as I crossed the gallery. I paused for a moment to slip my shoes back on at the door, and then I shut off the lights and closed up.

Upstairs, loud voices indicated the Grimaldis were still conducting their business, but I didn't have time to hang around and wait for a better time to leave. So I tucked my head down, gripped my bag strap tighter, and made a beeline for the exit.

I almost made it, too.

Right as I approached the door that would take me out to my car, a commotion startled me and I spun around to find Mr. Grimaldi's captive had escaped—somehow—and was running full sprint toward me. Or, toward the exit, but I happened to be standing right there in front of it.

The shock held me immobile, and I barely managed to gasp before a gunshot rang out. Wetness splattered my face, making me flinch, and then silence fell.

Then Mr. Grimaldi was shouting obscenities at his men, cursing them out for what was clearly someone's fuck up, and offering me his silk handkerchief.

"Tristian, I am so sorry," the terrifying old man apologized as I wiped blood from my cheeks. Holy shit. "This is so unprofessional, I'm terribly embarrassed. Jonas! Call Naomi and tell her to bring replacement clothing for Tristian!"

"No, no, I'm fine," I quickly reassured my boss, continuing to wipe my face off. Gross. Did I need an HIV test now? "Really, Mr. Grimaldi, that's kind of you, but I'm late for school." And my hands were shaking. The last thing I wanted to do was hang around and watch them clean up the dead body in the hallway. Especially with Dexter watching me like a piranha on meat.

"Tristian, you must let me—" my boss was saying, but I already had the door open and was making a speedy exit.

I kept his handkerchief but gave a bright wave to cover my internal panic. "Nothing to worry about, sir. I'll see you on Thursday. Have a great dead! I mean, day. Shit. Have a great day!"

My hurry to get into my car was so all-consuming, I didn't even notice I'd dropped my sweatshirt until I was five minutes down the road.

"Fuck," I whispered, looking down at my white blouse. My white, *blood-splattered* blouse. "God damn it."

Maybe it would wash out, if I had enough time to stop by the ladies' room before class with *Professor* John.

Tuesdays *sucked*.

seven

JOHN

The anticipation of seeing Tristian today had me all jittery. I badly needed to move up my timeline and recover those weeks I lost chasing Dr. Bailey like a fool, but Tristian was playing disinterested like it was an Olympic event. She also didn't seem to be the kind of girl who responded to an aggressive, forceful approach. More's the shame in that.

Would she even turn up for class today? She was technically my TA now, it was part of her job. Right? She *had* to show up.

In my excitement, I got there early. Then I had to wait, making casual small talk with a couple of the grad students who'd decided to start sucking up to the new professor early. I kept one eye on the door, though, and nearly swallowed my tongue when she sauntered in with about ten seconds to spare.

She wore black high heels, sheer stockings, a crimson-and-cream patterned blouse, and a matching wine-colored skirt that swayed way too temptingly as she walked across the floor to the TA desk at the side of the room. More than that, she wore an aggressive, distracted frown on her pretty face that made me desperate to know what'd happened before she came to class.

Politely, I excused myself from the students, telling them to take their seats before I moved closer to Tristian.

"Good afternoon, Miss Ives," I greeted her cautiously, studying her body language as she pulled out a laptop and booted it up. She flinched when I spoke, and it took all my control not to grab her and demand answers. "Are you okay?" I asked instead.

"Fine," she snapped, not even looking at me. Her spine was rigid, and her toe tapped nervously on the floor. When I said nothing more, just watched her, she blew out a breath and raised her eyes to mine. "Shouldn't you be starting the class, Professor?"

I frowned. Her cheeks were pinker than usual, but it wasn't her usual pretty blush when she spoke to me. It was more like she'd just scrubbed her makeup off and hadn't had time to reapply.

"I asked you a question, Miss Ives," I replied in a firmer tone. "Are you okay?"

Her eyes widened slightly, but she didn't look away. Nor did she answer immediately, and for a moment I let myself drown in her unusual pale blue eyes. Then she swallowed and gave a small nod.

"I'm fine," she lied. "Just tired. Do you need Dr. Bailey's notes for this seminar?"

She was brushing it off, whatever *it* was, and I made a mental note to work it out later. For now, she was here with me and seemed uninjured. That'd have to do.

"Sure, I'll take a glance," I agreed. Then, rather than having her send the file to my computer at the lectern, I just braced my hand on the back of her chair to lean down and peer at her screen.

Fuck the notes, I just wanted to get into her personal space, and her hair smelled just as amazing as when she'd flipped it in my face last week. There was a metallic, chemical undertone, though. Something I couldn't place. What *had* she been doing this morning?

Then, entirely unintentionally, I glanced at the front of her blouse. It was buttoned low, the edges of her white lace bra peeking out and pushing her perfect tits up like she was—

"Is that blood?" I asked, reaching out to swipe a spec of reddish brown from the swell of her breast before I could stop myself. Luckily she slapped my hand away before I could actually touch her, because *what the fuck was I thinking?*

She scowled pure venom up at me. "It's paint," she snapped, pulling her patterned shirt closed over her bust. Then I squinted harder at the silk fabric, which was suspiciously blood-colored itself.

Before I could form the question, though, she cut me off. "Do you have a particular interest in women's fashion, Professor Smith? I assume that's the reason why you're staring so hard at my designer blouse?"

Huh. Maybe I was being paranoid. And considering I'd just nearly touched her breast in front of more than a hundred students, I should *probably* ease off. For now.

Reluctantly I straightened up and shifted gears back into Professor mode. Maybe Tris had a student/teacher kink that I could lean into? Nah, she wouldn't make things so easy. I'd have to win her over another way. Starting with eliminating the competition.

Remaining focused on teaching grad students about iconoclastic representations in Western culture for the next three hours was pure torture. I kept Tristian in my peripheral vision the whole time, but she didn't glance up from her computer even once. Dammit. She was so far off where I needed her to be, and I was at a loss for how to catch *and hold* her attention long enough to pull off this heist.

To my surprise, though, she didn't immediately jump out of her seat when the class ended. Instead, she seemed lost in thought as she stared at her screen, like she hadn't fully registered that we were done.

"How was your date?" I asked, breaking her focus as the last of the grad students filed out.

She blinked in confusion, looking up at me as I moved closer. "Huh?"

I gave a half smile, getting a little hit of satisfaction when her attention shifted ever so briefly to my mouth once more. "Your date," I repeated. "Last night. Golf-prick Brad?"

She gave a huff of laughter. "I didn't have a date last night, and even if I did it wouldn't have been with *Chad*."

Why did that information please me so much? Stupid fucking Chad. "So what did you have on, if it wasn't a date?"

A small grin flashed across her face before she wiped it away. "Like I said yesterday, it's none of your business." She closed her laptop and slid it back into her bag before standing up to gather the rest of her things.

My mind scrambled for something else to say, something to engage her in more conversation, but...

came up blank. All I could focus on was how fucking short the skirt was as she bent over to retrieve a dropped pen, and how good she'd look bent over and—

Shit. *Focus.*

Seducing Tristian was a means to an end, nothing more. Would I enjoy it? Hell yes. But the second I was done using her, I'd be gone. In no way could I afford to let myself become attached to this prickly woman.

"I'll see you tomorrow, Professor Smith," she told me, slinging her bag over her shoulder and starting for the door without even waiting for me to reply.

"It's *John,*" I corrected her, clenching my jaw to stop myself from trying to ask her out again. That approach wasn't working on her. I needed to stop trying.

She didn't even reply to that, just extended her middle finger over her shoulder as if on reflex. Or maybe she thought I wasn't looking. Either way, it made me laugh.

I packed up my own bag, then ever-so-casually followed her at a distance again. This time she went into town and pulled up outside a clothing boutique. I decided to wait in my car while she went inside, thinking nothing much of it. She returned to her car only a few minutes later, though, wearing a new outfit and carrying a bag branded with the boutique's logo. She paused a moment, shoving the whole bag into a trash can, then climbed back into her car, wearing her new clothes.

It was such an odd thing to do that I let her leave without following. Instead, I waited until she was out of sight and got out of my car to retrieve the bag from the trash. A quick peek inside confirmed what I was already suspicious of. Her clothes she'd worn today were balled up inside.

"Designer pattern, my fucking ass," I muttered, rubbing the silk of her blouse between my fingers and noting how the dried blood flaked off.

What the *fuck* had happened to her before class? Clearly she'd had no time to go home and change, and I was torn between feeling horrified and insanely impressed that she'd just doubled down and pretended it was fashion.

I kept the blouse, climbing back into my car. If anything, it confirmed my assumption that she was working for the Grimaldis. How *else* would she be covered in blood that definitely wasn't her own?

Frustratingly, though, I had no idea where she'd just gone in her sexy new outfit. It couldn't have been home, or why would she *buy* clothes instead of just changing them? Crap. She must be meeting another date. Not Chad—she'd given a little nose wrinkle when she said his name earlier—so...someone else?

I hedged my bets and parked out back of the same bar I'd found her at the first night. Maybe it was a favorite of hers or something? And they served tasty wings, so that was decent incentive.

"Hey, you're back," a pretty blonde greeted me with a grin as I headed inside. "John, right?"

I studied her face a moment, then let an easy smile slip over my lips. "That's right, Krista."

Those eyelashes fluttered again. "You remembered!"

My gaze was already darting around the bar, though, and satisfaction surged when I spotted my beautiful TA. "I'm actually here to meet someone," I told the flirty bartender. Without sticking around for more small talk, I headed toward the table Tristian was sitting at, studying a menu. Before I got to her, though, a guy got there ahead of me.

I paused, watching as she greeted him with a lukewarm smile and kiss on the cheek. He slid into the booth right beside her, his hand disappearing under the table as he leaned in close. Was it on her leg?

"Professor Smith?" someone asked, jerking my attention away from Tris.

I turned to face the girl who'd spoken, recognizing her as one of my grad students. "Yes…?" I left the question hanging, waiting for her to fill in the blank with her name.

"Janie," she told me with a smile, "Janie Hartman. Um, are you here with anyone?" My brows rose at what sounded a whole lot like a proposition and she instantly blushed. "Oh, no, I didn't mean—I wasn't—Um, I just wanted to maybe buy you a drink and ask you some questions about some ideas I had for my thesis opening statement, and maybe the possibility of future TA opportunities?"

She was cute, Janie Hartman. Maybe twenty-five with honey blonde hair and an hourglass figure. She was taller than Tris, but still short against me. I wasn't interested in casual hookups, but maybe it'd water down the level-ten stalker vibes I was starting to exude around Tristian. So I gave a gracious nod and indicated an empty table close enough to Tris that I might keep an eye on her date.

"Of course you can, Janie," I agreed. "I love to talk Flemish portraiture over drinks." Since that was her area of specialty from my memory of student notes.

To my surprise, Janie was actually good company. She was intelligent and charismatic, easily sucking me into genuine conversation rather than the ruse I'd intended. So much so, I forgot I was keeping an eye on Tristian until she was standing beside my seat with a glare set on her face.

"John," she said on a sharp exhale, "can I speak with you for a moment?"

The temptation to say *no* and brush her off was so strong I could taste it. But ultimately, I wasn't in Whispering Willows to get laid by cute grad students. Tristian was my quarry, so I needed to play the game *with her*.

"Janie, I apologize," I said to my companion, turning the charm up to max factor. "Miss Ives just can't get enough of me during class, it seems." I meant that to sound every bit as suggestive as it came out, and Janie's eyes widened.

"I don't blame her," she muttered under her breath as she took a sip of her drink, and I held back a grin. Sliding out of my seat, I lightly touched a hand to Tristian's back—pretending like it was a crowded bar thing, when I really just wanted to touch her.

Her shoulders tensed, and she led the way across the bar to where it was marginally quieter beside the pool tables. She spun around to face me with her back to the wall, her arms folded under her breasts.

"Are you following me again?" she demanded, cutting straight to the chase.

I frowned in fake confusion. "Um…Tristian, you approached me. I was having a drink with Janie, so I didn't even know you were here." Lies.

She scowled, not buying my shit for even a second. I liked that about her, never second guessing herself. "In case things were run differently at your old university, Professor, it's prohibited for faculty to fraternize with students. Janie could get you into a lot of trouble."

I smirked, closing the gap between us and bending down closer to her face. I didn't touch her, not even a finger. But my lips were close enough to her ear that my breath would warm her skin as I spoke.

"Rules are meant to be broken, Miss Ives."

Her breathing hitched, and I resisted the urge to pin her against that wall and kiss her properly breathless.

"I don't know what game you're playing, John," she whispered, her voice shaking, "but if you think—"

"Yes you do," I corrected. "You're playing it, too. When you want to stop pretending you're not, you've got my number."

I forced myself to straighten up and shift away, my gaze tracking over her from head to toe. I didn't hide it, either, and a visible shiver ran through her. Perfect.

"I can see I'm distracting you from your date, though, so I'll take Janie home and leave you in peace." I smiled, and started to walk away, back to my table.

"I thought you weren't following me," Tristian spoke up, pausing me. "So how'd you know I was on a date?"

I didn't answer her, just continued back to Janie. A

few whispered words had her leaving the bar with me in minutes, but I wasn't in the mood to fuck around. As soon as we were out of the bar, I politely reestablished professional boundaries and drove Janie home.

There was only one infuriating woman on my mind when I got home to my bed, *alone*.

Tristian Ives.

eight

TRIS

That smooth-talking, lush-lipped, infuriatingly tall *motherfucker* ruined yet another date night. Despite how vaguely sure I was that Oliver was a great lay, the second John walked out the door with that slutty bitch Janie, I lost interest.

Okay. That wasn't fair. Janie was a perfectly lovely girl and I knew better than to villainize another woman to soothe my own weird jealousy issues. I wasn't even interested in John, so why the hell I cared who he went home with, I didn't know.

Maybe I was just concerned for my own job security? Yeah, sure, that was it. I wasn't *jealous;* I was *worried*. Because if John got fired for sleeping with a student then I might lose my TA position, and I really didn't want that.

That was the story I stuck to in my mind as I made a lame excuse to end my date—fully-clothed—and headed back to my loft apartment.

Hank was getting home at the same time as me, and he gave me a pointed look when I smacked the elevator call button just a touch harder than necessary.

"Bad date with the sexy Brit tonight?" he asked, arching a brow.

I glared back at him. "I wouldn't date that smug, arrogant prick if he was the last man on Earth."

Hank tipped his head to the side, clearly confused. Then I realized he was talking about my *date,* Oliver. Not John. Fucking hell, maybe I had an accent kink?

"Sorry," I muttered, "Um Oliver. Yeah, he's less interesting when I'm sober, to be fair."

Hank was too damn perceptive though. "Oh, I *see*... the mysterious John Smith is *British*? You left that part out the other night."

I rolled my eyes and changed the subject. "You're home late. Trouble at work?"

He shook his head. "Not at all, I just had a late meeting with my client from Australia." Hank was an interior designer, which was why our apartments were so gorgeous. He often worked with clients from all around the world, flying internationally more often than an arms dealer.

I just nodded, silently stepping into the elevator and pressing the button for our shared floor. He was squinting at me, his gaze like a laser beam.

"You seem tense, Ivy," he commented after a long moment of quiet. "Did something else happen?"

"Else?"

He gave me a warm grin. "Other than running into John."

I grimaced, thinking of the scene at RBD's and how I'd stubbornly refused to be late to class, so I pretended the blood on my blouse was part of the pattern. "Just a… colorful day at work."

Hank's brows hitched. "Oh?"

Giving him a tight-lipped smile, I shrugged. "You know how it goes. What happens at RBD's…"

"Stays there," he finished in a murmur. "I know." He didn't look even remotely reassured by that. If anything, he was *more* concerned despite the fact that I'd gone into my job with the Grimaldis with eyes wide open. I knew the risks and accepted them. Incidents like today, with the man being shot in front of me, were rare.

Our elevator doors opened, and Hank touched his hand to my arm gently as I moved toward my door. "Why don't you come in for some late dinner? I'm sure Nelson will be waiting up for me anyway."

"Undoubtedly," I agreed, "But no, I'm good. I need to

get into the studio tonight before I fall asleep." It calmed me down to paint. Grounded me. And holy shit I needed a shower; the brief cleanup I'd done before class with baby wipes really hadn't made me *feel* clean.

Hank still looked worried, so I grabbed him in a warm hug. "I'm fine, worry-wort. I promise. Tell Nelson to keep working on that ring. It's not his best work yet."

He gave a bark of laughter, squeezing me back. "You're asking for trouble with comments like that, Ives."

I grinned, bidding him a good night before letting myself into my apartment. The door clicked shut behind me, and I locked it on habit. A twenty-four-year-old woman living alone couldn't be too careful these days, and Nelson was a bear for making sure I stayed safe. Shit like locking my door just came as second nature these days.

Just being home in my own space eased a huge amount of tension out of my mind, and I breathed deeply as I headed for the shower. I'd tossed my blood-stained clothes in the trash, but I needed a full scrub down before I could really feel clean.

I paused a moment to turn on my stereo, pumping music through the whole apartment, then continued on to my enormous bathroom. There was no hurry to get out of the shower quickly, so I took my time scrubbing every inch of myself and washing my hair several times. I wanted to make sure *every* droplet of blood was gone.

Eventually, I turned the water off and stepped out to dry off. My long hair went into a twisty-towel to keep it out of the way, and I wandered my naked ass through to my art studio without bothering to get dressed. I freaking loved living alone.

I'd been working on a classical-style piece for a while, on and off as the mood struck, so I tugged the drop cloth off and prepped my paints and brushes. There was no better way to clear my mind and shed the violence of the day than painting naked with *Loveless* playing through the speakers.

This time, though, I couldn't seem to get my head clear. Every time I started slipping into the *zone,* John's infuriating face popped into my mind. His disgusted tone as he called my *Renaissance Lady* painting *awful.* Prick. Like he was even remotely qualified to cast judgment on the topic.

Professor of Art History didn't make him an *artist.* So…fuck him and his blatant lack of good taste.

And yet. There he was, crowding my mind and frankly *ruining* my favorite activity. So I quickly gave up and left my studio once more. Probably a good thing, since I needed to meet him at five in the morning for our first *mentor* session.

Groaning at the prospect, I climbed into bed and screamed into my pillow to let off steam. When that didn't work, I grabbed my phone and checked my messages. Sure enough, Chad had sent a dick pic. He'd sent several, daily, ever since I fucked him simply to spite John and his smug assumption that Chad would be crap in bed. He was right, but Chad wasn't taking the hint that I wouldn't be coming back for seconds. Thus, the dick pics.

I mean, fair call on his part. It was a nice dick, just a shame he had *no idea* how to use it. Poor thing. But he'd do for a visual while letting my imagination—and vibrator—do the rest of the work. Wetting my lips, I typed out a message to Chad, requesting a video. Not even a flicker of guilt touched me as I grabbed out my rabbit and waited for the response.

Sure enough, my phone pinged with a video less than a minute later. It was a five minute clip, so clearly one he had already prepared in his archive. Smiling to myself, I pressed play and slid my rabbit under the covers to blow off some steam in another way.

On the screen, Chad's hand stroked his thick length and I let my imagination wander. In my head, Chad was a nameless, faceless guy with *way* better conversation skills. He also knew what he was doing with that pretty cock.

A low groan escaped my throat as I fucked myself, letting the little buzzing rabbit ears do their magical thing on my clit. I pictured imagination-Chad pinning me down to the bed with his huge body, my legs spreading wider apart to accommodate his size.

"Shit," I gasped, my spine arching as my finger slipped, turning the vibrator up another notch of intensity. Imaginary-Chad was kissing me now, his lush lips consuming me, trailing down my jaw and sucking the sensitive skin of my neck. I was so close to coming, and my gaze flicked back to the video playing on the screen.

Real-Chad came all over his own stomach, jets of cum squirting from his dick, and imagination-Chad whispered dirty things in my ear.

My own climax hit me hard, and I shuddered through it, my toes curling into the mattress as imagination-Chad purred praise in his sexy accent.

Wait.

Chad didn't have an accent. Or lush, pillowy lips. Or...*fuck a goddamn duck!*

"No," I breathed out loud. "You did *not* just creep into my head while I got off!"

But...sure enough, there he was. Not imagination-*Chad* at all...but imagination-*John*. Crap!

"Doesn't mean anything," I told myself, tossing my

rabbit aside and wetting my lips. "Just means he's in my head, not that I'm attracted to him."

Sure. That seemed plausible.

My phone beeped, and I saw Chad's request for a reciprocal video from me. Fuck that. I closed the thread without responding and set my alarm for the morning. How in the hell I would be able to look *Professor Smith* in the eye after what I'd just done, I had no idea. But I didn't back down from anything, no matter how uncomfortable it might be. So I'd go and put on a brave face. And never, ever, *ever* let him into my head while masturbating again.

Sheesh. I needed to sleep.

nine

JOHN

Tristian Ives haunted my dreams after I left her at that bar with her *date*, and I found myself waking a full hour before my alarm was due to go off. Which probably wasn't the worst thing in the world, because I needed to squeeze in a workout before she arrived for our first mentoring session anyway.

I'd never been fond of exercise as a child, but after my grandfather took me in—when the authorities removed me from my father's care—I'd come to appreciate the importance of remaining physically fit. After all, I couldn't escape pursuit easily if I was winded and slow.

As it turned out, though, I wouldn't have time for a workout. I wouldn't have time for my *session* with Tris, either, which was more irritating than anything.

The email waiting in my encrypted inbox couldn't be ignored, though.

Blowing out a long breath, I calculated the time and distance required for the job I'd just been asked to do. If I left *right* now, I could be back within a few days. But where would that leave me on my task to seduce Tristian? Would my *Poppy Flowers* still be waiting when I returned?

"Dammit," I whispered, but scrolled through my contacts to find the number of one of my very best customers. She'd purchased from me more times than I could count, but this was a first.

"John, sweetheart, thank you for calling," the elderly woman said on answering my call. "I hope I'm not pushing the friendship too far with my request?"

I gave a short laugh. "Are we friends, Constance?"

"As close as people like us ever get, I think. So, can you help me out?" Straight to the point, as always.

I rubbed a hand over my face, thinking it over again. I was close enough, so it shouldn't take *too* much time away from Tristian—and The Game. "Of course," I replied, catching her tiny sigh of relief. "There is the small matter of payment, however..."

I enjoyed my work, but I wasn't a fucking charity. Okay, I wasn't *always* a charity. On occasion I did take a job that simply needed to tip the balance a little, or to help someone out who didn't have the means to pay. Constance D'Ath didn't qualify for that kind of discount.

"Whatever it costs, John, I'm happy to pay. It's taken me a very long time to track down this item, and it holds a lot of sentimental value to me."

That was what I liked to hear. "Alright. I'll be in touch when I have it secured."

"Thank you, John. I appreciate it."

Curiosity played a big part in my acceptance of Constance's job. After ending my call to her, I logged into my secure server to review all my prior transactions with the D'Ath matriarch. For the most part, she purchased artwork and jewels from me. But there was also a curiously high number of weapons among her purchases. Maybe she was a collector.

With as many things as I stole over my lifetime, it was easy to let them fade in my memory. Especially when they held no sentimental value to *me*. Most of the items Connie bought had only represented a dollar amount that allowed me to expand my network and upgrade my tools.

Of course, she didn't know about the priceless pink diamond I stole from her grandson's wife a few years ago. That one had been a personal challenge and one I was particularly proud of.

I packed a bag quickly, then hesitated when I started

to type out a message to Tris. I needed to let her know that our session today would be canceled and that I wasn't available to teach Dr. Bailey's classes for at least two days—something she'd need to cover. But instead I closed the message screen and put my phone in my pocket.

Ten minutes later, I found myself breaking into her loft apartment.

I nearly talked myself out of it six dozen times, but I was a man possessed as I unlocked her sixth floor window from the outside and let myself silently inside. I'd done plenty of surveillance on her building in the last few days, but this was my first time inside.

My brows hitched as I looked around the dark, open-plan loft. This was *not* student accommodation, not by a long shot. The Grimaldi family must have paid well.

The "bedroom" was in the corner of the building with a half wall acting as a headboard, allowing Tristian's huge bed to face the double height, seamless corner windows. It meant that I didn't lay eyes on her sleeping form until I was only feet away.

Then I froze. Fucking *froze.*

Tristian Ives slept naked...and had kicked the covers off entirely.

I swallowed hard, the small sound thundering in my

ears like a siren. I really, *really* shouldn't be here. Talk about playing with fire.

Was it the first time I'd crept around someone's house while they slept? God no. It wasn't even the dozenth time. But it was the first time I'd broken in without a *purpose*. I hadn't come to steal anything from Tris…or nothing tangible, anyway.

For several long moments, I just stood there, not moving, barely breathing. Staring. Then my gaze snagged on a familiar object tangled in her sheets and I cracked a smile. The painting hanging outside the Boles administration office was apparently more true to life than I'd guessed.

I needed to leave before I did something dumb and woke her up. Then how the fuck would I explain myself? I needed to just…go back the way I'd come, get in my car and *text her* like a normal person. Right?

Right. That's what I needed to do.

With astronomical effort, I forced myself to back away and slide back out the window I'd entered from. If nothing else, I needed to be gone before the sun came up and someone spotted my six-foot-five ass scaling the side of a building.

As I made my silent, stealthy escape, the distinctive sound of a cell phone alarm reached my ears, followed by a feminine moan that made me stiffen up…in more ways than one. Then, faintly, Tristian's sleepy shout.

"Fucking John Smith," she cursed. "Dream stealing fuck-bag!"

I grinned, but didn't hang around to hear any more. What did she mean by *that* though? Had she been dreaming about me? While naked? With her vibrator…? Oh man. Now I was really regretting accepting Constance's job.

Back in my car, I stared up at Tristian's window, watching like a stalker as the lights turned on. My phone was in my hand, the professional, polite message all typed out ready to send. But instead of sending it, I closed the thread and called one of my contacts to do some digging on Connie's job instead.

It was a decent drive from Whispering Willows to Shadow Grove, so I swapped out my car in the next big, anonymous city. One of my favorite things about visiting Shadow Grove was that a Porsche made me less noticeable than a Prius. New—bloody—money had been happily buying up properties under Timberwolf rule for several years, knowing it was "safe" territory. Like the Hamptons for criminals. It was cute and comfortable. I'd enjoyed my time there during the last Game.

I checked my phone far too often while I drove.

Would she text me? When she arrived at my house for our scheduled meeting time and found it empty…would she call? Or would she second guess herself and assume she'd got the time wrong?

Maybe she'd be seething mad and turn up at my class, ready to spit fire-balls and find me not there either.

I smiled to myself at that mental image. Something about Tristian made me *enjoy* infuriating her…like she infuriated me. Tit for tat and all that. I hoped she was utterly *furious* at being "stood up" and then she'd have to marinate on that feeling for days until I returned.

Or maybe she'd be concerned? Nah, doubtful.

My heart raced when my phone rang, but it wasn't her.

"Why are you leaving town, son?" the caller asked, not bothering to say hello. My irritation instantly shifted to ice cold, and I ground my teeth together. He was watching me, and in Whispering Willows. That meant he was closer than I'd realized.

"None of your fucking business," I snapped back, aware it was pointless to hang up. He'd just call again, and really, I had nothing better to do while driving. I might as well let this washed up old bastard help sharpen my focus.

He huffed a laugh. "You got a lead, kid? Maybe I

should tail you…let you lead me right to the painting, eh?"

I rolled my eyes. As if I'd ever be that stupid. Then again, I hadn't noticed he was watching me in Whispering Willows. "That's your problem, isn't it?" I sneered. "Always riding someone else's coattails and expecting to just cheat your way to success. How are you even still alive?"

His response was another laugh, louder this time, like I'd just cracked a crazy joke. Maybe he was drunk or fucked up on drugs. Story of my life. Or my childhood, anyway. Until he'd disappeared for a week and our neighbor reported me to authorities for living alone.

Igor's drug addiction had actually been the best thing he could have ever done for me. It was the reason Christophe had taken me in, raised me, and taught me his craft. Now all of a sudden Igor was back, and somehow he'd cheated his way into the final round of the Game. My father was full of fucking surprises.

"This is quite the conundrum, isn't it? Do I assume you've got new intel and follow you, or stay here in town with my eye on the Grimaldis, hmm? Maybe I just keep my eyes on that gorgeous teaching assistant of yours, huh, my boy?" he taunted, making my eye twitch with anger.

"I'm not your anything, Igor," I drawled, refusing to

let him hear the hatred I felt toward him. "But if you want my advice, I'd suggest you quit now while you're ahead. If the committee thinks you're even thinking about breaking the rules of The Game, you'll lose your collateral. I bet you won't have anything left after that."

My father was a decent thief but a terrible card player, and an addict to boot. Anything he stole would be simply funding his debts. I must have struck a nerve there, because he didn't laugh. Instead, he spat some empty threat and ended the call.

Of all the thieves in the whole damn world, it just *had* to be him in the final three. Then again, I should have seen it coming. Igor had a chip on his shoulder the size of Russia, after his father—my grandfather—had left him to be raised by his mother. Meanwhile, Christophe was off making his name as one of the world's best thieves, building his personal wealth to colossal amounts and never looking back.

After I was taken away from Igor by authorities, then raised by Christophe himself, things had gotten nasty. In Igor's mind, I had the life he was *supposed* to have had. Since my grandfather passed, I'd known Igor would be back. He wanted his pound of flesh out of the Valenshek estate, and I'd do anything possible to ensure he never got it.

Even if that meant walking over Tristian in the process.

I wish she would call.

ten

TRIS

Darkness should have been my first hint that John wasn't awake when I arrived for our first meeting. Or, shit, he wasn't even *home* because there was no way in hell he slept through the way I pounded on his door. Eventually, because it was getting embarrassing, I gave up and accepted the fact that either we got our schedules wrong, or he'd forgotten.

Frustrated, I decided to head over to the campus diner to get coffee and breakfast, and spent the next two hours working on my dissertation alone. Which suited me *perfectly* fine, to be fair. To say I was one hundred percent focused would be a lie, though. I spent half the time staring at my phone and wondering why the hell

John hadn't messaged me if he had something else going on.

He hadn't just overslept; he wasn't *home*. Which then made me wonder, where *was* he? At Janie's house? Fuck, I bet he was. He just had that smug man-whore energy that told me he'd probably already slept with half the students in his classes, since he only taught undergrad and graduate courses.

Gross. What an abuse of power. Dr. Bailey wouldn't *dream* of being so unprofessional. He was also pushing eighty, but that was beside the point. I'd bet money that Janie would get perfect marks for Art History this semester, too.

Or, shit, maybe not. I guess it would depend on how good she was in bed. John seemed like the kind of egotistical prick who'd lower a girl's grade if she had sub-par blow-job skills. Like maybe he only gave out an A+ if she paid extra attention to his balls or slipped a finger up his ass?

"Great," I muttered aloud, raking my fingers through my hair. "Now I'm thinking about John's balls and asshole."

"What?" someone said, making me startle. Then I tried really hard not to roll my eyes when I realized who it was that just interrupted my train of thought.

With a sigh, I mustered up a smile. "Hey, Chad. What are you doing here?"

He slid into the booth opposite me without an invitation. Groan. I knew asking for that video was going to bite me in the ass. Should have just stuck with good old porn websites.

"I was grabbing coffee before my first booking for the day, saw you sitting here all lonely like you were waiting for me..." His wink was loaded, and I felt nothing but distaste. Still, I had no one to blame but myself, so I drew a deep breath to rip off the Band-Aid.

"Listen, Chad," I said gently, closing my laptop to give him my full attention. "I think I might have given you the wrong impression."

His brows knitted together. "Uh, babe, trust me, you're giving all the *right* impressions. Don't even stress it. I know you're just crazy addicted to my body. I get it a lot."

I winced and tried not to look repulsed. If there was one thing that could *really* ruin a handsome guy, it was a shitty personality. Checking my watch, I realized I needed to head to class, anyway.

"Uh, yeah, that's not it," I quickly corrected Chad while packing up my stuff. "Look, don't take this the wrong way or anything, but—"

"Let me guess," he cut me off, sneering with an angry glint in his eye. "It's not me, it's you?"

Well…at least he was taking the hint. But that tone of voice pissed me off so I gave a harsh laugh. "Actually, Chad, it's you. So…bye." I hitched my bag over my shoulder and made a speedy exit, paying the waitress on my way out and telling her to keep the change.

Anxiety and anticipation swirled through my stomach as I made my way across the campus to my eight-thirty lecture with Professor Smith. I wanted to get there a few minutes early, so I could grill him on why the fuck he'd stood me up for our meeting.

The whole way, I psyched myself up to hand him his ass for messing me around. So much so that I was practically bursting with outrage and indignation when I burst through the classroom door, only to find he wasn't there either.

Frowning, I stood there staring at the empty desk and lectern for a minute, then shifted my attention to some of the students unpacking their computers and notes in the front row.

"Has Jo—uh, Professor Smith been in yet?" I asked, indicating the spot he was supposed to be occupying.

The guy just shook his head and returned to what he was doing.

I made my way over to the teaching desk, dropping

my own bag and pulling out my phone. Maybe he'd had something come up and needed to leave in a hurry? But surely he'd have called or messaged, and my phone showed neither.

What the fuck?

My irritation and anxiety built with every passing minute until eventually—when the class was supposed to start ten minutes ago—I accepted the fact he wasn't turning up. Gritting my teeth with fury, I pulled up one of Dr. Bailey's lessons on my screen and fumbled my way through the lecture totally off balance.

By the time the class finished, I'd flip-flopped between worried and irate so many times I was exhausted. My phone hadn't beeped. Not even once. What the *fuck*?

As I left the university, heading for my car, I pulled up his contact in my phone. I should call and make sure he was alive, right? What if he'd been in a car crash and was lying in a ditch somewhere?

It'd probably serve him fucking right if he was.

Ugh, okay uncalled-for. No one *deserved* that, but I seriously doubted that was what'd happened. He'd probably just hooked up with some stranger and lost track of time. In which case, I wasn't going to stroke his ego by calling to check up on him. Nope, fuck that. He can just wallow in guilt for all I cared.

Besides, I had more pressing concerns to deal with. Like returning to RBD's for work after the whole covered-in-blood incident.

My instincts screamed at me to run away. Just send in my resignation by email and never return to the Grimaldi estate. But my stubborn pride hissed at the idea like it was poisonous, so twenty minutes later I strode into RBD's like nothing had ever happened. I had to hand it to his cleaner, the hallway was *spotless,* and that in itself nearly made my confidence falter. He'd erased that man's death like...well, *exactly* like it'd never happened.

Swallowing my feelings, I stiffened my spine and continued past the ballroom without a second glance, keeping my eyes on my destination. I'd almost made it when I heard my name.

"Tristian, thank God you're here." Mr. Grimaldi's assistant, Naomi, came hurrying toward me with a garment bag slung over her arm. "This is for you." She handed over the bag. "And this, too." She held out a sealed envelope, waiting for me to take it.

My brows hitched, but she just shrugged. "I was told to make sure I put it in your hands, if you showed up for work. So..." She flapped the envelope, urging me to take it. Reluctantly, I relieved her of it and she flashed me a polite smile. "Thanks. Have a great day, Tristian."

I'd only ever spoken to Naomi in passing, but she was all business. So it didn't even slightly surprise me when she disappeared without any further explanation, leaving me to slip into the gallery with my hands full.

Once I was inside and the door was secure behind me, I let out a long breath and slipped out of my shoes. I tucked the envelope into my bag to investigate later. Whatever it was, it could wait. Not that I thought Mr. Grimaldi would be firing me…it was probably cash to politely request I keep my mouth shut about the dead man.

All the paintings were exactly as I'd left them, so I made my way into the workshop and started work. As always, it was easy to zone out, so when I eventually noticed someone knocking on the gallery door, I had no idea how long they'd been waiting.

"Shit," I whispered, realizing my shift was over already. Time had *flown.* "Just a minute!" I called out. Quickly, and carefully, I went through my routine of packing up my work station and ensuring everything was securely locked before I grabbed my bag and hurried across to the main gallery door.

My shoes were where I'd left them, so I slipped them on before opening the door.

"Oh," I gasped, instantly cursing myself for not ignoring the knocks. "Dexter. You startled me."

He was *right* there, giving me no space to exit the gallery without brushing up against him, so I just stayed where I was, blocking the door and holding it firm.

"Naomi told me she saw you earlier," he whispered, like that was a secret or some shit. "I had to come down and make sure you're okay, after—"

"Yep, totally fine," I cut him off. "Thanks for checking, though. I should get going."

Dexter didn't move. "What's the hurry? I thought maybe we could spend some time together..." He reached out and traced a finger down my cheek, making me flinch. He saw it, and his eyes narrowed.

"I have assignments to work on," I replied with a tight smile. "So, maybe another day."

He still didn't move out of my way, so I gritted my teeth and stepped closer so I could fully close the gallery door behind myself. As uncomfortable as Dexter made me, I wasn't going to abandon the gallery security.

"Count on it," he told me in a low voice, like I'd just offered to blow him next week.

"Dexter!" my savior, Mr. Grimaldi, bellowed from somewhere nearby. "Where are you?"

Dexter didn't immediately reply, still staring down at me as I shifted awkwardly from foot to foot. Then he gave a cold smile as he stepped back. "Here, sir! Just chatting with Tris."

Mr. Grimaldi came into view then, scowling at his youngest son. "Harassing her, more like. Leave my employees alone, Dexter, or we will have trouble."

Anger rippled through Dexter and I edged past him as quickly as I could, shooting Mr. Grimaldi an appreciative smile.

"Tristian, sweetheart," my elderly employer stopped me before I could scurry away. "Naomi said she saw you earlier. Did she give you the new blouse?"

I blinked stupidly for a moment, then remembered the garment bag. I'd hung it up in my workshop and forgotten all about it. "Oh, yes, she did. Thank you, sir, that's entirely unnecessary."

He huffed a sound of annoyance. "It was more than necessary after that distasteful scene yesterday, but I'm glad to see you back. I knew you were made of tougher stuff than some of my previous employees. Did Naomi also give you the invitation?"

"The…invitation?" So it wasn't a payoff. "Yes, of course. Thank you."

Mr. Grimaldi smiled wide. "Perfect! So, you'll be there?"

"Um…" My gaze flicked to Dexter, still glowering at his father. Fuck he scared me. "I'll do my best," I finally answered. I hadn't even opened the damn envelope so had no clue what I'd be agreeing to.

Mr. Grimaldi clapped his hands together, beaming. "Great!" His gaze shifted from me, to his son still hovering and staring, then back to me. "Let me walk with you out to your car, Tristian."

Thank fuck for that. I let out a slow breath of relief and accepted his offer, walking with him out to where I'd left my Corolla around the side of the house. He gave my twenty-year-old car a long look, then quirked a brow at me.

"This is what you drive, Tristian?" His accent on my name always sounded so exotic.

I smiled, unlocking the door. "Sure is. Thank you for the blouse, sir. See you Friday!"

Quickly, before he could say anything more, I slipped into my seat and pulled the door closed with a heavy *thunk*. Then I waved at him brightly as I reversed out of my parking spot and headed home. For the head of a crime family, Mr. Grimaldi was just a lovely old man.

eleven

JOHN

She'd fucking ruined my whole damn day. No, my *week*. Probably. Because there I was, in my happy place—stealing shit—and I couldn't even enjoy it because I was thinking about her. Tristian. Fucking hell, was this something Christophe had planned before he died? I wouldn't even put it past him to be fair. The old goat was constantly trying to set me up.

Constance's job was to steal a pair of matching two-hundred-layer twisted Damascus blades from a deceased estate. Her husband had been a hell of a bladesmith before he died and had often gifted his creations to friends or trainees. In this case, the owner had recently passed and his widow refused to sell them back to Constance.

So here I was, attending the man's wake to steal the weapons before they could make it to auction.

The luxurious penthouse home in Cloudcroft was dripping with wealth, and packed full of black-outfitted mourners. Most of them were well over retirement age, so I needed my head in the right zone to blend more seamlessly with the background and not stick out in anyone's memories of the day.

Easier said than done, some days.

I came in as a caterer, which made it easier to move around unnoticed—rich people had a bad habit of ignoring the staff—and also gave me a plausible excuse to be carrying a case of "cutlery" out of the party again later that evening.

Constance had been dead right about the wake being the best opportunity to snatch and run. The security was lax due to the number of people in the penthouse, all the items being auctioned were out of their display cases and getting packed up for transport, and best of all? The widow was drunk. Or drugged. Or both. Either way, she didn't seem to even know her own name let alone pay attention to the smartly dressed caterer stealing some blades. In fairness, they were far from the most valuable items available.

Value didn't matter to some of my clients, though. It wasn't about stealing for profit; it was stealing for sentimentality or pride. Those were often the most satisfying jobs. And the most amusing, given what some people asked me to steal…like potted plants.

My mind wandered back to Tristian as I rode the elevator back down to the lobby, the stolen blades secure in my cutlery case along with a pretty necklace I'd lifted off a woman's neck just for fun. When I'd broken into Tris's apartment, I had been wholly unprepared to see her sleeping naked. Now I couldn't get the memory out of my head.

I was so engrossed in my thoughts that I almost missed when a young girl lifted a wallet from an unsuspecting, suited man's pocket. Interesting technique but clumsy. It was a miracle she wasn't caught, and then she went and placed it in her shoulder bag. Silly.

Amusement sparked, and a flicker of excitement ran through me as I shifted closer and stole the wallet from her bag just as the elevator reached the lobby. She didn't notice—of course—and hurried out of the elevator car the moment the doors opened, thinking she was getting away with a stolen wallet from a wealthy man.

She'd taken the low-hanging fruit, that was for sure. This guy was wearing an Omega watch worth at least forty grand, and she'd gone for a wallet that he probably didn't even carry cash in. His cards would be canceled the moment he realized it was missing, too. Foolish child.

I brushed against the man as we both crossed the lobby, putting the wallet back in his pocket like it was never gone. It was tempting to take the watch instead, but the clasp already seemed flimsy and it was just too easy. There was no satisfaction in an easy theft for me these days, so I left it.

Instead, I took my case of stolen blades and strode down the block to where I'd left my car. I wanted to get them delivered to Constance ASAP, so I could get back to Whispering Willows and step up my game with Tris.

That call from my father earlier had increased the urgency for my task. Although I technically still had several months to steal *Poppy Flowers* and deliver it to the committee, all of that meant nothing if he got it first. Then there was still the third thief to worry about, and I hadn't seen her anywhere. Which was suspicious in and of itself.

I'd been playing it too safe, too patient. I'd won the Game so many times that I was getting too comfortable in my own skills and subconsciously arrogant. This one was different though. This one was more *meaningful* because my grandfather had set it up with his legacy on the line. His grand treasure. No way in hell was I letting my shitty deadbeat dad win that.

Tris would have to fall into line. Soon. Or I'd need to change tactics.

Constance wanted me to deliver her items to her at home, but thankfully she didn't live too far from Cloudcroft, and it was on my way back to Whispering Willows anyway. I drove straight there, pausing at the huge wrought iron gates to press the doorbell buzzer.

No one spoke, but the gate swung open a moment later, and I drove on up to the main house.

"John, how lovely to see you," the supremely elegant D'Ath matriarch greeted me as she opened the door. "Come through. Ana will make you a martini."

I smiled at her casual hospitality. "No, thank you," I declined. "I'm actually in the middle of another job, so I need to get back there quickly."

Constance gave a shocked gasp. "You didn't need to drop that to help me, John. I could have sorted this out another way or found someone else. Was it even a challenging task?"

I gave a short laugh. "Not even slightly. But I'm always happy to help out my best customer, Constance."

She led the way through to the sitting room where her wife, Ana, was indeed mixing a whole jug of martini. I wasn't as familiar with Ana, but we'd exchanged pleasantries in the past so I saw no harm in doing business with her now.

"Here we go," I murmured, placing the cutlery case on the low coffee table and popping the clasps open. Inside, the two beautifully crafted blades sat side by side, hilt to tip. "Hopefully I grabbed the right ones. He had a few different sets in his collection."

Constance shot me a grin and nodded appreciatively. "As if you make careless mistakes, dear. I'm forever appreciative for this." She pulled out her phone and wired my payment, the confirmation message vibrating in my pocket. "What's this?" She picked up the simple diamond necklace that had slipped down the side of the box.

"Ah, that." I reached out and took it from her, tucking it into my pocket. "Just a souvenir."

She arched a brow but didn't comment further as she closed the case up once more.

"Are you staying for a drink, John?" Ana asked, handing Constance a full martini glass.

I shook my head. "No, I have to get back on the road. Thank you, though."

The two old women exchanged a glance and Constance gave me a curious look. "We heard you're through to the final stage of The Game again...Is that the job you're on?"

Surprise rippled through me and my brows hiked. "I don't know what you're talking about. What Game?"

The two of them smirked knowingly. "Of course, silly us," Constance chuckled. "But if you *were* competing, we have our money on you for the win. If there's anything we could do to help..."

I almost dismissed their offer, but then my tongue stilled as I thought it through. Constance D'Ath was a very well-connected woman with plenty of ties to the criminal underworld through both her late husband and her grandson. So I tipped my head to the side and really thought it through.

"You've bought a lot of art from me over the years, Constance," I murmured, and she nodded. "You seem to have a finger on the pulse of black market paintings...an informant?" Because she was never surprised when I offered her a new procurement, no matter how valuable or hard to steal.

She just smiled and sipped her drink.

Ana sat beside her wife, her eyes glittering with interest as she cradled her own martini.

"So...hypothetically speaking, would you be able to tell me who possesses a specific painting?" Because I had no concrete evidence that the Grimaldis still held *Poppy Flowers*, just that they were the last *known* buyer.

Constance gave a small head shake and sighed. "I could try, but it's unlikely. My information tells me when key items of interest are *stolen*, not when they're kept. But I could certainly ask around in my circles, if it would help."

Damn. But interesting nonetheless. "Ah, I see. Well, if I ever need connections in art crimes, I'll know who to call."

She laughed. "Like they'd ever catch the infamous *Hermes*."

True. "I should go. I'll keep your offer of help in mind, but I certainly hope you haven't bet too much money on the Game outcome. These things can fall to pure luck sometimes."

Ana chuckled, shaking her head. "Bullshit. It's skill, and no one is better than Hermes, god of thieves, wealth, and *luck*." She winked, and I smiled back.

"It was lovely to see you both," I told them as I rose to my feet. "Please call if you track down any more of these that you need collecting." I indicated the case on the table.

Constance rose to her feet as well. "Please call *me* if you pick up anything that needs a new home."

Chuckling, I headed back to the foyer, with Constance walking alongside me. The front door opened before we got to it, and two heavily-tattooed guys walked in like they lived there.

The bigger of the two, with a short beard, halted in his tracks when he saw me standing there with

Constance, a glower furrowing his brow. "Who are you?"

His grandmother hissed a sound of warning between her teeth. "Mind your manners, Archer. This is a friend of mine, and frankly none of your business."

The second guy, with buzzed hair and soft gray eyes, gave me a curious look. "Have we met? You look familiar."

I bit back a grin. "Definitely not," I replied, then bent down to kiss Constance's wrinkled cheek. "Always a pleasure doing business with you, Connie." I breezed past the two tattooed guys, heading outside to my car.

"Who the fuck was that?" the bearded man asked again as I walked away.

Constance must have whacked him because there was a muffled *ouch* before she scolded him. "Mind your language, boy. And forget his face, if you know what's good for you."

I grinned, crossing the gravel driveway to my car and leaving them to their night. I was already thinking about Tris again, remembering all her perfect curves and the allure of dark ink on her back. I should have taken a closer look, because the missing details in my memory were driving me nuts.

"Hey, Hermes!" someone called out, and I was so distracted by Tris in my mind that I responded, turning to find the buzzed hair dude standing on the steps watching me. As I reacted, his curious frown shifted into smug satisfaction, because I'd just confirmed his guess. He was a smart one. "Nice car, man."

I flicked my tongue against my teeth, furious that I'd just been caught out like that. Rather than reacting further, I just gave a small nod and slid into my car. Fucking hell, this family...

Inconsequential. It was time to get back to Whispering Willows, and get a better look at what that tattoo on Tristian's back was of. I just needed to work out how to get her naked, first...

Turning out into the road from Constance's property, I checked my phone for the thousandth time. No new messages. She was *stubborn.*

twelve

TRIS

Three days. It'd been *three days* since John missed our mentor session, and I hadn't missed any calls or texts from him to explain his absence. He had missed all his classes, which I ended up having to cover, and at one stage on Friday I even went to ask the dean's assistant if she'd heard anything—making me late for work. Not because I was worried—fuck that—but because I was starting to feel like I'd hallucinated the whole six-foot-five beast.

I hadn't, but it only left me with *more* questions. Apparently he'd been in touch with the dean *three days earlier* to let them know I would be covering his classes for the week. Yet he couldn't be bothered to let me know? What an *ass*.

Weekends were usually mine. I liked to spend my

free time in the studio painting or just reading books and feeling inspired by art. But not today. Today I was panicking about potentially needing to juggle John's classes for another week, totally unprepared. So I'd reluctantly given up on my weekend of painting to plan out the lectures for the next week.

I'd left a stack of my textbooks in Dr. Bailey's office on campus, so I decided to work there where it was quiet and maybe I could focus. Instead, I found myself sitting there and remembering it was now *John's* office. And then my mind started going to dirty places thinking about him sitting in the same seat I was currently in... then thinking about me sitting in his lap. What his big hands would feel like on my thighs, pushing up my skirt, tugging aside my panties...

Fucking hell.

"Never going to happen," I muttered out loud, booting up my laptop and ignoring the way my own cheeks heated at my intrusive thoughts. John's mysterious absence had me thinking about him way more than I'd have liked.

For the next three hours, I worked on mapping out lesson plans for the next week and a half, not knowing when he'd suddenly show up again but not wanting to be so unprepared again. I hated being caught off guard like that.

Around lunchtime, I called it quits. I still had time to grab some food and head into my studio, so that's what I intended to do. I packed up my computer, put all the textbooks back on the shelf, and locked up John's office.

Turning on my heel, I smacked straight into a broad chest and hurt my nose.

"Ow!" I complained, rubbing my face and glaring *up*. "You bastard!" I spat the insult with venom, and his only response was a slight quirk to one brow.

"I missed you too, Tristian," John replied, his full lips curling. "Why were you in my office just now?"

My lips parted but no sound came out. All I could think about were those dirty thoughts I'd had, sitting in his chair. The brief fantasy of him fingering me as I sat in his lap…shit. My face flamed, and his eyes narrowed with suspicion.

"Where the hell have you been?" I asked instead, parking my hands on my hips and tilting my head back with indignation. "Three days you've been gone and not a damn word from you. Do you know how rude—"

"Aw, you missed me," he cut me off, smug satisfaction fucking *radiating* from him. "I knew I was getting into your head."

I swallowed hard. "Under my skin, more like."

Those kissable lips twitched again. "Cute. I'll take it. But we might have to save this exceptionally sexually charged banter for another time. I'm on my way to meet with the dean, and I probably shouldn't keep him waiting."

Outrage stunned me a moment. That was it? No apology, no explanation? "I take it the dean will want to know where you've been that was so important you had to disappear in the middle of the night, hmm?" Seriously, where the *fuck* had he gone?

He made a hum, like a laugh that got trapped in his chest. "No, actually. I believe he wants to speak about an anonymous complaint...someone apparently took offense to me *fraternizing* with one of my female students." He paused dramatically, his dark eyes drowning me and making it hard to breathe. "Inappropriately." In case I missed his meaning.

Struggling to find my words, I licked my lips. Fuck, why was I thinking about what it'd be like to *fraternize* with John again? He had to be at least ten years older than me, if not fifteen.

"You wouldn't know anything about that, would you?" he pressed, swaying forward into my personal space and making me lean back in order to hold eye contact. My back was basically against the door now, and *dammit* I liked it.

I shook my head slightly, denying it before I could decide to taunt him. "You and Janie weren't exactly subtle the other night," I pointed out. "In a student bar, too."

He stared down at me, his expression totally unreadable. Then all of a sudden he walked away and the vacuum of space opening between us made me gasp.

"Uh…where are you going?" I called after him. "We were talking."

"I told you," he said over his shoulder, not even pausing a moment. "I'm meeting the dean. See you Monday, Miss Ives."

What the fuck?

That big bastard had just rendered me speechless. I literally stood there in the hallway staring at space well after he disappeared around the corner, like my brain had just glitched and I was stuck on pause.

Eventually, though, I shook off the frankly uncomfortable interaction and headed for the parking lot. I definitely needed to go home and paint now. It was the only thing that might help clear my head of *Professor Smith* and his smug, sexy smile.

"I'm so screwed," I admitted to myself when I glanced in my rear view mirror. My cheeks still held a rosy flush and my lips were puffy where I'd wet them way too many times. Damn it.

I drove over the speed limit to get home, parking badly and tapping my foot impatiently when the elevator took more than ten seconds to reach me. Once inside the safety of my apartment, I could breathe easy again. I locked my door, kicked off my shoes, and went to the fridge for a coke. Then I carried my drink through to my studio and turned on some music.

The tension ebbed out of me with noticeable waves as I settled into my happy place, but my muse recoiled when I tried to pull out the vibrant yellows of my latest project. When I was feeling out of control with my emotions, like John seemed to always make me, I needed to listen to my creativity. Right now, it didn't want to work on the same painting we'd been doing for weeks.

"Something new?" I pondered out loud. Testing the theory, I moved my work in progress back into my canvas filing cabinet and pulled out a blank one. I placed it on the easel and squinted at it. "Too small," I decided, swapping it out for one three times the size.

The instant rush of happiness when I stared at the totally blank, three-foot square canvas said it all.

"New project it is," I murmured, turning to my shelves of paint tubes. "Now what colors, I wonder?"

thirteen

JOHN

Tris was so mad at me she'd been practically hyperventilating. There was also a suspicious edge of guilt in her eyes, making me wonder what *exactly* she'd been doing in my office. Then again, she really didn't strike me as the devious type, so she'd probably just been marking assessments or something equally boring.

Verbally sparring with her was better than I remembered. Brushing her off and walking away, while she'd be standing there with her jaw on the floor… perfection. I was still grinning as I let myself into the dean's office a minute later.

"John," he greeted me, glancing up from the papers he was reading. "Thank you for coming in on a

Saturday, I thought it best we get this sorted out smartly."

"Of course," I agreed, sitting down without waiting for an invitation. I hooked my ankle over my knee and raised a brow at the dean. "So?"

The old man frowned and cleared his throat awkwardly. "Well, as mentioned over the phone, there was an anonymous complaint made about—"

"You said it was a student complaint," I corrected him, enjoying the subtle power play as his eyes narrowed.

He cleared his throat again, looking down at the paper in front of him, then back up at me. "Did I?"

I smiled. "You did. But please continue."

The dean's eyes narrowed, his brow furrowed, and he read his printout again. "Yes, well, there was an anonymous student complaint about you yesterday, John. Apparently you were caught in a compromising situation with one of your students which, I'm sure I don't need to tell you, is firmly against the bylaws of Boles University and breaches your terms of employment."

"Is that so?" I murmured, completely unconcerned by this line of inquiry.

The dean stared at me like he couldn't understand why I wasn't *reacting* to this accusation. "Don't you have anything to say about it, John? This is a very serious accusation."

I shrugged one shoulder. "Not really. I presume you must have irrefutable evidence of this, er, what did you call it? Compromising situation? Could I see the photograph?"

He just blinked at me.

Satisfaction warmed me. "Ah, I see. So…no photograph? Video then?" I tilted my head, holding eye contact and waiting. "No video, hmm?"

He swallowed visibly. "Listen, John, I don't know how things are done where you're from, but here at Boles—"

"You don't require physical proof of an infraction? That seems like you're putting an awful lot of trust in this anonymous complainant, Lawrence." I tapped my fingertips on my knee, showing my irritation. "Do you have *any* proof worth my time coming in here on the weekend? Or are you simply wasting my time?"

His face flamed with anger. "So, you deny it then?"

I narrowed my eyes. "Deny *what* exactly? Having sex with Janie Hartman? Never happened. The girl saw me drinking alone and wanted to discuss her thesis, then I offered to escort her home. In case you weren't aware, Lawrence, it's a dangerous world for women alone at night. Besides, she's not my type."

He scowled. "So, this student was simply mistaken? You have never had, or never will have, inappropriate relations with a student?"

My mind instantly flashed to Tristian, naked in her bed. Then to how flushed and awkward she just was in the hallway as I got into her personal space.

"I never have," I agreed, smiling. "Is that all?"

He wasn't as senile as he looked. "And *will never* in the future, correct?"

I chuckled, rubbing at my jaw. "I can't make any promises like that, Lawrence."

His eyes damn near bugged out of his head. But, shit, I had *every* intention of getting Tris into my bed, and I'd rather not have to worry about university bullshit on top of that challenge.

"John, you can't sleep with the students!" The dean looked like he was about to have a heart attack.

Still, his poor heart health wasn't my responsibility. "I can, and I will. But *relax*, Lawrence. I won't make a habit of exchanging grades for blow-jobs. There's only one student that I plan to *fraternize* with, and I'm confident she won't be making any complaints."

His mouth flapped like a fish out of water as he tried to wrap his head around my blatant audacity. Eventually, his eye twitched and he expelled a long breath. "John, if you're sleeping with your TA then—"

"I'm not," I corrected. "Yet. But when I do—because trust me when I say that it *will* happen—you're going to look the other way if any nosy, anonymous complaints are made by jealous, frustrated peers. Am I clear?"

"Why on *earth* would I—"

"Because I know, Lawrence." I leveled him with a steady gaze. "I *know*."

He just stared back at me for a moment, studying my face like he was convinced I was bluffing. Then I smiled and waggled the foot I'd hooked over my knee, drawing attention to it. Dean Lawrence paled instantly. Then wet his lips as he met my eyes once more.

"That..." he said carefully, quietly, "is not illegal."

I shrugged. "I never said it was. But I get the feeling it's something you'd like to be kept quiet, isn't it? Tell you what. You turn a blind eye to me seducing my pretty little TA, and I'll make it worth your while."

Interest piqued in the dean's face. "Oh, I see." He pursed his lips. Then licked them. "What shoe size would you say you are, John?"

I smiled. "I take that as an agreement, Lawrence. Have you heard how Dr. Bailey's mysterious illness is going? As much as I'd love him to recover, I do find myself growing quite attached to Boles University already."

Dean Lawrence sighed, shaking his head. "There's

been no progress, unfortunately. I hear a new specialist is coming to see him next week, though. The whispers from his nurse are that he might have been poisoned, if you can believe it? Who would want to poison an old man?"

"Who indeed?" I pushed up from my chair, ending our chat. "I need to be going. I have papers to grade and a TA to seduce." I shot the dean a wink on my way out of his office. "Pleasure doing business with you."

I sauntered out of the building with a spring in my step and a renewed purpose. Ultimately, I didn't give two fucks if Boles took offense to my sleeping with a student, so long as I walked away with *Poppy Flowers* at the end of it all. And to be fair, it wouldn't exactly be a hardship to fuck Tristian Ives. The girl was perfect, right down to her bratty mouth.

My mind wandered to her *again*. What was she doing this weekend? Would she be working at the Grimaldi house again? Or did he give her the weekends off? If so...what would Tristian do with her free time, I wondered?

Subconsciously, I'd already made up my mind to break into her apartment again tonight. But I pretended I was exercising self-control as I headed into town to do some shopping rather than knocking on her door and forcefully breaking the palpable tension between us. Surely it was driving her nuts, too?

It took me a while to get all the things I needed in town, so I picked up Chinese takeout from a cute little restaurant around the corner from Tristian's place. Was I quietly hoping I'd run into her? Absolutely. So when it didn't happen, I had to go home disappointed.

In the solitude of my campus housing, I forced myself to eat and then meditate. Between Tristian and my father, my emotions were all chaos, and I needed to find my control once more. After that, I went for a run.

By the time I got back, showered, and changed, I had no patience left. I needed to see her…

It took *all* my better judgment to wait it out until two in the morning before breaking into her loft apartment again. I always found two AM the best time to go creeping around in the night. Midnight was just too early, especially for people who habitually dated Tinder matches and had no classes in the morning.

I entered through the same window I'd used last time, bracing myself as I listened for any sounds that could indicate she was awake. Or with company. That idea filled me with a weird, cold anger that made me pause. What the fuck did I care if she'd taken another Tinder match home? It made no difference to me, so long as she was still open to my advances and not locked down in a monogamous relationship.

And yet. The idea of finding another man in her bed made me see red.

Swallowing my unexpected rush of emotion back, I padded softly through her dark home, heading straight for her bed to check if she was there. I hadn't come to steal anything, I just wanted to check on her. Was that weird? Maybe. But given she was my best lead in getting my hands on *Poppy Flowers*, the compulsion to see her didn't raise any alarm bells. I *always* kept close tabs on my targets, getting to know them as thoroughly as humanly possible without tipping them off to my manipulations. This, admittedly, was a step further.

But...she was different. Somehow.

A gut deep wave of relief washed through me when I saw her lying there, fast asleep and *alone* in her big bed. She was naked again—was this a habit for her? This time she was sleeping on her stomach, her cheek squashed into the white pillows and her inky waves splayed over her body in the most tempting way.

My hand balled into a fist as I fought the urge to sweep her hair aside and reveal her back tattoo. All I could make out was a lotus flower. Infuriating!

Forcing myself to look away, I turned my attention to her bed. Last time I visited, she'd left her rabbit vibrator tangled up in the sheets like she'd fallen asleep after some quality self-care. This time, I didn't see it anywhere, so I silently opened her bedside drawer. Yep, there it was.

How often did she use it, I wondered. Would she notice if it went missing? Would her mood change, without convenient self-supplied orgasms?

As if possessed, my hand moved before my brain even finished the thought, lifting the vibrator from Tristian's drawer and tucking it into my jacket pocket. The familiar, addictive rush of excitement ran through me as I slid the drawer closed once more and Tris continued to sleep.

Smug as fuck, I took one last, *long* look at my prey, then quietly retreated.

We had a mentor session first thing Monday morning, pre-dawn. I could hardly wait to see what sort of mood she'd be in by then. Maybe her self-control would snap, and she'd make the first move. That'd be exciting.

Shit. The exit out of her window was a whole lot harder than it'd been on the way in. In more ways than one. Damn that temptress.

fourteen

TRIS

John was invading my brain in the worst kind of way. After our brief interlude outside his office, he refused to get out of my head all weekend. Hell, I even woke up Sunday morning after a particularly filthy dream about him and reached for my rabbit.

To my intense frustration, it wasn't in my drawer. Nor was it caught up in my sheets or under my bed or… shit, I'd bet anything I'd accidentally sent it to the laundromat with my bed linens the previous morning. Ugh, talk about embarrassing when they found that bouncing around in the washing machines.

My Sunday was supposed to be for painting and my dissertation, but I made an exception to run into town and buy a new rabbit from the one and only sex shop within Whispering Willows. The guy at the counter made a less than professional comment about my choice of Sunday morning activities, but I ignored it and hurried home again.

The mood for self-care had passed, but at least I had a replacement rabbit for later when I'd inevitably feel the urge after painting. It wasn't *every* time I painted... but this new one I'd started seemed to get my heart racing. Not to mention John's constant presence in my head. Yeah, better to have the new rabbit than do something dumb like try to act out my little school office fantasy during a teaching meeting.

I groaned out loud. We had a mentor session first thing Monday morning...my schedule, so no one to blame but myself. Then again, after he'd just ghosted me for three days last week, maybe John could use a dose of his own damn medicine.

Smirking to myself, I turned off my alarm for the morning, and poured a glass of wine. If I was going to poke the arrogant bear with a stick, I may as well make the most of it.

One entire bottle of wine later, I fell into my bed without even bothering to wash up. I was way too tipsy to handle showering without help, and I really didn't want to do something stupid...like call John.

Shit. He was in my head again.

Groaning, I very deliberately turned my phone *off* to remove the temptation and risk of somehow accidentally calling him. Tossing it onto the floor beside my bed—not even plugging it into the charger—I reached for my new rabbit instead. Thank fuck I'd run that errand, because a nice quick orgasm without masculine baggage and bullshit was *exactly* what I needed.

SOMEONE WAS SHAKING ME AWAKE.

What the fuck?

"Who—? What—?" I mumbled, groggy with sleep and last night's wine. "What's going—?" The fuzz cleared from my eyes and I stared up into a pair of deep brown eyes that did *not* belong in my apartment. "John?!" It came out as a strangled shriek of outrage.

All at once, I scrambled for my sheet to cover myself since I always slept naked, and then I looked around like somehow I could work out why the fuck John was in my *home*...while I slept. Naked.

"Good morning, Grumpy," he said in that deep, rumbly voice that instantly made my pussy clench. Fuck. John was here and I was naked in bed and wine was still clouding my brain.

"What—?" I cut off as my voice croaked, so I wet my lips and tried again. "What in the ever loving *fuck* are you doing here, Professor Smith? How did you even know where I lived? *How did you get in*?" I was meticulous about locking my door, and the elevators had security swipe access.

He just arched a brow in amusement, slouching back in the armchair he'd apparently dragged over from my living room. How long had he been here without me knowing?

"You didn't show up for our session this morning, Tris," he said in that hypnotic voice. "I was worried."

Oh, that was sweet.

Wait. No. Not sweet, *creepy*.

"How'd you get in here, John?" I demanded, gritting my teeth as I held the sheet to my chest tighter. Not that it probably mattered, since I had a habit of kicking my bedding off while I slept. He'd probably already had a good look.

He ran his thumb over his lower lip, drawing my attention like a marshmallow to fire. "You left the door unlocked," he finally replied. "Which, I might add, was very irresponsible. Anyone could have come in here and robbed you blind while you slept. Or worse." He gave me a pointed look and I clutched my sheet tighter still.

I frowned. "I never leave my door unlocked."

He just squinted back at me. "Well, explain how I got in here. I assure you, Tris, I can't teleport…no matter how useful that skill would be."

Okay, sure. He had a good point. It wasn't like my Art History professor was going to literally break in just to wake me up. Now that I thought about it, I couldn't be positive I'd locked the door. My head had been all fogged up when I got back from the store, so it was *possible* I'd forgotten.

"Okay well, as you can see, I'm perfectly fine."

His lips tugged up at the corner. "That you are."

A tense silence hung in the air. Had he meant that to sound like it had? No, shit, that was my dirty wine-soaked mind at work. Fuck, where had I left my new vibrator? I tried to glance around subtly but couldn't see it anywhere. Maybe I'd put it back in my drawer.

"So, you can leave now," I prompted, giving John a hard look. I really needed him to leave.

He just slouched into the armchair further, like that was even possible. "Why would I? We have a session booked. I'm a busy man, Tristian. If you want my *mentorship* then you'll need to stick with our agreed schedule."

My jaw dropped. The *audacity*.

Seething, I tightened my jaw and straightened my

spine. "Fine," I growled. "Go and wait in my living area while I get dressed, then we can start."

He gave a low chuckle, rubbing a hand over his slightly stubbled cheek. "No, we've already wasted half an hour. I'm not waiting even longer while you take a forty-minute shower and put on makeup. You can get changed while we talk or you can stay naked. It makes no difference to me."

A small sound of disbelief squeaked from my throat as I stared back at him. "You're joking," I accused in a strangled voice. Fucking hell, why were my nipples so hard?

John shifted his big frame, leaning forward and resting his elbows on his knees as his intense stare held me captive. "I don't joke about academics, Miss Ives." His gaze lowered, running over my sheet and the way my fingers clutched it in a white-knuckled grip. "Unless you're uncomfortable. Are you?"

I needed to swallow before I could find my voice, but I had a sneaking suspicion that admitting he made me uncomfortable would be a victory for him. So I just drew a deep breath and mentally steeled myself to play his game. "Not even slightly," I lied. "I just didn't want to make *you* uncomfortable...*Professor Smith*."

His lush lips twitched with a barely restrained smile before he carefully schooled his expression. "Good, we're on the same page then. Everyone is perfectly comfortable. Shall we begin?" He reached over and plucked one of my textbooks from the floor beside his chair, flipping it open.

Prick. He wanted to engage in silly little power games? He'd picked the wrong girl.

"Sure, go for it," I agreed, wiggling forward on the bed until my feet touched the ground directly in front of where he sat.

He glanced up, his eyes narrowed suspiciously. "What are you doing?"

My smile was pure innocence but the eyelash flutter might have been overkill. "I just need to use the bathroom," I answered, standing up and relishing the way he leaned back to maintain some space between us. "I'll just be a minute. Can't risk a UTI, you know?"

Then I dropped my sheet. I only allowed myself a moment's satisfaction at the way his eyes widened and his breathing stilled, then I sashayed past him to cross over to my bathroom. I didn't turn to check if he was watching me walk away; we both knew he was.

In the safety of the bathroom, I decided that maybe a cold shower might be a wise idea. Except...John would hear the water running and know exactly how affected I was by that exchange. Shit, I couldn't have that. I'd have to settle for splashing cold water on my face instead.

Okay, fine. My face and my cunt because she was throbbing like I'd been watching live porn.

I delayed as long as I could, then tossed on a silk gown. It wasn't an admission of defeat, but there was no way in hell I could stay fully naked and not crack even slightly. Besides, the thin gown would be *more* distracting to him, especially if I only loosely belted it. He'd never know if it was about to slip in the right direction.

When I jerked the bathroom door open, I squeaked a sound of shock to find John standing *right fucking there*.

"You okay, Miss Ives?" he purred, smug victory all over his face. "Do you need another minute to sort yourself out?"

Oh. Come on. That wasn't even slightly subtle.

I shrugged, shaking my head. "Nope, I'm fine. Can I make you a coffee? It is awfully early, after all." And I was a touch hungover.

He gave me a long look, his dark eyes taking in my robe with an appreciative glance. "Sure. Black, no sugar."

I needed to brush past him to get out of the bathroom, but the effect was leagues apart from when Dexter had cornered me in a similar way. With John, I was fighting the urge to touch him—despite how infuriating and arrogant he was—and with Dexter... well, I was just plain scared.

John's presence was so huge I could feel him following me across the open space to the kitchen but I didn't acknowledge him while I hunted out some coffee mugs and turned on my cute little pod machine. Nelson always turned his nose up at my pod coffee—he was a barista-espresso man—but they were quick and easy and infinitely better than watery filter coffee.

"So, I guess we need to start from scratch," I commented as I poured a long black for John. "You have no idea where I'm up to on my dissertation, and I—"

"Actually, I'm fully caught up," he corrected, taking the mug from me when I held it out. His fingers brushed mine, and my brain short-circuited a moment. "It would be terribly unprofessional if I showed up to this session unprepared, wouldn't it?" He sipped his scalding coffee, his eyes glittering.

I gulped a breath, focusing on making my own coffee by adding milk to my cylindrical frother. "God forbid we be unprofessional," I muttered, all too damn aware of my own nudity under the silk robe.

John said nothing, despite the fact he had to have heard me. I just laser focused on making my coffee, because my brain was pounding. I'd kill for some ibuprofen but didn't want to show any weakness.

My stomach had other ideas, rumbling so loud I felt it in my toes.

Fucking hell. Talk about sexy, Tris. Not that I needed to be sexy for John…but still. I ignored it, pouring my velvety milk into my espresso and lifting the mug to take a sip. Then it rumbled even louder and John gave a vexed sigh.

"Did you eat anything last night, Tris?" he asked, judgment dripping from every word.

I gritted my teeth, spinning to face him. "Yes, I did," I sassed back. "I had fruit."

He wasn't fooled, his dark lashes narrowing around his too-observant eyes. "Wine isn't fruit, Miss Ives." He crossed to my fridge, pulling the door open like he lived here. "Well, this is depressing."

Irritation flared hot in my chest. "I thought you were here to mentor me, Professor Smith, not offer uncalled-for commentary on the state of my fridge."

He arched a brow in a way that did naughty things to my insides. "I can't concentrate if your stomach insists on making that racket." He pulled an armful of my paltry ingredients out of the fridge and dumped them out on the counter.

"John, you can't just—" My protest cut off with a squeak as he wrapped his hands around my waist and hoisted me to sit on the counter.

"I can," he corrected, his mouth hovering just inches

away from mine like he was thinking about kissing me. "Or are you going to tell me to stop?"

Fuck. Why did that sound so damn loaded?

My stomach answered for me, grumbling hard enough to chatter my teeth, and John's lips twitched in another one of those infuriatingly smug half-smiles.

"That's what I thought," he whispered, then patted the top of my ass like he was telling me *good girl*. "I'll cook, you can fill me in on your ideas about the evolution of female sexuality from the Renaissance through the Neoclassical era. That *is* your research topic isn't it?"

I wet my lips, ready to tell him to go fuck himself as he moved to my stove to pull out a skillet. Instead, though, the only response that escaped my voice box was a meek, shocked, "Okay."

Pathetic. The second he left, I was hunting out my new rabbit and putting my hormones back where they belonged.

fifteen

JOHN

Leaving Tristian's apartment—through the front door this time—an hour later, I could safely confirm that I had *no clue* what we'd discussed. At least not anything academic, anyway. How could I possibly retain that kind of information while she was all but naked, within arm's reach of me?

My only excuse for the reckless decision to wake her up this morning had to be temporary insanity. I wanted to see how she was going to react, but nothing had actually prepared me for her rising to the challenge. I'd one hundred percent expected her to be embarrassed and demand privacy while she got dressed. But nope, not Tristian Ives.

Fuck me, the way my dick got hard when she

dropped that sheet...right when I thought I had myself under control, too.

She'd kicked me out right on our scheduled end time for the session, explaining that unless I wanted her to show up for class in that robe, I needed to let her shower and change. I definitely did *not* want her wandering around Boles in that robe, so I conceded.

I hummed a happy tune as I rode the elevator down, finally feeling like I'd made *progress* with prickly Miss Ives. It was about damn time, too.

When the doors slid open to the ground floor, an older man in a three-piece suit stood waiting for the elevator directly in front of me. He frowned at me, then glanced up at the display above the door.

"Hello," he said with heavy suspicion. "Who are you?"

Shit. I hadn't realized Tris had such nosy neighbors. Most people in apartment buildings didn't even give a new face a second glance in passing.

"John," I replied, offering a friendly smile. "Have a nice day."

I tried to pass, but he put a hand on my arm to halt me before I could make my escape. The elevator closed again behind me, too, cutting off that exit.

"John, hmm?" the man repeated, sounding *entertained*. "You wouldn't happen to be Ivy's new friend, would you?"

I squinted my confusion. "Ivy? Oh, Tris." Tristian *Ives*. "I wouldn't say we're *friends*. Yet. But I'm wearing her down, I think."

The old guy barked a laugh. "Oh, you think, do you? Well, you're here…so maybe you are. I'm Nelson, by the way, Ivy's neighbor." He extended a hand, and I shook it. Something told me he was more than just a neighbor, and a new plan started forming in my head.

"Nelson, it's nice to meet you." It really was.

"Ivy told us you're filling in for Dr. Bailey while he's unwell," he said, confirming my suspicion that they were closer than neighbors. "Did she show you her assessment piece that she's been working on?"

My brows rose. I hadn't even thought to ask to see her studio, despite the splatters of paint on her hands and wrists I saw while she slept. Once she'd woken up, all full of fire and barbs, it'd evaporated out of my head.

"She didn't," I admitted. "We had an appointment scheduled for this morning, and when she didn't show up, I grew concerned. Turns out she just overslept." Naked. That was definitely an every-night thing and something I thought about way too damn often.

Nelson frowned. "That's not like her. I hope she wasn't up late with Oliver again."

Jealousy nearly choked me. "Who is Oliver?"

Nelson just waved it off. "Some guy she met on one

of those silly phone apps. The two of them practically shook the whole building down last weekend, I had to hunt out my noise canceling headphones just to get some sleep." He chuckled, but there was a calculating gleam in his eye. "Gosh, she'd kill me if she heard me say that to you...her *teacher*. I assume your visit this morning was, er, academic?"

Was this old guy fishing for gossip on Tristian's sex life? I couldn't decide if I was outraged or amused.

I gave an easy smile. "Academic, yes. Unfortunately." I grinned wider, and Nelson's brows rose knowingly.

"Ah, I see...well...John was it?"

"Yes," I confirmed, "John Smith."

Nelson gave a short laugh, then shook his head. "Right. Well, how have you been finding Whispering Willows so far? Have you got any family or friends here in town?"

"I don't. It's just me, all alone in the university accommodation. I can't even cook well, can you believe it? Hopeless." I gave a disparaging laugh, playing along with the opening Nelson was clearly about to offer.

He gave a short nod. "Well, then. You'll have to come by for dinner tonight. I happen to be an *excellent* cook, and I know my husband would love to meet you. He and I have visited all the great art galleries together, back when we were younger. We'd love to talk shop with you over Beef Wellington…if that works for you?"

Perfect.

"Oh, I don't know," I hedged. "I would hate to impose…"

"Nonsense, it's no imposition at all. We'd be happy to have you, John." Nelson reached out to call the elevator once more, and the doors opened almost instantly. "Seven o'clock sound okay? We're on the same floor as Ives, the only other apartment."

I nodded, giving a small salute. "Yes, sir. I'll see you then."

He gave me a nod of approval as the doors closed, and I grinned to myself. If Tris wanted to play hard to get, I was going to take any and all opportunities to tip the scales. Dinner with her neighbor sounded just delightful.

Tucking my hands into my pockets, I chuckled as I sauntered out into the street. My fingers wrapped around the silicone toy I'd stolen from Tris's bed while she was "freshening up" this morning. It definitely made me do a double take when I'd seen it peeking out from under her bed. Did she have two? Or had she somehow bought another on a Sunday?

Either way, it was mine now. And I'd stalled long enough that she had no time to search for it if she wanted to make it to class on time. Yeah, this job was fun for all the wrong reasons.

I had a literal spring in my step as I returned to Boles and headed for the classes to prepare for the eight-thirty lecture that I'd witnessed Tris deliver just a week ago. She arrived just five minutes after me, looking cool, calm, and composed. Like she hadn't just played a game of sexual tension chicken with me all morning.

"Good morning, Professor Smith," she greeted me with a sultry smile, her voice loud enough to be overheard by the students already arriving. "How lovely to see you back. I do hope you're recovering well from that nasty case of syphilis you mentioned."

I nearly choked on my own breath. "What?"

"Oh, whoops," she covered her mouth, looking around us like she was checking if anyone overheard. Funny. They definitely did. "Sorry, was that a secret?" She used a stage whisper that made me want to bend her over my knee and smack her ass.

"Sit down, Miss Ives. There's a stack of assignments on your desk to mark." I pointed toward her desk at the side of the room and glowered a promise of retribution. She just smirked and fluttered those heavy dark lashes of hers. Fuck.

When I glanced over to the students, I found several

girls staring with shocked expressions and a few guys snickering and murmuring to each other. Great.

Good thing the only person in Whispering Willows that I actually wanted to sleep with was the very same one smiling smugly to herself as she perched on her seat and opened her bag. Fuck, was she wearing thigh-high stockings? She was. I could see the band at the top when she crossed her legs and her skirt rose.

Her knowing gaze met my eyes, and I realized she'd caught me looking. Screw it, if she wasn't already getting the hint maybe I needed to be less subtle. So I took another long look at her legs, and shot her a wink with my back to the students.

My reward was the slight widening of her eyes and faint pink touch to her cheeks. It was a good start.

For the next three hours, I found every opportunity possible to hold her attention. Questions, eye contact, casual touches. By the time the class let out, I was ready to hoist her up onto the desk and rip her panties off...so hopefully she was feeling the same way.

"Can I take you to lunch, Tris?" I asked as she packed up her laptop and notes. She was seated, her skirt bunched up enough that those thigh-high stockings and suspenders were all I could focus on.

She paused what she was doing, looking up at me with a skeptical expression. "To discuss the lesson plans

I spent half my weekend mapping out? Or because you want to get into my panties?"

I gave her a sly smile. "Does both work for you?"

Her lips pursed and her eyes glittered as she held back a smile. Then zipped up her bag and slid it over her shoulder as she stood. "Sorry, I've got plans, and I'm not wearing any panties. I'll email the lesson notes to you, though...Professor."

I rolled my eyes as she walked away, the stubborn brat. She was only calling me that to try and maintain an illusion of professionalism that *never* existed to begin with. Also...what the fuck did she just say about her panties?

"What sort of plans?" I called after her, not willing to let her off so easily. "Plans with *Oliver*?" Oops, where did that come from?

She paused, spinning around on those way-too-high-for-class heels. "How do you—" She broke off shaking her head. "Never mind. And it's none of your business. Have a nice day, Professor Smith. Don't follow me."

I smiled, because I was absolutely going to follow her. Tristian was turning me into a stalker on top of a thief, and I still had her vibrator in my pocket like a sick little trophy. I could hardly wait for dinner with her lovely old neighbors tonight. I bet they'd have plenty of stories to tell, and maybe I could find a reason to knock on her door afterwards.

Chuckling, I packed up my own bag and sauntered out of the class. Anyone who didn't know me better would genuinely think I was infatuated with Tristian Ives. I wasn't, though. She was just a means to an end. To *Poppy Flowers* and my grandfather's legacy.

Nothing more.

sixteen

TRIS

Work was particularly painful. Not only did I have John on my mind every damn minute, I also hadn't been lying about not wearing any panties. It'd been an impulsive decision while trying to speed-dress in the paltry amount of time he'd left me to get dressed this morning, but now…it didn't seem so clever. Particularly after I got cornered by Dexter again.

I worked myself up even more on my drive home, raging silently about how his advances were officially past the point of mildly uncomfortable and straight into harassment zone. Most days, Mr. Grimaldi ran interference and I could slip away. Today he'd been nowhere to be seen.

My emotions were running so high that I needed to

take a moment in the elevator and just *scream* into my balled up jacket. By the time I got to my floor, I was no calmer. If anything, I was worse because my hands were shaking and my skin was all pebbled with cold.

"Fucking hell, Tris," I whispered aloud, "pull yourself together."

I was way overreacting. Nothing had *actually* happened. Dexter had been his usual self, making his interest in me as more than an employee perfectly clear. This time, without his father around to redirect his attention, he'd gotten a little handsy before I'd managed to escape out to my car. That's it. Essentially *nothing*... yet I couldn't seem to convince my lizard brain of that fact.

Bypassing my own apartment, I went straight to Nelson and Hank's. I needed to not be alone right now, and the two of them never failed to make me feel safe. And they could always be counted on to cheer me up, even if I did have to take cheap shots at Nelson's perfectionism to get a reaction.

I knocked on their door—because I'd learned the hard way not to barge in unannounced—then opened the door when I heard Hank call out for me to come in.

"Ivy, sweetheart, we didn't expect you tonight!" Hank said, coming over to the door to greet me as I came inside.

I wrinkled my nose. "You didn't? I come over practically every night. And I had a really awful day at work so I need company. And wine. I'm mostly here for your wine."

His brows were high. Really high. What the hell? Had I just interrupted him and Nelson having quality time again? No, he was fully dressed.

"Well, you're always welcome for wine, Ives, but you haven't come by this early in ages," Hank pointed out. "You've been all about the Tinder dates."

I rolled my eyes and groaned. "Yeah well that's ruined now thanks to fucking *John*. I swear to God, Hank, that arrogant, egotistical, *smug* piece of shit man is ruining my life. I had to awkwardly dump Chad in a café the other day because he suddenly gives me the ick. Then, on top of all *that* I had to deal with fucking Dexter without Mr. Grimaldi there to run interference and..." I shuddered.

Hank gave me a sympathetic wince, having heard all about Dexter from me on multiple occasions. Still, he gave me a small, teasing smile. "Who was Chad?"

I threw up my hands. "Doesn't matter *now*." I nearly told Hank about John showing up in my apartment this morning, but then I'd have to admit that I'd left my door unlocked and that would earn me a whole lecture about personal security, and I was already feeling too fragile.

He was kind of hovering in front of me, and it just struck me as odd.

"Um, did I interrupt something?" I asked, suddenly feeling awkward. "I feel like I did. I'll go."

"No, don't go!" Nelson called out. "Come and join us for dinner, Ivy. Hank's being silly."

Hank grimaced, and I wrinkled my nose at him in confusion as I dropped my bag and kicked off my shoes. He didn't explain himself, though, so I skirted around him and headed for the dining room.

Then stopped dead in my tracks.

"What the *fuck* is he doing here?" I demanded, glaring *death* at the smug, sexy piece of shit sitting at Nelson's dining table with a glass of wine in hand.

"I'm sorry," Hank whispered. "Blame Nelson, not me."

Nelson just pulled out a chair at the table for me, indicating that I should sit. "Don't be so dramatic," he scolded. "Tris was just venting about her bad day. I'm sure she doesn't really think…er…"

John raised one brow. "That I'm an arrogant, egotistical, smug piece of shit? Yes she does. But that's okay, she's no angel herself."

My cheeks flamed with embarrassment at being overheard, even though I felt no guilt for what I'd said. It was all true, but how dare he imply that I was as bad as him?

"Sit down, Ivy," Nelson urged. "Hank will pour you some wine. Dinner is almost ready."

It was on the tip of my tongue to make an excuse to leave. But no, fuck that. This was *my* territory, and I refused to let John push me aside like he was man-spreading all over my life. So I narrowed my eyes in a glare at him and plonked my ass down at the table.

Hank and Nelson let out an audible breath of relief when I did, and I shifted my accusing glare to Nelson. "How'd you two meet?" I asked from behind gritted teeth.

"We met in the lobby this morning," Nelson informed me with a prissy look, "as John was leaving *your* apartment."

Okay, yes, I could see how that didn't look great given how early it was. But he didn't have to invite him over for dinner, for fuck's sake. John was *such* a smug fuck.

I said nothing, accepting the full glass of wine that Hank just poured me.

"Who's Dexter?" John asked when the silence stretched. "And what'd he do to get you all worked up?"

I glowered. "None of your fucking business, Professor."

Nelson scowled and shook his head. "Language."

I rolled my eyes and took a huge mouthful of wine.

"Come help me plate up," Hank suggested, nudging Nelson. "Now."

I scoffed as the two of them retreated to the kitchen, leaving John and me alone at the table. "Subtlety isn't their strong suit," I muttered, watching the two old men whispering to each other as they dished out dinner.

John leaned forward, his big hands resting on the table. "Who's Dexter, Tris?"

Like a dog with a fucking bone. "Why? You worried about more competition?"

His lips twitched. Fucking hell, why was that so alluring? "I didn't realize I was competing. Good to know, though. And no…not worried about that. Just wanting to understand you better."

My run-in with Dexter, and the way his behavior was escalating, had me shaken enough that John's claim to want to *understand* struck me as genuine. Caring. It was what I needed, and an ounce of defensive anger slipped from my shoulders.

"He's my employer's son," I answered honestly, toying with the stem of my wine glass, "and not someone who hears *no* very often."

John didn't react. He just stared at me, impassive, then nodded. "I see."

That was it. *I see.*

I blew out a frustrated sigh and raised my glass to gulp more wine. Maybe I needed to get a nice alcohol buzz going so I could forget the clammy feeling of Dexter's hand on my thigh.

"Okay, dinner is served," Hank announced in an overly cheery voice, carrying two plates of food over. Nelson was right behind him, carrying two more, and he gave me a hard look as if to say, *don't be such a bitch, Ives.*

We'd be having words later, my nosy neighbor and I.

For a while, I kept quiet and just ate my food—Nelson was an incredible chef—and drank my wine. Hank refilled my glass several times, and I carefully avoided meeting John's gaze for as long as possible. Which was actually harder than it sounded, considering he was seated directly opposite me.

Eventually, he must have grown bored with the light, casual conversation about abstract art that Nelson was carrying, and decided to start a fight instead.

"Another one?" he commented when I reached for the wine bottle. "Don't you have work tomorrow morning?"

My hand stilled and my gaze snapped to his. "Excuse me?"

He wet his lips, his eyes glittering with amusement. "I said—"

"I heard you, John. I just wanted to provide an opportunity for you to find your better sense and retract the question." I held eye contact with him as I picked up the wine bottle, then poured my glass, filling it up way higher than the swell of the glass so that I could finish the bottle. Only once it was very clearly empty did I place it back down on the table. "Last I checked, you were neither my keeper nor my lover, so why the hell would I care for your thinly veiled judgment?"

"Not yet," he shot back so quickly and full of promise that I choked on the sip of wine I'd just taken.

Nelson cleared his throat dramatically. "Would anyone care for dessert? Maybe?"

I should have done the smart thing and excused myself. I was already more than tipsy and seeing John sitting there making casual friends with *my* family had only exacerbated my already foul mood. But the challenge was crystal clear in his eyes as he accepted Nelson's offer for dessert. He thought he could chase me away.

"I'd love some," I finally responded. "Maybe it can sweeten up the sour company tonight."

That comment earned me a kick to the ankle from

Hank, and a bark of laughter from John. Sick son of a bitch probably thought I was flirting with him. Dead wrong. I didn't care how hot he was, I'd rather call Chad for a second chance than cave to John Smith's inflated ego.

For now, though, arguing with him was soothing my panicked mind and healing the little mental wounds Dexter had inflicted so carelessly. So I stayed, even knowing it was likely to all blow up in my face.

seventeen

JOHN

Tristian was in a vicious mood, and it absolutely should not turn me on as much as it did. There was something utterly intoxicating about the way her dark lashes narrowed around her eyes as she glared daggers across the table. I needed to adjust my hard dick way too many times for polite dinner company.

Dexter. The youngest Grimaldi son. That was who had ruined her day and put that haunted look in her eyes. It was gone now, after a whole bottle of wine and plenty of distraction from me deliberately antagonizing her, but it'd nearly gutted me when she first walked in. She'd looked *scared*, no matter how quick she'd been to cover it up.

What the fuck had Dexter Grimaldi done to terrify my beautiful prey like that?

How could I convince her to tell me? To *trust* me?

I was at a loss. So I contented myself with simply helping her push it aside, to take up all the real estate in her consciousness and let her heal through redirection of emotion. She wanted to scream and yell at Dexter, to spit insults at him, maybe even inflict pain? She could do that to me, and it'd do nothing to deter my interest.

Hank glanced uncomfortably between Tris and me as his partner went to fetch dessert from the kitchen.

"So, um, John," he said, attempting to break the nearly suffocating tension across the table. "How long do you think you'll stay in Whispering Willows? I think you mentioned you're just covering Dr. Bailey's classes until he's well?"

I shrugged. "He might die."

Hank's brows shot right up to his hairline, and his lips formed a small O at my callous comment. Shit, hopefully they weren't friends with the old professor.

"Let's all pray for a full recovery, hmm?" Tris offered with a heavy dose of snark. "Like tomorrow. Then you can fuck off back to Finland."

A slow smile played over my lips. "You've been researching me, huh?"

She stiffened, a flash of panic at outing herself crossing her face. Then she shrugged it off. "You're the hot new professor at Boles, John. People talk. What did you expect?"

Oh, she thinks I'm hot. Excellent. As if her body language cues hadn't already alerted me to that information. Particularly her reaction to me waking her up this morning. Fuck that'd been enjoyable.

"Tell me about your job, Tris," I coaxed, hoping the wine was working its magic to loosen her lips. Shit, I meant, to make her chatty…but now I was thinking about a whole other set of lips and needed to shift in my seat *again*.

Apparently not, though, because she just sneered. "Bite me, John."

Christ, she had no idea how badly I wanted to do just that. Right on that peachy ass of hers, leaving my teeth marks in her pale skin like a brand.

"Tristian!" Hank scolded, looking outraged.

She instantly flushed red, her whole aggressive demeanor shifting to embarrassment. It took me a second, then I realized neither Hank nor Nelson had called her by her first name even once since I'd met them. It was always Ivy or Ives. Never Tristian. This must be the equivalent of a parent using their child's middle name.

"Sorry," she muttered—to Hank, not me—then drew

a deep breath before returning her pretty eyes my way. "I work at the university, Professor, as *your* TA. Remember? And I do it because I need the medical insurance. Birth control is worryingly expensive these days, but it's rather preferable to the alternatives."

Her smile was as sweet as arsenic and I tried really hard not to grin back at her. "I meant your other job, Tris. The one you rushed off to after class this morning."

"And the one you badly need to quit," Hank added quietly but not *that* quietly.

Tris shot him a warning glare. "It's not up for discussion." To me, she gave a closed-off look. "I do cleaning and restoration work for a local family's private collection. It's an excellent job, and I despise being late, so yes I do *rush off*, as you say."

I tried to act surprised, like this was new information to me and not the sole reason why I was pursuing her romantically. She, above anyone else, had the best access to the Grimaldi art collection and legitimate reason to be removing paintings from their frames.

Framed paintings were a bitch to steal *with* their frame. So bulky and hard to hide.

"This must be an impressive personal collection to have you employed full time," I commented, carefully keeping my interest professional. "Do they have a lot of old paintings?" Since there was no reason to clean or restore *new* art, it was a fairly redundant question. Which she was quick to point out.

"No shit, Sherlock. For a middle-aged man with a PhD you're not super smart, huh?"

I almost choked on the sip of wine I'd taken, and Hank gave her a sharp elbow to the ribs. He looked ready to scold her properly, so I quickly laughed to show I wasn't offended by her spice.

"Middle-aged man?" I repeated, still chuckling. "I'm offended. I don't think I look a day over thirty-five."

"Thirty-two, maximum," Hank assured me, nodding.

Tris wasn't amused, rolling her eyes. "How old *are* you, John Smith?"

I smiled. Then changed the subject back to her work. "What are you working on at the moment? Anything I might know?"

She wrinkled her nose. "If I told you, I'd have to kill you." It was a joke, but also…not. "I signed an NDA when I was employed by Mr. Grimaldi," she explained.

Of course she had. He'd have to be an idiot not to require that of all staff, or he'd have the art crimes douchebags crawling all over his mansion looking for stolen paintings. Not that the Grimaldi family were thieves; they were just rich and knew who to buy from.

"Sounds exciting," I murmured, watching her raise her glass to her mouth. The way her rose-pink lips caressed the delicate crystal rim held me enraptured until Nelson returned with a full size cake on a fancy glass cake stand. It was beautifully decorated with chocolate scrolls and powdered sugar, and I'd bet anything Nelson had made it himself.

Hank hopped up from his seat to fetch plates, and Nelson produced a gorgeous knife to cut the cake with.

"That's an impressive blade," I commented, leaning over slightly to take a closer look. "Is that a scaled down replica of the Sutton Hoo sword?"

Nelson beamed. "It sure is. Good eye."

Tris rolled her eyes again, scoffing into her wine glass like that would somehow muffle the sound. Nelson heard it, of course, and scowled at her.

"Ivy was just telling John about her work at RBD's," Hank informed his husband when he returned carrying plates and utensils.

Nelson seemed shocked at that, so I was going to take a guess that he was well aware about the Grimaldi family and their "business" ventures. "Is she now?" he murmured, serving big slices of cake onto the plates Hank held ready.

"Calm down," Tris muttered, "John truly doesn't care about my work. He's just offended that I haven't fallen for his charms so is now laying it on thick enough to suffocate me into submission."

A laugh caught in my throat, making me cough on the sip of wine I'd just taken. Shit, now I was trying to picture Tris as submissive in bed, and the image wasn't working. She was too…caustic. Not to say it wouldn't be fun to try…

I'd zoned out while indulging that brief fantasy, and when I tuned back in, Nelson was whispering something in Tris's ear that had her eyes sparking with fury.

"She's not wrong," I offered, sensing Nelson was scolding her for being rude to his dinner guest. "At least, about me being offended that she hasn't fallen for my charm. I *am* actually interested in your work, though." I addressed the feisty woman herself as I said that, locking eyes with her across the table. "Unlike *Chad,* I actually have common interests with you, *Ivy*. I'd very much like to hear more about this gallery you're working at." So very much more. Like how secure it was, and what the locks were like.

Nelson gave Tris a less-than-subtle nudge, and she painted a fake smile across her lips.

"Like I said," she murmured, still holding eye contact with me, "if I told you, I'd have to kill you. And blood is such a pain to get out of silk."

"Yes, I imagine you'd know," I commented quietly. Her eyes widened, and those perfect lips parted in surprise. I liked taking her off-guard like that. "This cake looks incredible, Nelson," I enthused, changing the subject before she could panic about me figuring her out. "Did you make it yourself?"

Nelson puffed up with pride as Hank distributed the plates, then sat down. "I did, indeed. I enjoy making things. Creating. Ives gets that from me."

"Oh, you're related?" I glanced between the two of them, not seeing the resemblance.

Tris gave a scoff, muffled by her mouthful of cake.

"They're not," Hank corrected. "They just act it. Did you leave any family behind in England?"

"Finland," I corrected, since that was where I most recently lived and worked *visibly*. Only very new or very stupid criminals left no paper trail of their own existence. The effort required to remain completely anonymous was entirely counterproductive. "And no. No family, no wife or girlfriend." Another heated look toward Tris. She didn't flinch or blush, just rolled her eyes. So sassy.

"Subtle, John, real subtle. Maybe next time just flop your dick out on the cake and see if anyone wants to suck it."

She didn't even attempt to say it quietly, either, and for a moment no one else spoke. For me, I was trying hard not to laugh, despite how horrified Hank and

Nelson looked at her less-than-polite dinner conversation.

"Ivy, that was too far," Nelson growled, shaking his head. "Even for you. John is *my* guest in *my* home, and you need to apologize."

Her jaw dropped, her cake fork forgotten in her delicate fingers. "*Me* apologize? He's the one who manipulated his way in here just so—"

"Ivy, *stop*," Hank said with quiet command. "Do you hear yourself? The man didn't manipulate anything, and no offense, sweetheart, but I don't think he's desperate enough to keep pursuing you when this is how you speak to him."

Oh *ouch*. That one had to sting. Little did Hank know, I was a sucker for the bad attitude on Tris.

"It's fine, really," I offered, trying to smooth things over. "I'm not—"

"I'd rather wipe my ass with a box jellyfish than apologize," Tris informed her pseudo-family. Then to me, she offered a sarcastic smile. "Kiss my ass, Professor Smith."

Tempting. So fucking tempting.

"Tristian," Nelson snapped, giving her a harsh glare.

She glanced down at her wine glass, her long fingers curling around the stem. But Hank put a hand on her wrist, shaking his head silently. Damn, was she thinking about tossing that at me? She was *really* fired up tonight, and it couldn't possibly be all directed at me. What the fuck had this Dexter creep done to her?

Her jaw tightened, then she drew a deep breath. "Thank you for dinner, Nelson." She stood up, shoving her seat back a touch more aggressively than necessary. "I've overstayed my welcome, it seems."

Hank gave a groan and whacked Nelson lightly with the back of his hand as Tris stormed out of their apartment.

"What?" Nelson hissed. "She's being a bitch and it's uncalled for."

"Jesus Christ," Hank sighed. "I'll go talk to her."

"I'll do it," I interrupted, pushing back my own seat. "After all, it's my fault she's upset. The least I can do is apologize to her myself."

Nelson rubbed his eyes. "No, that's nothing to do with you, John. She's having a hard time at work, and her standard coping mechanism is to lash out. It's my fault. I should—"

"No, really," I cut him off, already on my feet. "I insist. After all, she and I still need to get along in an academic relationship. Better we mend some bridges now. Thank you so much for dinner, it was lovely."

I was already halfway out of their home when Nelson replied, but I wasn't listening. My focus was entirely on chasing down Tris and getting some answers about what had happened to her today.

One way or another, I'd make her open up to me. Maybe once we established some trust, she would let her walls down.

eighteen

TRIS

What the fuck had John brainwashed Nelson with? How in the hell had he somehow snared my old neighbors in his web of charm and smug arrogance so fucking *fast?* Yes, he was hot. There was no denying the man's physical attributes. But good *God,* that personality left a lot to be desired.

Logically, I knew that John was only the straw that broke this camel's back. His small irritations and smug self-confidence were not *that bad* on their own. But compounded with that unpleasant *encounter* with Dexter this afternoon? Too damn much.

I practically kicked my own front door open, tossing my bag on the floor hard enough that I winced to hear my phone hit the ground. Whoops. I paused in my rage to crouch down and fish the device out and check if it was broken. Thankfully, the case had protected it, because I really didn't need to go forking out for a new phone right now.

My tantrum slightly dampened, I kicked off my shoes and padded through to my kitchen. I was tipsy, no question about it, but not so drunk I couldn't go for another glass of wine. At least just to try and calm myself down. Maybe I needed a bubble bath or something.

Nodding to myself, I headed through to my enormous bathroom and set the bath running before heading back into my kitchen. Then I pulled up short when I found I was no longer alone.

"What the *fuck* are you doing here?" I demanded, wishing I'd kept my heels on. Not that they put me anywhere near the same height as John, but I'd take any advantages I could get. "How'd you get in?"

He cocked a brow as he pulled a bottle of wine from my under-counter wine fridge. "You left the door open," he replied. "Again."

I scowled, glancing over at the door that was now closed properly. Now that I thought about it, maybe I didn't shut it. I got distracted with my phone hitting the floor, then just…forgot. Fuck. I needed to get my shit together before I started making mistakes in areas that would matter. My home security didn't count. Not even with John constantly breaking in.

"Okay well, thanks for pointing out the flaws in my routine today," I snapped, folding my arms under my breasts and glaring daggers. "You can leave now, I'm not in the mood for any more silly games."

His lips tugged into one of those infuriatingly sexy smiles. "Silly games? Is that what we're playing?" It should be illegal for a man that looked like John to have an accent that could turn legs to jelly. He kept his eyes on me as he poured us both a glass of wine, not spilling a single drop. Fuck that was hot.

I needed to swallow hard before I could reply. "John…get out of my house. I'm not in the fucking mood."

He handed me a glass, his fingers brushing mine as I took it without thinking. "What happened at work today, Tris?"

Irritation flared hot inside my chest, followed quickly by the nearly overwhelming stale taste of fear that Dexter had conjured up. Fuck, right when I'd nearly pushed that handsy creep out of my mind for the night.

"None of your goddamn business, John. Now for the

third time, get *out* of my house." I slammed my wine glass down too hard on the counter, breaking the stem and spilling wine and glass everywhere. I didn't care, though, too focused on running from the slippery memory of Dexter's hands on my thighs.

John didn't leave. Of course he didn't. I'd have been shocked speechless if he'd actually done as I asked, but instead he stepped forward and grabbed my wrist as I went to slap him.

"Tristian," he said quietly, his eyes intense. "What happened?"

I gritted my teeth, trying to pull my hand free. "You happened, John," I snarled back, redirecting my fear into pure bitchiness. "You keep breaking into my home and—"

"It's not breaking in when you leave the door open," he cut me off, giving a twitch of a smile. "But continue."

What the fuck was I saying?

A sting of pain in my hand distracted me, and I glanced at it. Apparently I'd cut myself when I broke my wineglass, because a small line of blood trickled down the pad of my palm and over John's fingers where he gripped my wrist. Not that it seemed to bother him.

"John...please," I tried again, some of the heat and anger deflating out of my voice. "Leave me alone."

His brow furrowed slightly, like he was trying to

judge whether I meant what I was saying. Then he glanced at my bleeding hand. "I can't leave you like this, Tristian. At least let me fix your cut."

I scoffed. "It's barely a scratch and you know it. The concerned doctor bit is way overplayed, you'd have to try way harder than that to win me over."

His gaze flicked back to my eyes. "Ah, so there's still a chance…"

Oh shit. I'm in trouble now.

"You're dreaming," I replied with a weak laugh. "You're my professor and my dissertation advisor. Nothing more."

His lush lips tilted. "You and I both know that's not true," he said, calling me on my bullshit. "But if that's how you want to play it…" He shrugged, releasing my wrist gently and stepping away. "I guess I'll see you tomorrow."

Panic rippled through me. Did I *really* want to be alone right now?

"That's it? You're just backing down?" I narrowed my eyes. "I don't buy it. You're not a quitter, John Smith."

He tossed his head back, barking a sharp laugh. "You're right," he agreed, his dark gaze returning to me with blazing heat. "I'm not. But I'm also not the kind of guy who forces his attention on a woman who has asked me to leave. Three times, no less. Get some sleep, Tris, I'll see you tomorrow."

Indecision and annoyance tore me to shreds inside as he started to turn to leave, and my tongue refused to make any words. Then he hesitated and turned back around. Two steps and he was right there in front of me.

I inhaled sharply as he leaned down. He was aiming to kiss my *cheek* and logically I knew this. I knew it, and was okay with it, and yet for some *insane* reason I found myself turning into him just as his lips brushed my cheek.

Time fucking *stopped* as his lips touched mine ever so lightly, and he froze.

"Tristian..." he murmured with an edge of warning.

He was right. What was I doing? I literally *just* told him I wasn't fucking interested, and here I was initiating a kiss? Yup, apparently I was. My better judgment flew right out the window as I leaned in to kiss him properly.

He gave me no more opportunity to change my mind. His fingers slipped into the hair at the back of my head, holding me firm as he kissed me back. Waves of hot desire washed through me as I moaned and parted my lips, allowing him access to kiss me deeper. Holy shit, my useless Tinder dates lately had made me forget what it was like to be *really* kissed, because the way

John's full lips devoured my mouth nearly made me come.

Melting into his strong grip, I let him lift me *one handed* until my legs wrapped around his waist. His huge palm gripped my ass, his fingers hooked under the edge of my skirt where it'd bunched up and my horny brain immediately started fantasizing about what it'd feel like to have those strong fingers plunged inside my throbbing pussy.

I tugged his lower lip with my teeth, like I'd imagined way too many times, and the groan he gave went straight to my clit.

This was a bad idea, no freaking question about it. But was it *really*? John was only filling in for Dr. Bailey temporarily, so technically he wasn't *my* teacher. Right? And he wasn't sticking around Whispering Willows forever, so there would be no harm done. Surely. Just some mind-blowing sex for a few weeks and then he'd return to Finland and I could go back to the two-pump-chumps on Tinder.

Shit broke on the floor as John sat me on the counter, his lips trailing down my jaw and kissing the side of my neck. Holy hell…that mouth ought to be illegal. He wasn't gentle with it, either, his teeth nipping my skin more than once as he left his mark right over my pulse point.

"Shit, Tris," he whispered, his hand skating up the outside of my thigh, under my skirt. "I thought for sure you were bluffing..."

I gave a sultry chuckle, because I *still* wasn't wearing panties. I did have stockings and suspenders on, though, which had been deliberately to tease John after he'd so rudely woken me up this morning. But apparently Dexter had taken my choice in clothing as an invitation.

Cold disgust lanced through the burning arousal and I sucked a sharp breath, pushing John away slightly.

"What's wrong?" he asked, immediately sensing the shift in my mood.

I swallowed hard, tasting the acid of fear on my tongue once more. Fuck.

"Nothing," I finally forced myself to say, shaking my head. "Um, this was a mistake. You need to go."

He frowned down at me a moment, still taller even with my butt perched on the counter. It wasn't an outraged kind of scowl at me changing my mind, though. It was more of a concerned expression, and that was worse. I'd have rather he acted like any other douchebag man left with blue balls and be an asshole about it, but no. John just *ignored* his huge hard dick between us and stroked a thumb over my cheek in the most painfully *caring* gesture that made me want to cry.

"Okay," he finally said, wetting his lips. It was so

damn tempting to lean in and kiss him again, but that was only going to continue giving him the wrong idea. So I gave a short nod and tugged my skirt back down as he stepped away.

He only moved away far enough for me to close my legs, but then braced his hands on the counter either side of my hips. "Tris...you can talk to me."

I shook my head because I really couldn't. He had *no* idea who I really worked for—Luther Grimaldi the mafia boss, not Luther Grimaldi the nice old art collector—and what happened to the people who crossed his family.

"There's nothing to say," I lied, my voice cracking with weakness. "It's late, I should sleep..."

His brow tightened again, then he gave a small nod. "Sure. I'll see you tomorrow." This time when he kissed my cheek, I remained exactly where I was. My only reaction was to let my eyelids drop shut, desperately holding back the tears heating the backs of my eyeballs.

When I opened them again, I was alone.

For a minute, I just sat there on my kitchen counter, staring across my apartment at the closed front door. Then the sound of running water reached my ears, and I gasped out loud.

"Fuck!" I screamed, racing back to my bathroom where the tub was overflowing all over the marble floor

and soaking the carpet of my bedroom. As if my day needed to get worse.

I turned the taps off, yanked the plug out, then just collapsed onto the drenched floor to cry. At least my tears couldn't make things any wetter than they already were.

nineteen

JOHN

Just because I left her apartment—as she'd asked—didn't mean I left the building. Not immediately, anyway. I closed her front door softly behind myself after leaving her sitting there on the kitchen counter like she was being held together by tissue paper, but then I just stood there leaning against her door for the longest time.

I heard her shout a curse a moment after I left, but then…nothing more.

Eventually I had to accept that she wouldn't come running after me to finish what we'd started—what *she'd* started, much to my shock—and reluctantly left her building. I wasn't going home, though. Not now…I had someone I needed to pay a visit to.

As I made my way downtown, I couldn't stop

thinking about Tris. Kissing her had damn near short circuited my brain. I was no stranger to using women to get what I wanted, but this particular job was coming dangerously close to making me lose focus. I'd *so* badly wanted to carry her through to her bed and really explore those suspenders properly…and she'd *wanted* me to. Hadn't she?

I licked my lips, tasting the memory of her kiss. Fuck, my dick was still hard, too.

Was she worked up and frustrated right now? Was she desperately searching her apartment for the new rabbit I'd stolen this morning? Smiling to myself, I imagined how enraged she might be when it was nowhere to be found.

Then again, she'd been so upset when she told me to leave, I might be the furthest thing from her mind. What had flipped her mood so abruptly? It had to have been when I mentioned her lack of underwear.

Which seriously made me question, what the *fuck* did Dexter Grimaldi do to my little Venus de Milo?

I pulled into the busy parking lot outside a club on the outskirts of town, locking my car and tucking the keys in my pocket as I sauntered to the entrance.

"Sorry, friend, we're full," the bouncer informed me, putting a hand out to stop me passing by.

I arched my brow. "On a Monday night? Is there something special going on?"

The bouncer was shorter than me, but broader. Mostly fat, I'd guess. "Yeah, it's called being the only strip club in a town full of horny college kids." He chuckled, his belly shaking. "And the girls ain't half bad, either."

I glanced past him, but couldn't see anything past the host station. With a sigh, I pulled out a hundred dollar bill and offered it to the man. "Will this help?"

He took it from me, then had the gall to hold it up to the light and check if it was authentic. Satisfied, he tucked it in his shirt pocket and reached for the velvet rope across the doorway. "My mistake, looks like we do have space for one more. Welcome to The Slippery Lips, friend."

The inside of the club was nothing special. It was just a cheap rip-off of one of the Copper Wolf venues in Shadow Grove that had been making a big splash in the entertainment market. Girls in skimpy outfits prowled the floor, giving lap dances or providing "conversation" for patrons while one dancer had her time on the stage.

I casually leaned against the bar as I searched the dark interior, searching for a certain Grimaldi who was known to frequent this club. Among all their other shady businesses, The Slippery Lips was a good front for washing dirty money, and rumor was that Dexter ran the joint. And enjoyed the perks of that position.

"Can I get you a drink, big man?" a sultry waitress asked, leaning across the bar to touch my arm. "You look thirsty."

I smiled politely back and ordered a whisky on the rocks. "Is your boss here tonight?" I asked when she placed my drink down on a coaster.

She tipped her head to the side, seeming uncertain. "Which one?"

"Dexter," I answered, and caught her slight grimace of distaste before she covered it up. So Tris wasn't the only one who had an issue with the youngest Grimaldi.

The girl nodded across the room. "He's over there. Sin is in town for the night I think."

Curiosity sparked at that. Sinister Grimaldi was Dexter's older brother and the heir to the Grimaldi family businesses. He spent most of his time working on acquisitions and mergers…hostile takeovers to grow the company in his father's name.

I thanked the waitress, paid for my drink, and headed over to a vacant table closer to where the Grimaldi brothers were sitting with a group of men that seemed to be lower level muscle. Dexter was in the throes of a lap dance from a petite woman, his hands gripping her ass as she swayed and ground against him in time with the music.

Slightly further away, the older Grimaldi brother sat scowling into his drink, ignoring the girls floating around their group, eager to please the bosses. He looked positively uncomfortable, which was curious since I knew he frequented other strip clubs and brothels on business. Maybe he was just feeling awkward about the way his brother way practically fucking that woman in front of everyone.

The music shifted and the girl in Dexter's lap performed an almost inhuman back bend, flipping herself over to wiggle her crotch right in his face a moment before righting herself once more.

I sipped my drink to hide my smile, watching the private show with new interest.

It took her a few minutes, dealing with Dexter's wandering hands like a professional, but eventually she locked eyes with me across the dark club. Her brows rose ever so slightly in surprise, and I smirked, saluting her with my drink.

She continued dancing, not missing a beat, but with the hand she'd wrapped around the back of Dexter's neck she extended her middle finger.

I chuckled, sipping my drink and letting my gaze wander around the room once more. My confrontation with Dexter would have to wait for another night. It was poor form—and against the rules—to knowingly sabotage another Game player while working a mark. At least now I knew who I was up against.

Only three contestants competed in the final round of the Game, all of us vying for the same prize. It wouldn't be the first time I'd gone head-to-head with Tink in a Game, and it also wouldn't be the first time I beat her. She was a tough opponent, though, I'd give her that much. Tiny, pretty, and trained as a contortionist from childhood, she was my dead opposite.

I finished my drink then pushed to my feet. I'd leave her to work Dexter over because he was a dead end on *Poppy Flowers.* Only two people currently held security clearance for the Grimaldi gallery, and one of them had her tongue down my throat an hour ago.

Past the main floor of The Slippery Lips strip club, there was a gaming lounge set up with a handful of card tables. I gritted my teeth as I made my way over to the blackjack table and tapped a guy on the shoulder.

"Leave," I told the man. "Now."

"What? I'm not—" the guy glanced up at me. And up. Then winced at my murderous expression and nodded. "Yeah, you know what? Texas Hold 'em might be more my speed tonight." He gathered his chips and scurried away, leaving his seat vacant.

"Was that necessary?" the smirking card dealer asked. "There were other seats, if you really wanted to play."

He was right. The guy I'd scared off was the only one who'd been at this particular table. I sat my ass down in one of the empty seats and folded my fingers in front of me. "Hi, *Dad*. How unexpected to see you here." I arched a brow, my implication clear. He'd always had a nasty gambling habit, so his posing as a dealer in the Grimaldi club was so predictable it was embarrassing.

There was no guilt in his smile. "You know how it goes, son. The best cover story is just one step away from the truth. Isn't that what you're doing, too?"

My jaw tightened. "My position at Boles is—"

"I wasn't talking about teaching, Ivan. I was talking about the way you're seducing that tasty little brunette. Who is she, anyway? Someone working for the family?"

I swallowed back my emotions. He didn't know Tristian's connection to the Grimaldis, which meant he was *way* behind the game. Not shocking, he was probably just planning on following Tink and me until he could cheat the win. As if the council would ever allow that to play out…but Igor was a dirty cheat at heart and knew no other way.

My response was a tight smile. "It's John. Ivan died a long time ago, old man."

His expression darkened somewhat. "Of course. Well

good luck with whatever your angle is. Seduce the girl for…something?"

"Oh sure, let me just tell you my whole plan so you can win the Game." I rolled my eyes, the sarcasm heavy in my voice. "You must think I'm stupid. This isn't *my* first rodeo." But it *was* his, suspicious in and of itself.

My father just shrugged, shuffling the cards in his hand. "Well, suddenly there's something worth playing for." The Valenshek Legacy. My grandfather's enormous wealth, hidden away and awarded to whoever won *this* Game. He loved to make things difficult, that was for sure. "I have to admit, Iv—sorry, *John*—I never thought you were the kind of man who could pull this off."

Irritation prickled at my spine. I never should have approached him. "Pull *what* off?" I gritted out. "This is my fifth Game, and I've won all four previously. Why would this be any different?"

My father's smile turned cold, calculating. "Not the Game,I meant your *angle*. Making a poor innocent girl fall in love while you use her for selfish gain?" He clicked his tongue disapprovingly. "That's low, even for a thief. Have you thought how heartbroken she'll be when she finds out she got *used?*"

That struck a chord, way too deep. I swallowed before answering. "You're misinformed, per usual. That's not even remotely what my angle is, and your silly amateur mind games are pathetic. Good luck working *this* angle, though." I indicated his uniform and sneered. "Nice to see you won't be providing any real competition for me."

I pushed back from my seat and strode out of the gaming room before he could get another word in. Tink caught my eye as I passed, her brow raised in silent question, but I ignored her and continued out of the club. My *fucking* father had gotten under my skin, and I was *furious* about that fact.

What the hell did I care how heartbroken Tris might be when she worked out what I'd done? I'd be long gone, and never returning. She was tough enough; she'd be fine. It wasn't like she even *liked* me, let alone was at risk of falling in love.

No, that wasn't my angle. I didn't need—or want—her to love me. I just needed her to let her walls down *just enough* to give me what I needed, and then I was gone in a puff of smoke. Just a memory of a good time… I hoped.

So why then did I drive away with a sick sense of dread in my belly?

twenty

TRIS

Dinner at Nelson's with John had been...*ugh*. A bad idea only scratched the surface of my mixed-up feelings toward that whole cursed encounter. Not only had I been drunk, bitchy, and aggressive, but I'd also nearly announced exactly what Dexter had done to me. Which was nothing, comparatively. Wasn't it? I mean, it could have been worse.

Regardless, if I told Hank and Nelson what was really going on, they'd make me quit. And I had too much invested in my position with Mr. Grimaldi to throw it all away now over my own inconvenient sense of personal space.

And then there was that kiss.

It was the wine. Obviously the wine was to blame. I

would *never* have made a move on John Smith otherwise…would I? I mean…sure, I was attracted to him, but there was more that had to go into decision making than just pure chemistry. Like his shitty, infuriating personality for starters.

But…goddamn, that *kiss*. If I'd had panties on, they'd have been set on fire.

Then of course I went and ruined it all by having a panic attack.

Thank *God* he'd left when I asked him to, so no one had to witness my meltdown. When I'd woken for work this morning, though, it had taken a whole lot of makeup to put my face back together. Even so, Mr. Grimaldi commented on my bloodshot eyes when he passed me on my way to the gallery.

I'd been so nervous on going back to work that I needed several attempts to unlock my workspace. My palms were just too sweaty to get a clear read. But eventually I made it inside and could breathe slightly easier until it was time to go.

There was no zoning out and losing time for me this time. The looming threat of Dexter hung heavy over my head for my whole work shift, and I decided to leave ten minutes earlier than usual. If for no other reason than the fact I needed to pull my shit together before class with John.

I held my breath as I opened the gallery door, peering out carefully before fully exiting.

To my intense relief, I didn't see a single other person as I hurried out to my car. Adrenaline rushed out of me as I drove away, making my hands shake and cold sweat sluice down my spine. I fucking *hated* that feeling. I needed to get a damn grip and stop letting Dexter inside my head. He was a nuisance and nothing more.

With my extra time, I swung by my apartment for a lightning-fast shower to chase away my lingering fear, and a fresh set of clothes. I dressed up, using my sexual tension with John as fuel for my tough exterior.

By the time I got to campus, I was running a tiny bit late. My short skirt swung around my thighs as I hurried down the quiet corridor toward the lecture halls. My focus was consumed by how much I hated being late and frantically playing out all the various scenarios for how John might treat me today. We'd kissed...*I'd* kissed *him,* and then when things got heated I'd spiraled into a panic attack and kicked him out. Was he going to be weird? Or act like nothing had happened? Or...angry? I didn't know which option was worse.

Someone grabbed my arm just before I reached the lecture hall, yanking me off balance and making me exclaim when my center of gravity tipped. I didn't hit the floor, though, as a strong arm picked me up and dragged me into a small, dark space. A closet. I was in a closet with—

Oh. *Ohhhh.*

The way John's lips crushed mine erased all my anxious scenarios of how he would act around me. Hell, it erased all thoughts entirely as I parted my lips and kissed him back with an edge of desperation. His huge hands grasped my butt, lifting me up as my legs wrapped around his waist, giving him easier access to kiss me considering our height difference.

It was still a bad idea, but right now it was exactly what I needed to clear my head of anything other than my intense need to fuck my professor.

He moaned as I bit his lower lip, his hard length grinding against my core. He had my back against the door, trapping me with his huge body. To my surprise, it didn't panic me in the least. It made me feel…*safe.*

Shit, I couldn't be developing actual feelings for John. That was the *worst* possible scenario, and totally absurd. He was annoying, arrogant, entitled, and rude. No, I wasn't catching feelings, I was just sexually frustrated and his thick cock trapped between us was promising to rock my world.

"Tris…" he murmured against my mouth as I rocked my hips and tugged his shirt free. "We have a class to teach."

Words failed me and I gave a small sound of disagreement. Fuck the class, they could take the day off. Right?

He broke away, grinning like a damn Cheshire cat. Then he kissed me again, softer this time and it wreaked absolute fucking *havoc* on my heart.

"I just wanted to make sure last night wasn't a hallucination." His voice was a sexy deep rumble that sent shivers through me and made me squirm again. *Damn it, John, make me come.*

He didn't, though. He simply set me down on my feet once more and brushed a teasing kiss over my cheek. "To be continued, Venus."

And then he was gone. Fucking *gone*.

I was speechless. Did he seriously just…?

For a minute—or longer—I stood there staring at the closet door where John had exited. I needed to process my jumbled thoughts. First there was my intense frustration at being left high and dry—metaphorically only; I was all kinds of wet physically—and then the confusing, intoxicating desire for the arrogant son of a bitch. Finally…outrage and anger. How dare he play with me like that? He knew full fucking well what he was doing, yanking me into this little closet for what was hands-down the hottest make-out session of my whole damn life.

Also, who the fuck did he think he was with that cutsie nickname? Given our shared education in art history, it wasn't hard to work out he was naming me after Venus De Milo. I liked it way more than I should.

Except now he'd left me in a janitor's closet, all worked up and desperate for dick, while he strutted back into the lecture hall like nothing happened. Or, so I assume. I was too paranoid to leave the closet just yet. Fucking hell, I'd bet anything my makeup was like something out of a Halloween special now, too.

"Shit," I breathed out loud, bracing my hands on one of the shelves as I fought to get my breathing steady once more. My pussy was throbbing. Distracting me. After my panic attack last night, I hadn't bothered hunting for my new rabbit, but now I was seriously wishing I carried a bullet in my purse or something.

No way could I go into class like this. John would be counting on it, too, the smug fuck. He was probably in there right now, hiding his boner and waiting to see me walk in all flushed and horny.

Licking my lips, I slipped a hand under my skirt and rubbed my clit through the damp fabric of my panties. It wasn't my preferred method, but it was a hell of a lot better than letting John call the shots. Closing my eyes, I let my mind slip back to that kiss from just minutes ago while my fingers went to work.

It always took longer to do things manually, and required more imagination, but thankfully John had left me with plenty of fresh mental images to draw from. The touch of his big hands, the press of his fingers into my flesh, the full softness of those lips…It was all too easy to picture what it'd be like to have that mouth all over my body, kissing, sucking…I'd bet money that he ate pussy like a pro.

That was the mental image I needed to find my climax, and I gripped the shelf tight as my body tensed and trembled, my knees going weak.

It wasn't *the best,* but it would do the trick. It'd ease the burn of arousal enough that I could go into the lecture hall calm and collected, not panting all over the professor like a bitch in heat. Then maybe after class I could get something more *penetrative* than my little rabbit clit vibe from the local sex shop. After all, a girl couldn't have too many toys.

Smoothing my skirt back down, I took some slower breaths to calm my racing heart. I'd still need to stop by the ladies' room and fix my makeup, but then I could stroll on into class and show John that he's outmatched. I could not, and *would not,* be played like that. Regardless of who started things last night.

I should have been more annoyed than I was, but when I saw how badly he'd smudged my lipstick I was just...turned on. Damn it. Instead of outrage, my belly was buzzing with excitement and the fizzy warmth of anticipation.

Kissing John while drunk had ripped the tourniquet off, and now this thing between us was gushing out like blood from a severed artery. I had to hope it'd die off just as quickly...before either of us caught real feelings.

If it wasn't already too late.

twenty-one

JOHN

My focus was shot all to hell as I started the lecture. Tris hadn't come in yet, and my mind was still back in the closet with her. It'd taken a monumental amount of effort to leave her like I had, and I'd damn near changed my mind the instant I put her down. But I could already see where her head was at. She thought she could fuck me once and *clear her head*.

That was far from my intention. I needed to really make sure the hook was set before I reeled her in. And that, unfortunately, meant not giving in to the suffocating tension between us. Not yet.

When she *finally* entered the hall, I couldn't keep my eyes off her. Shit she was gorgeous, and that beauty was only heightened by the puffiness in her lips. Knowing I'd done that made me stumble over my words and lose my train of thought.

Tris picked it up for me, smooth as fucking silk as she took over my presentation for the next two slides, giving me time to pull myself together. I ended up needing to hide behind the lectern to adjust my pants. I doubted the dean wanted to hear complaints about me walking around a class with my hard dick acting like a divining rod.

"...right, Professor Smith?" Tris was saying, tilting her head toward me in amusement. What the fuck did she just ask? I had no clue, because I was too busy thinking about my dick.

She inclined her head ever so slightly, and I took it as a hint that I needed to agree. "Yes, exactly," I quickly replied, flashing a smile to the students while I pretended I had even the faintest clue what I'd agreed to. Glancing up at the projector screen, I recognized one of my prepared slides with a small theory exercise. Tris must have just told them to do said exercise.

"Are you okay, John?" she whispered, stepping closer with her back to the students. It meant none of them could see the devious grin on her lips, or the glint of evil in her eye. "You seem...flustered."

Understatement of the fucking year. It would seem like my plan to get her worked up and panting for me had backfired. Spectacularly. Here I was, gripping the edges of the lectern like it could somehow ease my blue balls, and she seemed totally fucking composed.

Wetting my lips, I swallowed back the need to bend her over a desk right in front of the grad students. "Fine," I lied. "Just thinking about how *hard* this lesson is."

Her smile widened. "Is it?" Like she didn't already fucking know.

"I don't think this is hard at all," someone in the front row interrupted. Clearly I hadn't lowered my voice like I'd intended. "In fact, it's kinda easy compared to the stuff Tris was teaching. No offense, Professor, but you're a big softie compared to her."

Tris was biting her lower lip, her shoulders shaking with silent laughter and I glared daggers at her.

"Thank you, Mr. Pembroke," I replied to the opinionated student. "Good to know. Miss Ives, don't you have assignments to mark?" I nodded to the huge pile of work on her desk, recently turned in by another of my classes.

She just smirked and sashayed her sexy butt over to the desk. I was coming dangerously close to losing the upper hand with her…something I needed to rectify *soon.*

The rest of the lecture was pure torture. Plain and

simple. I ended up letting the students leave early because I was thoroughly disinterested in teaching them much of anything.

"Ending the class early," Tris commented from her desk as the last of the grad students filed out of the hall. "That's unlike you, Professor Smith. You usually love to listen to yourself talk."

A few remaining students snickered a laugh, but I waved them off, waiting for them to leave and the door to close before taking Tristian's bait. She was still marking papers, her spine straight and her legs crossed, but I couldn't help noticing the way her pen wobbled as I drew closer.

"Well, it occurs to me that we were in the middle of something," I said quietly, teasing my fingertip down the bend of her neck from behind, watching her skin shiver and react. Her pen slipped on the paper she was marking, leaving a line of ink.

"Were we?" she asked, oh so innocently. "I don't recall. Now, if you don't mind, I was—"

"Let me remind you," I cut her off, grabbing her by the waist and spinning her to sit on the desk. The stack of assignments toppled to the floor, scattering everywhere, but it was worth it to hear the breathy gasp of lust that escaped her lungs.

My plan had been to kiss her again—or maybe more

—but before I could get close enough she planted her heeled shoe on my chest, pushing me away.

"Not so fast, Casanova," she scolded, keeping me at arm's length. Or *leg's* length, as it was. "I don't know what that little closet scene was all about, but I don't appreciate being played."

My eyes widened. "I told you—"

"Uh huh, weak excuse at best. You know what I think?" She leaned back on her hands, keeping her high heel planted against my chest. It hurt, but I still leaned into it to test how determined she was. Very, apparently.

I licked my lips again, appreciating the view she was presenting with her leg up like that. "What do you think, Venus?"

Her lips ticked up with a smile at her new nickname. It suited her, I thought. Beautiful…but as hard and unyielding as marble.

"I think you're trying to dickmatize me until I'm so desperate that I can excuse your crappy personality and inflated ego." Her words were designed to hurt, but there was nothing but lust and amusement in her eyes.

"My ego is perfectly in proportion with the rest of me," I informed her, reaching down to grasp my erection through my pants.

She followed my gesture with her eyes, her tongue darting out to wet her lips. "Huge, apparently." She cleared her throat, shaking her head slightly as she returned her gaze to my eyes. "I hate to be the bearer of bad news, John…but yours isn't the only dick in town."

Her leg flexed, pushing me away far enough that she could hop off the desk. She picked up her bag and tucked the strap over her shoulder as my brain frantically processed what she'd said.

"Venus, you better not be saying that—"

"Sorry, Casanova, I can't chat. I have a date." Her wink fucking *slayed* me, and then she was sashaying out of the class with that short skirt swaying like a red flag in a bull pen.

My jaw dropped. "Tristian, don't you dare—" I started to protest, but she was already gone, flipping me her middle finger as she disappeared out the door. "*Fuck,*" I exclaimed to the silent room. Everything in me demanded that I run after her, but just glancing at the mess of assignments scattered all over the floor made me pause.

Damn it.

Damn *her*.

I knelt down and quickly tidied up the mess, putting the papers all back on the desk before packing up my own things to leave. She *had* to be messing with me. No way was she going to meet another Tinder loser after that kiss earlier. No freaking way. Fuck knew I couldn't fathom the idea of fucking anyone else right now.

That in and of itself should have set off alarm bells in my head, but it didn't. It was just the truth.

I needed to follow her. I needed to *know*.

"Ah, John, just the man I was looking for." My jaw tightened as I glanced over my shoulder, finding Dean Lawrence striding along the hall toward me, a smug smile on his weathered face. "A word in my office?"

I groaned inwardly, then turned to face him with an impatient expression. "A quick one, Lawrence, I'm in a hurry."

His answering smirk was way too smug for my liking, and a cold thread of worry tightened around my lungs. "Of course. Come along then."

He led the way into his office which wasn't far from where we were, and waved me in ahead of him. When he closed the door, he flicked the little lock and I raised a brow.

"Lawrence, if this—"

"You said you were in a hurry, John, so I'll cut to the chase. I appreciated you delivering on our little agreement last night. Very much appreciated it." He licked his lips in a creepy way.

I held back a snort of laughter that was threatening to escape. I didn't judge others for their kinks, because it was no harm to me what revved the dean's engine. If anything, it just made controlling him easier.

"No thanks necessary, Lawrence. If that's all...?" I gestured to the door, clearly wanting to leave.

His smug, greasy smile was back. "It's not. I'd like some more."

I sighed. "No. Now, if there's nothing else, I'll be going."

Dean Lawrence cleared his throat, then turned his computer monitor around and hit play on the video he already cued up. Mother *fucker*.

"I see," I murmured, watching myself and Tris on the screen. It was nothing pornographic, just CCTV footage from the lecture hall. But it was definitely a compromising situation, with her foot on my chest and her skirt all hitched up around her waist like that. Shit.

Lawrence stopped the clip. "I'm glad we're on the same page, John. Use polish this time, please."

I rolled my eyes and stuffed my hands into my pockets. If I had *any* hardness left after sparring with Tris, it was well and truly gone now. "Sure. Color?"

The dean swallowed audibly. "Purple," he replied, his voice breathy. "With glitter."

I jerked a nod, then let myself out of his sweat-stinking office without another word. Technically, I held more power than he did here. His fetish getting out to the public would do much more damage to his professional life than my tryst with a student. But that split second of decision made me second guess myself. I couldn't call his bluff, because regardless of how little I might care...Tris would. And I couldn't jeopardize that...not yet. Not when I was finally getting somewhere with her.

Besides, as far as blackmail went, the dean wasn't asking for anything outrageous or humiliating.

Now that I'd well and truly lost Tristian's tail, I gave up my plan to follow her and instead went home to my staff cottage. Maybe I could work off some steam in the shower, while picturing her spread out naked underneath me.

Or hell, maybe I'd just sit in my dining room and jerk off on the print of her Renaissance Woman self-portrait. Yeah...that'd do the trick. Next time we crossed paths, maybe I could keep my head clear and stop acting like a horny teenager.

twenty-two

TRIS

I hadn't been lying when I told John I had a date to get to. I just failed to mention that my date was with a brand new rechargeable boyfriend. Unlike my usual mini rabbit—the bang bang bunny—which just worked the clit, I'd upgraded to a Big's Bunny, the "girthy" edition. Even so, I got the distinct impression John's dick would put my new toy to shame.

Still, I spent *way* too long indulging in self-care that afternoon while painting. I chalked it up to the fact that I was painting naked again…and that John had seriously got into my head with that make-out session this morning.

Eventually—when my pussy was actually aching—I showered, dressed, and shifted my focus to assignments and my dissertation. Much less sexy, but only just thanks to my egotistical professor having his fingerprints all over every piece of work.

My stomach rumbled aggressively at me sometime after dark, and I yawned. Come to think of it, I'd missed lunch, so it was no wonder I was hungry. My fridge was embarrassingly empty, though. I spent far too much time eating my meals at Nelson and Hank's place these days. Which wasn't an option today, since I was still furious at them for inviting the devil into their home last night.

"Take-out it is," I muttered to myself, putting my shoes on. I'd rather walk two blocks for Chinese than cross the hall to speak to Nelson right now. Traitor.

If I was being honest with myself, I was mad at him for more than just playing buddy-buddy with John Smith, the insufferable prick. I was also nursing a grudge about Dexter. Nelson was the reason I worked for the Grimaldis…but I also knew he'd make me quit if he found out what was going on. So I was pissed at Nelson for putting me in that position and pissed that he was forcing me to keep my mouth shut about it. Basically just mad as hell on all fronts.

So I raked my fingers through my messy, damp hair and power walked my cranky butt over to Royal Orchid, where they made the most excellent honey sesame chicken. I called my order in on the way over but was fully prepared to wait when I got there.

The restaurant was busy, which wasn't unexpected, but it did make me wish I had some friends that I could be texting or calling while I waited. Hank and Nelson were my only real friends, and they were both old enough to be my grandfathers. I just never made the time—or effort—necessary to build lasting relationships with girls my own age. Always too busy in my art studio.

Now, though, I seriously craved someone to talk to about things. Mainly John. I needed a peer perspective on the headfuck that was Professor Smith.

I was so caught up in my own head, thinking about how mad I was at the world and feeling sorry for myself, that I ran straight into a woman exiting the Royal Orchid with her hands full of take-out boxes.

"Oh shit!" I exclaimed, reaching to steady her, but she somehow managed to keep them all stable. If it'd been me, they'd be all over the sidewalk by now. "I'm so sorry, I wasn't paying attention."

"You're fine," she assured me with a laugh. She was smaller than me, her hair an edgy platinum bob and her eyes a deep mossy green. "No harm done. Thank God. I'd have cried if I needed to wait for Charlie to cook me another Kung Pao Chicken when I'm this hungry."

"Oh, good choice," I enthused. "It packs a punch, though."

She grinned. "Oh, I know. I've only been in town a month and I think I've eaten here at least a dozen times already. So tasty."

I smiled, agreeing. "I'll let you go. Sorry again for nearly ruining your meal."

"We're good. I'm Katinka, by the way." She somehow held onto her huge pile of food while extending a hand for me to shake.

"Tristian," I replied, taking her hand. "Are you a student at Boles?"

Her laugh was like bells. "No, God no. I'm working at The Slippery Lips over on East Street." *Oh.* I nodded awkwardly, and she laughed again. "Geez, I'm a stripper, not a prostitute. No need to give me that face."

My cheeks instantly heated. "I wasn't judging, I just…"

"Didn't know what to say? Totally fine. I sucked at academics, but I'm crazy bendy, so it was either stripping or the circus. And, don't tell anyone? But stripping pays *way* better." She grinned, full of the type of unapologetic self-confidence I envied. Not that I was a wilting flower myself, but I faked my strength while hers seemed totally authentic.

I shrugged, smiling back. Her energy was infectious.

"I dunno, as small as you are, you always could have become a thief. I bet that pays well."

For some reason she found that *all* kinds of funny and nearly dropped her food when she laughed so hard. "You're right, Tristian," she finally chuckled. "Maybe I need a career change. But for now I guess I better keep shaking my ass on stage for sweaty old men."

"Well, it was nice meeting you, anyway. I better see if my food is ready." I nodded to the front door that we were still standing in front of. "Have a good night."

"You too, Tristian," she replied with a warm smile. "Hopefully I'll see you around."

Unlikely, given I had never stepped foot in The Slippery Lips the entire time I'd lived in Whispering Willows…but it was kind of a shame because Katinka seemed like the sort of girl I could be friends with.

As I let myself into the restaurant my stomach tightened at the wave of delicious smells that hit my nose. Yum. My mouth was already watering. I approached the take-out counter, but the woman working told me my order was still another five minutes or so away and to take a seat.

There was a small waiting area divided from the main restaurant by a couple of potted plants, but I didn't even make it to the vacant seat before spotting a familiar face in the restaurant. Make that *two* familiar faces.

John locked eyes with me, his expression totally unreadable. Then he quirked one brow…invitation or challenge? Fucking asshole.

I swallowed my anger back and pasted a smile on my lips as I approached the cozy table for two.

"Professor Smith. Fancy seeing you here." I totally ignored his dinner date, keeping my eyes locked with John's.

He leaned back in his chair, casually resting his elbow on the back like he knew how good that made his arms look. "Don't act innocent, Miss Ives. Admit it, you're following me."

I rolled my eyes, all kinds of irritated. "In your dreams."

"Frequently," he replied, his gaze heating.

A small cough reminded me that we were not, in fact, alone. So I forced a laugh and shook my head like it was a joke. Somehow. "Sorry, how rude of me to interrupt your dinner. I was just collecting take-out. I'll leave you to it. Nice to see you again, Janie."

"Yeah, you too, Tris," she replied with a brittle smile and a clear *fuck off* look in her eyes.

I gritted my teeth and turned my back on them, fury sparking along my spine as I walked away. Was he fucking serious right now? Just today he was dragging me into a supply closet and trying to fuck me on a desk after class. Now here he was having dinner with Janie fucking Hartman? Prick.

The fact that I'd lied and told him I had a date was beside the point. Because it was a lie. He was *actually* here with her…and now I wanted to stab him with a damn fork. Repeatedly. In the jugular.

Womanizing bastard.

It took *way* more effort than I'd really prepared for just to sit my butt down in the waiting area with my back firmly to the restaurant. The six minutes it took before my name was called at the take-out window were pure hell, and then my night got six million times worse.

The kind of catalyst event that drove regular people to become supervillains.

I'd forgotten my wallet and couldn't pay for my dinner.

twenty-three

JOHN

The urge to grab Tris before she walked away was nearly overwhelming. It took all my effort to clench my fist on the table instead and simply watch her sexy, yoga-pants-covered ass retreat back to the front of the shop.

"Are you sleeping with her?" Janie *fucking* Hartman asked with clear envy. "Because that'd be totally against the university rules. You could get fired if anyone found out."

"Oh yeah? Then why are you trying so hard to suck my dick, Janie?" Okay. Maybe not my most tactful moment, but Tris had knocked me off balance.

Janie gasped her outrage, pressing a hand to her chest. "Professor Smith! I am *shocked*...that you don't think I'd treat anything between us with the utmost discretion and privacy."

Good lord.

"Janie, I appreciate the offer—" I really did not "—but Tristian and I are not sleeping together." Yet. "So this is highly inappropriate."

The waitress started to bring over my meal, but I quickly asked her to box it up for me to take away instead. I had better places to be.

"What did you say to her?" Janie asked with wide eyes, making me realize I'd spoken to the waitress in Mandarin.

My focus was on Tristian's dark hair over at the takeout counter, though. She was stressed out about something, raking her fingers through her hair and her shoulders slumped.

"Janie, a word of advice? It's rude to invite yourself to eat with someone else, particularly your professor. Did it occur to you that I wanted to dine *alone* tonight?" I leveled a hard glare at her, and she wilted. "Like you pointed out, I could lose my job for fraternizing with students. No offense, sweetheart, but I'm not risking it for you."

She flinched, and rightly so. It wasn't even a thinly veiled insult. But I was annoyed that Tristian had misconstrued what was happening here, since Janie had sat herself down uninvited just minutes earlier.

"Professor Smi—"

"Shush, Janie," I cut her off, standing up. "Your desperation is showing."

Leaving her there, I strode over to where Tris was still speaking with the hostess at the counter. I just managed to catch enough of their conversation to understand what was going on, so before Tris could leave I placed a hand on her waist and politely asked the hostess to charge her meal with mine, which was being boxed up for takeout. In Mandarin, of course, which saw Tris jerking her head up to stare at me.

"I like how impressed you look right now," I murmured as I handed over my credit card to pay. "I need to surprise you more often."

"I'm not impressed," she grumbled, taking her bag of food when the hostess passed it over. "I'm embarrassed. I can't believe I forgot my wallet. I was sure I picked it up on my way out the house."

"Maybe you had other things on your mind," I suggested, flexing my fingers where I still held her waist. Just in case she'd somehow forgotten our extracurricular activities already.

Her scoff was somewhat insulting as she slipped out

of my grasp. "Thank you for paying, John, but you really should get back to your date. Good night."

She slipped out the door just as my own bag of food came out of the kitchen, so I collected it then followed. I didn't call out or catch up, but she knew. I knew she knew.

After half a block, she whirled around and glared daggers. "Stop following me, John. It's creepy."

I pointed to my chest, glancing around as if confused who she was talking to. "Me? Follow you? Aren't you the one who turned up at my dinner table?" I tipped my head to the side, offering a playful half smile. "Besides, maybe we just happen to be heading in the same direction."

Her eyes narrowed further. "Bullshit."

I shrugged. "Maybe I just want to make sure you get home safely. It's dangerous out here at night, you know?" She just stared straight through my lies, making me feel awkward all over again. "What are you doing for the rest of the evening, anyway?"

She pursed her lips, like she was considering feeding me a fabrication. Then sighed. "Studying. My professor actually still expects me to turn in updates as well as mark assignments."

"He sounds like a twat," I commented, deadpan. "An insufferable, arrogant, overwhelmingly handsome twat."

She broke eye contact as she tried to hide a smile, clearing her throat. "Yes, well. That twat is in charge of my academic future right now, so I really should get back to studying. Good night, John."

I continued following when she started walking, and she quickly lost patience.

"Seriously?"

I smiled. "It just occurred to me, you haven't had any proper one-on-one time with your dissertation advisor in *weeks*. Not since Dr. Bailey's health started to decline."

Tris scowled. "We had one yesterday, when you broke into my apartment and woke me up."

"One doesn't make up for all those weeks of missed time," I countered, "and the door was open. It's not breaking in unless I break something."

"If you're suggesting a mentor session *now*, you're crazier than you look. Go home, John. I've got shit to do and delicious honey chicken with veggie fried rice to eat." She lifted her food bag to remind me, then spun on her heel and continued walking home.

I followed.

"Janie must be fucking awful in bed if you'd rather stalk me to get away from her," Tris muttered, loud enough for me to hear.

I chuckled, reaching into my own bag to grab a

spring roll. Yum. "Is that jealousy, Miss Ives? Green is particularly sexy on you, I must admit."

She muttered some curses under her breath, and I happily munched my spring roll as I followed her the rest of the way to her building. When I tried to follow her inside, she put a hand on my chest to stop me.

"What do you think you're doing?" she asked, her brows raised with a clear challenge.

I smiled my very best innocent smile. "My food is getting cold, with all this manly protection I was forced to do. Can't I borrow a fork?"

A small chuckle escaped her. "You really can't take no for an answer, can you? Does it hurt your ego, John? Being turned down? I bet it's new."

"I don't know what you're talking about, Tristian. I'm only concerned about your academic results."

"And my safety, walking home alone," she added.

I nodded. "And that."

Her eyes narrowed. "And your cold food."

I grinned. "That, too."

She pursed those pretty lips again, squinting up at me. "You can help me with my dissertation and that's it. Then you're gone."

I held up my bag of food. "And eat?"

Her eyes rolled. Again. "Fine." She stepped out of the

way, letting me in as she pressed the elevator call button. "But only because it's a crime to let good food go cold."

Victory was so close I could taste it.

I kept my mouth shut as we rode the elevator up to her floor, then waited as she unlocked her door. The suspicious look she gave me as I entered her apartment was unmissable, and totally entertaining, but I still didn't push my luck.

"Do you have anything to drink?" I asked, setting my bag of food down on her kitchen counter and going straight to the cabinet storing her plates. If she noticed that I already knew where to find them, she said nothing.

"I have wine," she replied, putting her own food bag beside mine and folding her arms. "Although that sounds like a terrible idea considering how last night turned out."

I chuckled, pulling out two wine glasses. "I'd say it turned out pretty great."

"Just so we're clear," she said with an edge of determination in her tone, "this…thing. Whatever game you think you're playing tonight? It's not going to work. Last night was a moment of insanity, and not one that I intend to repeat."

I poured us both a glass of Shiraz. "And what about today?"

"Entirely forgettable, clearly," she lied, giving me a sarcastic smile. "Either way, I'm not fucking you tonight. Or any night, for that matter. You're bad news and you damn well know it."

She had no idea.

"Tristian..." I sighed, shaking my head as though uncomfortable. "I never intended for you to fuck me tonight, and to be honest I'm a little offended that you think that's all I came up here for. Yes, I'm attracted to you. But I've never been interested in winning a woman over by wearing her down...I'd much prefer enthusiastic participation from my bed partners. I really just wanted to help you study."

Liar.

She wasn't buying my shit for even a second. "Uh huh. Sure. One more time to really get my point across. I'm *not* going to fuck you tonight."

Amusement rippled through me. "You're not going to fuck me tonight. One hundred percent understood, loud and clear." I offered her a glass of wine. "Shall we eat?"

Suspicion rolled off her in waves, but she took the glass anyway and watched as I plated up our food with ease, not needing to search around her kitchen for anything. I'd already poked around enough while she was asleep to know where she kept all her things.

To be fair, I wasn't feeding her lines she wanted to hear. I fully accepted that I wasn't getting laid tonight. She most definitely wasn't in the mood, which might have had something to do with the curious new hot pink device sitting on her painting stool when I glanced into her studio. Spoiler alert, it wasn't a paintbrush.

But more to the point, my *plan* with Tris didn't entirely revolve around bedding her. Yes, that was one way to slide past the emotional barriers and gain her trust, but I needed more than that if I were to use her access for *Poppy Flowers*. I needed to know *her*. So tonight, that was my plan. Gain a better depth of understanding about who Tristian Ives was, and what keywords she might pick for a password.

And then…maybe tomorrow *I'd* fuck *her*. Not the other way around.

Crap, now my dick was getting hard again. *Think quick, John.* "Tell me about Nelson and Hank," I suggested, grabbing the most logical topic of conversation and the least boner-inducing one at that. Old men didn't do it for me, but as far as I could tell they were the closest thing Tris had to family in this town. They were a solid place to start.

Reaching into my pocket, I turned on my voice recorder.

twenty-four

TRIS

As I sat across the table from John, sharing a strangely intimate meal, all I could think about was *where the fuck had I left my vibrator?* Not because I needed to use it—we'd had enough self-care time all afternoon—but because I would be beyond mortified if John saw it. And it'd totally ruin my cool, calm, collected vibe if he knew I'd spent the afternoon masturbating like a sex addict.

Thank fuck I did, though. No way could I keep my paws to myself if I was still riding that sexual tension high from this morning.

John seemed genuinely interested in *getting to know me* while we ate, which freaked me out. I didn't open up to anyone outside of my elderly neighbors, I sure as shit wasn't trusting John as far as I could throw him. And he looked heavy. So I fed him some bland bullshit that barely even scratched the surface of my history with Nelson and Hank.

"Why do I get the feeling you're not telling the truth?" he eventually asked, slouching back in his chair and spreading his legs wide. I *hated* when men did that on public transport, but it was stupidly hot in this setting. Like he needed extra room for his massive cock.

Crap. *Wrong train of thought, Tris.*

"Why would I feel the need to lie?" I responded, standing to take our dirty plates to the kitchen simply to stop myself thinking about John's cock any longer. "It's not like I'm some kind of deadly assassin working for a secret society." I chuckled to myself, thinking about what a shitty assassin I'd make.

John drained the last of his wine, then joined me in the kitchen. "Nah, you don't have the right vibe for the Mercenary Guild. You're too…human."

I scoffed. "Oh, I bet." Funny guy. Like such a thing even existed. "I thought you were going to help me with my dissertation tonight, not deep dive into my personal life."

"Speaking of," he took the opening that I hadn't intended to provide. "How was your date this afternoon? Can't have been good if you're out getting Chinese for dinner *alone*."

I opened another bottle of wine. "You can't help yourself, can you? Maybe I should ask how your date was with Janie, but I already know the answer seeing as you're here…with me."

"Touché," he murmured, holding his glass out for me to refill. "What are you working on right now?"

His eyes held mine as he sipped his wine, and a hot flush of heat rippled through me. "Um, my dissertation. We already established this."

He smiled, then headed in the direction of my studio. "I meant, what are you *painting?* There are splatters on your right forearm."

I frowned, peering at the limb in question. Sure enough, just below my wrist there was a red and gray smudge of dried paint, which was flaking slightly. How I'd missed that when I showered, I had no clue.

Then suddenly I remembered where I'd left Big's Bunny and gasped. "Wait, John, you shouldn't—" But it was way too late; he was already inside my painting studio, standing in front of the canvas I'd left on the easel. Shit. Shit, shit, shit. Was it still there on the chair? Or had I moved it? Why couldn't I remember?

Biting the inside of my cheek, I hurried over to the studio and tried to subtly peer around John to check for the hot pink bastard. Relief washed over me with intensity when it was nowhere to be seen. I must have taken it into the bathroom to wash. Or maybe even tossed into my bedroom drawer. That sounded more likely.

"Tell me about this," John prompted, peering at my latest project.

I tipped my head to the side, looking at the abstract splashes of color then glancing up at John. "Why don't *you* tell me about it, Professor? You had some pretty strong opinions about my painting at Boles."

He tilted his face toward me, one brow raised. "This is a vastly different style from the *Literary Woman* self-portrait, Tris."

I smirked. "I'm full of surprises, John. My style changes depending on my mood…and the assignment. That one at Boles was a custom request while I was going through a neoclassical phase of study."

He nodded slightly, turning his attention back to the painting I'd been messing around with. "And right now you're in an abstract phase?"

"Apparently," I muttered, mostly to myself. "This was just a…therapeutic project. I've actually been working on still life lately."

John studied my unfinished piece a little longer. "Something feels very familiar about this. Kind of…I'm not sure. Masculine? What is your muse for this?"

I bit my tongue, refusing to look up at him for fear of

betraying the truth. "Uh, cats," I said, picking the first thing that came into my head that wasn't *you, John.*

"Cats," he repeated, frowning at the painting.

"Yes, John, *cats*. It's a portrayal of the staccato nature of feline affection. Obviously." I scowled as I doubled-down on my bullshit. "It's a work in progress." Grabbing a drop cloth, I tossed it over the artwork to hide it from view before he could notice that the moody golden brown in the corner was the exact shade of his eyes. "So...shall we look at my dissertation work?"

He hummed a response but continued looking around my studio, the nosy fuck.

"What type of still life?" he asked, picking up one of my sketch books and flicking through. "Fruit bowls? Flowers?"

I folded my arms under my breasts and gave him a hard look. "I thought you were here to look at my research, not browse my art."

Placing my sketch book back down, he shot a quick grin in my direction. "I'm just curious, that's all. Last time I was here I didn't get a chance to see your work."

No, because I was busy climbing his body like a monkey in a tree.

"Come on, Casanova," I drawled. "Textbooks are this way." I exited the studio and breathed a small sigh of relief when he followed me over to the coffee table where I'd left all my notes earlier.

I picked up the pretty floral notebook that I drafted all my key points in and handed it to him. "Here, take a look over these. I just need to use the bathroom super quick."

Scurrying into the bathroom, I frantically searched around for anything embarrassing. I scooped up my dirty clothes from earlier, tossing them into my laundry basket, but didn't spot Big's Bunny anywhere. Thank fuck, it must be in my drawer. And John had *no* reason to be in my bedroom, so I was pretty sure I was in the clear.

That was a relief. Talk about a close call.

"All okay?" the big sexy fuck asked when I returned to the living room. He was seated on my couch, making it suddenly seem so much smaller than I remembered.

I nodded, taking the single seat perpendicular to the couch. "Yep. So…am I on the right path with my notes?"

He glanced at my notebook in his hands, then squinted at me. Then gave a pointed look at the empty couch space beside him.

Stubbornly, I pretended I wasn't following his train of thought and just blinked innocently while waiting on his response.

He quirked a brow at me, then sighed and tossed my

notebook aside. "We shouldn't try to discuss academics after wine. It's just begging for mistakes to be made. Tell me about how you got into painting."

I wrinkled my nose, tucking my foot up onto my chair so I could hug my knee. "Why do I feel like you're interviewing me for something, John?"

His smile faded slightly. "Does it? I'm sorry, that wasn't my intention. I just find that it helps me as a teacher to understand what motivates my students. Where their true passion lies, whether it's in the actual art theory, the practical, or the history." He leaned forward, bracing those delicious forearms on his knees. "Help me get to know you better, Tristian."

Why did my name sound so freaking sexy on his tongue? It had to be the accent. That was the only explanation for it.

I swallowed hard, all my bullshit fakeness flying out of my head. Something about the intense way he started into my eyes had me totally unable to lie.

"Nelson got me into it," I admitted, my voice soft. "I met him the first time when I was six. In a casino. My mom had a really bad gambling habit and just took me along with her then forgot I was there. One night, it had to have been after midnight, I got lost while hunting for dropped quarters. Suddenly everything looked the same, all bright lights, loud noises, and strangers. My mom was nowhere to be seen and I panicked."

I paused for a breath, remembering that fear of abandonment like it was yesterday, and John shifted forward in his seat, closing the expanse between us somewhat.

"Is that when you met Nelson?" he asked quietly, a worried frown marring his brow.

I nodded. "He found me curled up and crying underneath a closed roulette table. I told him what had happened, and he helped me find my mom. She didn't even notice I'd been gone." *Bitch.* "Then a few nights later he saw me there with her again. He bought me chocolate milk and asked questions that made me feel… I don't know. Visible. Then a few hours later he came over with a bag from the casino gift shop. It had a coloring book in it and a tin of beautiful colored pencils. It was the most incredible thing I'd ever owned."

"That was kind of him," John murmured. "Did you see him frequently from then?"

I shook my head. "No, not for years. I colored every page in that book, then managed to get some blank paper to start drawing the pictures for myself. Eventually, though, the pencils ran out and my mom wouldn't replace them."

He scowled. "Let me guess, the rent was months

overdue already and your power was about to be shut off?"

I gave a small laugh, releasing my knee to reach for my wine on the table. "How'd you know?"

John grimaced. "I know gamblers. So how'd you reconnect with Nelson?"

I took a huge, unladylike mouthful of my wine and swallowed hard. "In the same casino again. This time I was around nine, I think? He found me in the bar, drawing pictures of the patrons with a blue ballpoint on serviettes. He remembered me and sat talking to me for a while. Mostly asking shit about my mom and why a kid my age was in a casino bar. You know, normal concerns."

John scrubbed a hand over his hair. "Yeah, I know. So what happened to your mom? How'd you end up living with Nelson?"

I smiled, then sipped my wine again. "I don't live *with* him, we're just neighbors. Technically Hank is my landlord, though."

"Ah yes, I remember him mentioning that he's an interior designer. He did a beautiful job on this conversion." John's gaze scanned my open-plan loft with appreciation, and my insides warmed with pride for Hank.

"That night when I was nine, Nelson gave me a

business card and told me that if I was ever in trouble and *needed* someone to keep me safe, to call the number on it. I tucked it into my drawing things and pretty much forgot all about it until I was eleven and running away from home. I was dumb, naïve, had *zero* plan…but I refused to go home. Then I found Nelson's card in the bottom of my bag and figured I had nothing to lose." I shrugged, finishing my wine with another mouthful. "The rest, as they say, is history."

John studied me for a long, quiet moment. Then he drew a deep breath and let it out slowly. "So…we have more in common than I realized."

That surprised me, and I reassessed his body language. He was concerned for me, yes, but he was also tense and slightly defensive. "Your mom, too?"

He shook his head. "My dad. My mother died when I was four. Brain cancer."

I gasped softly. "John, I'm sorry…"

"I barely remember her," he admitted with a sad smile. "But she was my father's *whole* world. He didn't love anyone like he loved her…including me. He spiraled into addictions and gambled away my mum's entire fortune before I reached high school. Which was impressive, seeing as she was from a very wealthy family. She'd lost touch with her parents when she married my dad, but when my grandfather found out…" His words faded as he stared into space for a moment.

I gave him silence, not wanting to butt in on a moment of internal reflection.

He flashed me a lopsided smile with only a hint of warmth to it. "Christophe raised me after he found out, and it was honestly the best thing that could have happened to me. He taught me everything I know. He made me into the man I am now *despite* my father."

There was a depth of emotion in his voice that surprised me, and I craved more information. I might not admit it, ever, but I wanted to understand him better, too. This felt like the first glimpse of the *real* John Smith, and I didn't want it to end.

"I'm glad you had that," I told him with sincerity. "Even if he did raise you to be an arrogant prick who can't handle rejection." Whoops there went the tender moment.

John tossed his head back with a laugh, then shrugged. "He wasn't perfect by any means, and I'd dare say his ego would dwarf mine. You'd have *hated* him."

Oh shit.

"How long ago did he die?" I whispered, realizing he was using past tense when speaking of his grandfather. The man who had raised him when his shitty father failed. When I thought of losing Nelson, or even Hank…

it was like a knife to the guts. I couldn't even begin to understand.

John's eyes dipped to the floor and he swallowed. "Six months ago," he said, his voice husky. "He's the reason I'm even here, funny enough. Playing his games even after he's gone."

Confusion furrowed my brow. "How so?"

John's lips parted, then his eyes jerked up to meet mine like he'd just realized what he'd said. Then he forced a smile to curve his full lips. "Sorry, just... moping. Losing him was unexpected, even as old as he was. He was just one of those guys that seemed immortal, you know?" He glanced at his watch, then ran a hand over the back of his neck. "It's pretty late. I should get going."

He was already on his feet and heading for the door before I could think of a plausible reason why he should stay. Aside from *I don't want you to leave,* I had nothing. And I was way too stubborn to offer that level of vulnerability when he was still playing jealousy games with Janie Hartman.

"John," I blurted out as he opened my front door. He paused, turning slightly to look back at me. I took a few steps closer, awkwardly playing with the hem of my sweatshirt and feeling way out of my depth. "Thank you..." *For being real with me. For sharing something so personal and making me feel less exposed with my own honesty* "...for dinner, I mean. I'll pay you back."

A sad smile flickered over his lips. Then he crossed the space between us and cupped my cheek with his huge hand, tipping my face back. His lips met mine softly, but went no further.

"There," he murmured. "Paid."

My breath caught in my chest, and I damn near drowned in his gaze. Then he released my face and started out the door once more, making my insides swoop like I'd just crested a rollercoaster.

"Oh, out of curiosity," he said from the doorway, his hand on the frame as he glanced back. "What was the name of the casino?"

I frowned. "The Royal Pelican. Why?"

He nodded once. "No reason. Good night, Venus."

The door closed before I could respond, so I whispered *good night* to no one.

twenty-five

JOHN

Sweat dripped down my spine as I burst out into the street below Tristian's apartment. My heart was racing and my breath shallow, and I just needed…*fuck*. Why the hell had I bared my soul like that to her? However brief, it still left me feeling *naked*. And that pissed me off.

I needed to speed up my plan. I needed to complete this heist, steal *Poppy Flowers,* and get the *fuck* out of Whispering Willows before I could lose my head. Or my heart.

Just thinking of the useless organ made my chest hurt, and I rubbed the heel of my hand against my breastbone. Tris just had a way of making me forget… and that was something I couldn't afford to do.

Especially not now when my grandfather's legacy was on the line.

Stuffing my hands into my pockets, I glanced up at the top window of the building. Warm light spilled out, and I found myself imagining what Tris was doing now. I'd up and left so abruptly, was she confused?

"Stop it," I hissed to myself, forcing my eyes away from her window and setting off down the street. I'd parked at the Royal Orchid, two blocks away, so I set a quick pace to get back there. I couldn't help smiling to myself as I walked, feeling the stolen vibrator tucked into the back of my pants, disguised by my shirt. The sheer *size* of this one had proven a challenge to conceal, but where there was a will, there was a way.

I'd almost started laughing when she came into th studio and started looking around. She'd been relieved when it wasn't there, but what was she going think when she worked out it wasn't *anywhere*?

Taking it was reckless, and foolish. Sooner or la she would put the pieces together and realize I stealing her toys. But I quietly hoped it would take more thefts before she figured it out.

Meanwhile it was doing wonders for my smug to think she would be getting more and more fru by the day. Although she could clearly get the jo manually, if her rapid recovery after the supply closet was a hint.

Pushing Tris out of my mind—as much as humanly possible with the taste of her kiss still on my lips—I refocused on my task at hand. Soon I'd have the keys I needed to steal *Poppy Flowers*, so I needed to do my due diligence on how secure the manor really was.

It was a tricky thing, testing security systems. They needed to be poked at and activated. But if you did it too much, you risked the whole system being replaced or upgraded, throwing the entire plan back to square one.

I parked my car a good mile to the south of the Grimaldi house and popped the trunk. I always kept some spare supplies in my car, so I quickly swapped my clothes for blacks and pulled on a pair of gloves. Only morons left fingerprints when they didn't intend to.

Once I was ready, I lifted the hood and hid my keys so I wouldn't risk jingling while creeping around the Grimaldi property, then set off into the trees. My eyes needed a minute or so to adjust to the thick darkness, but it wasn't long before I could walk more confidently without a light.

There was no rush to get there, so I took my time and marked out a mental map of my path. It was late when I arrived at the edge of the property itself, but some lights were still on in the house, and a pair of security guards walked the grounds casually, chatting about a football game and barely paying attention.

"Complacent," I whispered to myself, watching as the men passed by where I stood only a dozen feet away. "Looks like no one has tested the Grimaldi security in far too long." Which was only going to work in my favor.

Once the guards passed, I tossed a stick against the fence to check if it was electrified. Nothing sparked, and I wasn't surprised. If no one had ever tested the defenses, why bother maintaining them?

I waited another minute while the guards' voices trailed off into the distance, then scaled the fence with ease. Now that I was inside the property boundary, I needed to move quickly and avoid detection by both the guards *and* the cameras. Just because the Grimaldis failed to electrify the fences didn't mean they'd turned off the CCTV. That'd just be stupid.

Keeping my pace casual and unhurried—unsuspicious—I searched out the camera points, calculated their angles and then slipped into a blind spot. Raised voices from inside the house caught my attention, and I shifted closer to hear them better.

Sure enough, as I found a new hiding spot beneath a window and behind a particularly thorny rose bush, the conversation sparked my interest again. Tristian. They were talking about Tris…and it sounded like someone wasn't happy with her.

No, wait. They weren't happy *about* her…or more to the point, about something that'd happened concerning her and the other participant of the conversation. I'd put money on that being Dexter.

What the fuck had happened? What had he done to put that *fear* in her eyes last night?

Against my better judgment, I waited there and listened. This was *not* what I'd come to do tonight, and yet…Tristian Ives was fast eclipsing all other priorities in my life, and that simple fact filled me with dread. I couldn't let her fall for me…it wasn't fair, when for me she was merely a means to an end.

So why then was I filled with rage on her behalf, ready to blow my cover and fight Dexter Grimaldi for her honor?

Maybe it was grief messing with my head? She'd somehow got me to open up about my grandfather, and it was like ripping the surface off a fresh scab. Christophe was the only person I'd ever come close to loving, so maybe it was all just getting mixed up in my head now.

"…been over this a thousand times, boy!" The angry words spilled out of the window as I crouched there, desperate for more information. That had to be Luther

Grimaldi, head of the family and Tristian's employer. "You're not to touch her again, am I clear? If I find out..." The rest of the threat became muffled, but my blood was already running cold.

Again. He'd put his hands on her? I'd put money on that being against her wishes, too, considering the mood she'd been in after work.

Fuck. Here I was planning a nice, easy art theft. Now I'd be leaving a body behind when I left, because the urge to murder Dexter Grimaldi was so hot I actually found myself halfway out of the rose garden before I caught myself.

"Stop it," I scolded myself, keeping my voice barely louder than a whisper. Nowhere near loud enough to be overheard and caught. "She's not worth losing the Game for."

Somehow, saying it out loud made that statement even more hollow than it'd been inside my head, but I shook it off. I had to. Whatever was going on with Tris and Dexter, it was her issue to sort out. She could always quit her job if it was that bad, couldn't she? It wasn't like she was scraping her pennies together, living in Hank and Nelson's beautiful building. Not to mention, her pay from Boles for working as a TA.

If she was keeping this job, then it couldn't be as bad as I was imagining.

Could it?

No, Tris wasn't a victim, and she wasn't weak willed by any stretch of the imagination. No way in hell would she put up with abuse just to keep her paycheck, no matter how healthy it was. She'd have kicked him in the balls and phoned in her resignation.

That was the story I sold myself as the voices of Dexter and his father faded away out of the room and I released my pent-up breath. *This* wasn't my objective; *she* was merely a distraction. A means to an end and a huge distraction.

Repeating that to myself, I set about my task of testing the manor security. Above all else, I had to keep my head in the Game. Christophe had left *everything* to the winner of this event, and while I could possibly stomach seeing Tink take it home, I'd rather die than give it to Igor.

With that in mind, I poked and prodded the house until eventually I tripped the alarms. Then I timed how long the response took, and in what form. How many guards, what kind of weaponry, then followed silently as they decided it was a false alarm. I needed to know what they'd do *after* a false alarm. Would they tighten security and run checks on all the camera feeds? Or just go back to playing cards in the break room? All these little pieces of information were invaluable in planning my escape once I had my prize.

It was nearly dawn when I returned to my car, but I had a plan.

Now everything depended on *her*. Tris. She was the missing piece in my puzzle, and I would make her fall into place...one way or another, even if it hurt her.

Or me.

twenty-six

TRIS

Dinner with John had been…weird. Weirdly *comfortable,* if I was being totally honest, like we were actually finding common ground with one another. I'd spilled my guts about my shitty mom, totally without meaning to, but he'd kind of reciprocated by telling me about his grandfather.

But then he'd freaked out and left.

When I woke up the next morning, I had a message in my voicemail from Mr. Grimaldi. He said he was dealing with some business and to take a few days off work. That wasn't the part that was unusual; he'd done this once before, and when I'd returned the whole house smelled of bleach. But something about the timing of this gave me an uneasy feeling.

Mr. Grimaldi advised that he'd be in touch when he

wanted me to return, but for now I should enjoy some time off. Like I wouldn't spend every spare second of my day panicking that something terrible had happened… or was about to. Still, it gave me time to catch up on my academic work so I couldn't protest too much.

The only downside to *that* plan? John was being weird.

For a *whole fucking week* after that gentle kiss as he left my apartment, he treated me like he was my advisor…*and nothing more.* At first I thought he was just playing silly games, making me second guess this whole thing between the two of us. Then I thought he was maybe trying to make me make a move on him…which I refused to do because fuck him for trying to manipulate me.

The more time that passed, though, the less certain I was of that assumption. What in the fuck *was* going on, then? I couldn't shake the uneasy feeling of coincidence with Mr. Grimaldi giving me time off work and John going cold after trying to fuck me on top of a desk last week.

It was stupid. They didn't know each other, and the two things had nothing to do with one another…but it sat uncomfortably that the timing coincided.

The one silver lining to having a week off work was that I hadn't seen Dexter. Over the weekend I'd found the party invitation Mr. Grimaldi had given me—along with the new blouse—and realized it was only a week away. So after yet another awkward class with John on Tuesday afternoon, I hurried out to the parking lot with plans to go shopping. Knowing the Grimaldis, it would be a black-tie affair, so I needed a new dress to wear.

I'd been late when I arrived, deliberately waiting until the last second to enter the lecture hall, so I'd had to park way over in the back of the staff parking lot. It took me a few minutes to walk there, fidgeting with my keys the whole way. I was *trying* to think about what sort of dress I should buy, but all I could focus on was whether John would see it…and what color he'd like the most.

"Pathetic," I groaned to myself when my car came within sight. "He's not going to see it, Tris."

The invitation had included a plus one, but I wasn't taking one. It was pointless when all I needed to do was show my face to keep my employer happy and keep up appearances. Worst case, I could probably take Hank.

That idea made me smile. Maybe I could convince Dexter that Hank was my sugar daddy or something? If he thought I was unavailable, surely he'd lose interest.

Ugh, who was I kidding? That wouldn't stop him. His own marriage sure as fuck wasn't.

"Tristian!" Someone grabbed my elbow, making me scream in fright.

I jerked free of their grip, spinning around in a panic to find some guy from the football team with a weak smile on his face.

"Whoa, sorry," he said with a forced laugh, "I didn't mean to scare you. I called out a couple of times, but you didn't hear me."

My frown deepened. "Okay?" I just…wasn't in the mood. I recognized this douche from a few years ago. He'd asked me out and I turned him down, not wanting to deal with relationship drama within school, and his friends gave him shit. Then he'd called me frigid like *that* was mature. Asshole.

"Are you in a hurry to get somewhere?" he asked, giving me a once over. "You look good, by the way. Like…hot as fuck. The whole student teacher thing is all kinds of—"

"Did you need something?" I interrupted, not wanting to hear his thoughts on my clothing choice. I only dressed to impress one person, and I was embarrassed to admit that it hadn't even been for *me.*

His eyes dipped to my cleavage again. "Yeah, you dropped this back there." He held up my sketchbook. "Figured you would want it."

My lips parted in surprise, and I glanced down to

find my bag was halfway unzipped. Crap. "Yeah, uh, thanks..." I reached for the book, but he held onto it when he should have released. "Um, is there something else?" I tugged on the book, trying to make it obvious that he needed to let go.

"Actually, there is...I was wondering if I could take you for a drink sometime? Some of the guys thought you were hitting it with the new prof, but I'm not buying it after how he talked to you in class just now." He tried to give me an endearing smile, but it just came off as smug.

I swallowed, remembering how cold and *professional* John had been during class. Then gave a tight smile and jerked my sketchbook free of his grip. "Sorry, I'm seeing someone." I stuffed the book into my bag as quickly as I could, avoiding the guy's eyes. I couldn't even remember his name, and all I could think was the condescending way John said *Chad*. Now every slightly rude, self-centered guy was *Chad* in my head. Dammit.

"Ah, that sucks," New-Chad said, rubbing the back of his neck. "Maybe if things don't work out, you can give me a call."

I grimaced, then felt like a judgmental bitch for it. "Maybe," I agreed weakly. "Thanks again. I should...go." I jerked a thumb over my shoulder in the direction of my car, and the football douche gave a nod.

"Sure. Got it. See you in class, Tristian." He gave a small wave and walked away, leaving me standing there with frazzled nerves. Hell, I didn't even realize he was *in* my class, and if that wasn't a clear indication of how much focus John sucked up, I didn't know what was.

Okay, that wasn't fair. John had only been at Boles for a month, and the year was nearly over. I had no excuses.

Blowing out a sigh, I raked my fingers through my hair and continued toward my car. What was I thinking about when he'd scared me? Clearly it was something important if I hadn't heard him call out my name. Oh. That's right. I'd been fantasizing about John escorting me to the Grimaldi party like a scene out of a chick flick.

Groaning at my own pathetic obsession, I pressed the unlock button on my key and reached for my door handle. My fingers barely brushed it before a hand clamped over my mouth and a large body crushed me against the door.

Fuck! Douchebag?

A wave of familiar smell reached my nose, and my knees nearly gave out. I'd rather it had been douchebag.

"Have you been avoiding me, Tris?" Dexter growled in my ear, his tongue wetting my lobe and making me shudder with disgust. "You haven't showed up for work all week, beautiful. Did I scare you off?"

I tried to shake my head, since his hand was still clamped over my mouth. His other hand slipped between my shirt and skin, his fingers finding my breast and squeezing painfully hard.

A whimper escaped me, and Dexter moaned, crushing his hard dick against my backside.

"Oh yeah, you like that, huh? I knew you were one of those girls." His fingers mashed my boob again, sending pain shooting through my chest. Was he kneading bread? Oh my fucking God, that hurt. "You'd better have been lying to that little shit just now, Tristian. I told you last week, I'm done with our flirtation. I'm claiming what's mine this weekend at the party, you understand? No one fucking tells me what I can and can't have. Not you, you filthy little whore, and not my father." His hips rocked against my backside again, and his breath came in short pants like he was about to come in his boxers. "Am I understood?"

His hand was still over my mouth, so I just nodded.

For a moment, his response was just heavy breathing. Then he licked the side of my neck and chuckled. "Good. Wear something pink for me, Tristian. Pink like I bet that wet pussy of yours is. Fuck I can't wait to see it."

He jerked against me, grunting, and vomit crept up my throat.

"Don't forget, babe. Friday night, you're all fucking mine."

One more vicious boob twist and he released me, his footsteps fading away across the concrete as my knees buckled and tears tracked silently down my cheeks.

My knees hit the hard ground, but I barely even registered the pain. I was cold all over, uncontrollable shivers shaking my limbs as I wrapped my arms around my knees and hid my face behind them.

Once again…it could have been worse. He could have done worse. And if he was to be believed, he fully intended to at his father's fancy party on Friday night. Why? Why wait until then and not just get it over with? He had ample opportunity just now…unless he was worried I would scream if he let his hand off my mouth.

I wanted to think I would have…I wanted to believe I was the kind of girl who'd scream so loud the entire campus could hear me. Like I would have fought him off, kicking and clawing, making it as physically difficult as possible.

But I wasn't. I'd frozen and let him touch me…just like I had last week when he'd caught me after work. I'd just…done nothing. Because I was scared, and because I knew he was no ordinary predator. He was Dexter Grimaldi, youngest son to a mafia don who I'd *just* witnessed shooting a man a scarce fortnight ago.

Something told me that if push came to shove, Mr. Grimaldi would protect his name, his son, and I would just disappear.

So I just sat there beside my car, curled up in a ball as I sobbed my heart out because I was *terrified*...and because more than anything, I hated myself for not being the girl I wanted to be. Deep down, I was weak, and Dexter knew it.

twenty-seven

JOHN

Keeping my distance from Tris all week was pure fucking torture. After that night at her apartment when she opened up to me about her mother and I realized how eerily *similar* our stories were…I knew I needed to take a step back.

She did *not* make it easy, though. At first it was flirty comments and smiles, then she realized I was pushing her away and she got vengeful. Those outfits she wore to our mentor sessions couldn't have been an accident. Damn woman was trying to break me rather than make a move herself, and it was working.

The distracted way she'd just rushed out of class while wearing those skintight black jeans and high-heeled boots was the last straw. It'd been a week since I kissed her, and I was craving her lips like a drug. I needed to rethink. Regroup. Reassess. *Something*. But I couldn't keep going like this.

Also, when I broke into her apartment again the night before while she slept, I'd spotted the invitation to a party at the Grimaldi house on her table. I'd been at this game long enough to know my perfect opportunity when it arose, and *that* was it. I'd use the party as my distraction and lift the painting. This time next week, I'd be long gone from Whispering Willows, so surely I could give in to desire for just these last few days?

To my frustration, though, a student approached as I packed up my computer and stuffed it into my briefcase.

"Yes?" I snapped, terse as all hell, then regretted it when she flinched. As convenient as this cover identity was, I actually liked teaching. "Sorry. I'm just in a hurry. What can I do for you, Miss Jewel?"

The painfully shy girl clutched her bag to her chest like a shield, avoiding eye contact as she shifted her feet. "I'm sorry, sir. I just wanted to ask for an extension on the research assignment? My grandma is—"

"Yes, fine," I quickly agreed, not interested in yet another sick grandma story. At least ninety percent of them were bullshit, but this particular student had an otherwise flawless record. She could get some grace without spilling her family history. "Just turn it in when it's done."

Her eyes widened in surprise, but I was barely paying attention.

"Is that everything, Miss Jewel?"

Her lips parted and she blinked, confused. Then she frowned. "Um actually, no. I'm sort of struggling with…" I stopped listening. I just nodded and hummed like I was listening, then quickly suggested she book an appointment to chat in my office when I had more time. Next week. When I'd be gone from Boles and a new teacher would take over.

By the time I managed to get out to the parking lot, I figured Tris would already be long gone. She'd had a determined look on her face like she had somewhere to be, despite the fact she'd not gone to work at the Grimaldis even once all week. Something about it made me uneasy. The fact that they'd given her leave right after I poked at the security had me worried that they were making upgrades.

I needed to take a little drive and check out what was going on. Maybe I could play the part of dumb, lost foreigner and ask directions at the gatehouse. Yeah, good plan. My car was in staff parking, so I slid into the driver's seat and started to reverse out of my spot when I paused.

Was that Tris's car? Further down the lot, almost as far from campus as possible…It definitely looked like her shitty Corolla. But she had to be long gone by now. That student had delayed me nearly ten minutes leaving the class, and Tris had been in a hurry.

Curiosity spiked at me, though, so I put my car back into park and got out.

What was my excuse if she was in her car? Maybe she just got a phone call and her car was crappy enough that it didn't support Bluetooth calling? She definitely seemed like the law-abiding type, so she wouldn't risk talking on her phone while driving.

As I drew closer, disappointment filled my chest. The car was empty. Maybe she got a ride with someone else? But who? Was she seeing someone else already? Shit, I was getting jealous like we'd actually been dating. We never even slept together, so why was I acting like I owned her?

Maybe because I wanted to.

I almost walked away when I heard a small sound that cut straight through my chest.

Panic rippled across my skin as I spun back around, my gaze searching for the source of that noise. *Who was crying?*

My fears were confirmed a moment later when I found her, curled up in a ball on the dirty concrete between her car and the next.

"Tris," I breathed, sinking to my knees and reaching

out a tentative hand. My fingers barely brushed her hair, but she flinched like I'd kicked her. It was enough to make her look up, her puffy eyes barely cracked. But when she realized it was *me*...

The air knocked out of me as she launched herself into my arms. Not that I was complaining, I wrapped her up tight, holding her to me as my back rested against the wheel of a Jeep. Her whole tiny body trembled as I stroked her hair, and it took every ounce of my willpower to just sit there and hold her, rather than hunt down whoever hurt her...and strangle them with their own intestines.

She didn't need me running off to prove my masculinity right now, though. She needed comfort and safety and *that* was what I could give her. We sat there on the ground for a while, not speaking a single word. When her trembles eased and the tension in her body seemed to lighten, I held her securely to my chest and got to my feet.

"John—" she protested, pushing back slightly with a frown. "I'm capable of walking."

I didn't set her down, because I didn't feel like she was uncomfortable or scared of me, just prideful and stubborn. "Tristian," I murmured, carrying her across the parking lot in the direction of the staff cottages,

"You could be capable of flying and I'd still be carrying you."

She had nothing to say to that, and thank fuck for that. Because I was dangerously close to losing my cool, and I *needed* her to let me take care of her right now.

My cottage wasn't far away, and I was fairly sure no one saw me carrying my raven-haired TA into my private quarters. But even if they had, it wouldn't have stopped me. Fuck Boles and their rules, and fuck my teaching career if that's what it came down to. It was a convenient and enjoyable cover identity, but I wasn't incapable of starting a new one.

Neither of us spoke as I carried her inside, closing and locking the door behind us. I left the key in the door, making sure she saw it so she didn't think I was trapping her, then deposited her on the lumpy couch.

She immediately drew her knees up to her chest and a flare of fury lit me up inside. Someone had hurt her. Someone had put that hollow look of fear in her eyes, and I'd bet I knew who.

"Wait there," I muttered, pushing up my sleeves and heading for the kitchen. She didn't protest, and that only worsened my mood. The Tris I knew would have snapped back that she wasn't a dog to be told to sit and stay, but not now. Now she just hugged her knees and stared blankly at the worn out carpet under my coffee table. Shit.

Dexter Grimaldi was going to pay for breaking my girl.

When I returned to her, it was with a cold bottle of tequila and two shot glasses.

"Day drinking?" she croaked, raising her sad eyes from the carpet to frown at me.

I shrugged, sitting beside her and pouring both shots. "Why not?"

She sighed and took the little glass I offered her. "Why not, indeed?" She didn't even wait for me to pick up mine before downing the whole thing and handing me the empty vessel.

I watched her wince and gag, then wave her hand at me to refill the glass. What a queen.

I obliged, then took my own shot with her this time.

"Wanna tell me what happened?" I asked quietly, pouring us another.

She coughed, covering her mouth with those delicate fingers of hers. I had this overwhelming need to watch her paint, especially while she was working on that abstract piece that was *totally* inspired by me. Fucking *cats*. What a weak lie.

"Nope," she croaked. "I wanna drink your expensive tequila and pass out. That work for you, professor?"

"Fine by me," I agreed, handing her another. "But only a real prick lets a girl drink on an empty stomach. Pizza work for you?"

She nodded, eyeing her third shot like it was the answer to all her problems. "Cheese. Or Hawaiian."

I eyed her with confusion. "That's all?"

"Yup." She tossed back the shot. "It's what I like."

"Fair enough," I murmured, pulling out my phone to order on the local pizzeria app. "Can I get one truthful answer from you, Tris?"

She handed me her shot glass with a frown. "I'm not lying. I like boring pizza, and there's nothing wrong with that."

I rolled my eyes. She was a damn lightweight. "Not that. *This.*" I gave her a pointed look. "Was it Dexter again?"

Fear tracked across her face, and she wet her lips. "What do you mean, *again?*" I just stared back at her, and she grimaced. "I can't talk about it."

Don't explode, John. Keep your cool. She needs calm and comfort, not macho aggression.

"Tris, if he hurt you then you need—"

"To keep my mouth shut," she cut me off with a death glare. "I get that you're new in town, John, but some people are above the law. He happens to be one of them. Let it go."

Let it go? *Let it go?* Hell. No.

"Tristian," I growled, ready to push the issue with her.

She glowered back at me. "John. Stop trying to play therapist and pour the damn shots."

My hand tightened around the neck of the tequila bottle like I wanted to strangle Dexter Grimaldi. Tristian's idea of just pretending nothing had happened worried me more than I cared to admit, and for some reason I just couldn't *let it go.*

Fuck, did that make me Ana to Tristian's Elsa?

"You need to talk to someone, Tris," I insisted, holding the tequila hostage. "Why not me?"

She stared at me for a long moment then spluttered a laugh. "Why *not* you? Better question would be *why you,* John. We're not dating, we're not friends. We're not even *fucking,* so seriously, why on earth would I confide in you?"

I wasn't backing down that easily. Not now, when we potentially only had a few days left. "Because for some reason, you don't want to confide in Nelson and Hank," I replied, keeping my tone soft and caring, despite how badly I wanted to yell at her. "And if you can't talk to them...who else is there?"

She inhaled sharply like I'd just slapped her, but it was the truth. I'd watched her enough to know she had no close friends, no family, literally no one to confide in outside of her elderly neighbors.

For a moment, I thought she might crack and open up to me. But then she clenched her jaw and nodded. "Good point," she said with bitterness. "Excuse me, I need to pee."

She got up, wobbling a bit on her feet, then hurried to my bathroom before I could find the words to apologize. Not that I'd said anything untrue, but just because it was true didn't mean it was kind. Nor that it needed to be said. Fuck's sake, why did I keep pushing her away even while attempting to draw her closer?

"You've lost your edge," I muttered to myself, downing a shot of tequila. It was good stuff, Don Julio 1942, but even expensive tequila burned a little. Fucking Dexter. I was *sure* he was responsible now. She didn't need to admit it when the truth was all over her face.

My phone was already in hand, and I found myself scrolling for a number of someone who'd sort him out for me. Permanently. He may be above the *civilian* law, but there were much bigger, darker authorities out there, and plenty of them owed me favors.

I nearly placed the request, but I hesitated. It was only a few more days until I got my hands on that painting...if I had Dexter killed now, the party would be canceled- and I might lose the Game.

All bets were off once I'd won, though. Perhaps Dexter could wait.

The sound of running water from the bathroom snagged my attention, and I put my phone down once again. My imagination was running *wild* with the lack of information. Mentally the time calculations were ticking over, and with that I was running through all the possibilities of what'd happened while I was held up in the classroom.

It'd been ten minutes, at most. Maybe less. And no one else was around when I'd walked out there at all, so he couldn't have had more than a few minutes alone with her. Was that long enough to—?

No. No, she was still fully dressed, her jeans buttoned and her boots laced up on her feet. He'd scared her, though, no question about that. So what did it really matter what he'd physically done? He'd gotten inside her head, and that was bad enough.

Fuck, I wished she would just come out of the bathroom and *talk* to me.

I wished she would trust me, and that was the most selfish thing I could possibly ask...because I had every intention of taking her trust and using it for my own gain.

Tris deserved more, but I couldn't make myself stop.

twenty-eight

TRIS

Once I got into the bathroom, the floodgates opened. Tears started rolling again and I had to turn on the taps to hide the fact that I was crying. I didn't *want* to tell John what'd happened and I sure as fuck didn't need his pity.

I only let myself cry for a minute before pulling my shit together, but then I needed to sit there on the closed toilet seat and wait for my eyes to lose their red puffiness, because my stupid pride wouldn't be okay if I went back out there like this. It didn't matter that he'd literally found me sobbing in a ball on the ground. This was different.

So I sat there like a stubborn asshole until John knocked on the door and told me the pizza had arrived.

"Thanks, I'll just be a second!" I called back, standing

up to check my reflection. My makeup was basically all gone already, but damn it all to hell my eyes were still puffy and bloodshot.

John knocked again, softly. "Tris? I'm just making a call outside, but the pizza is on the table and there's Visine in the mirror cabinet."

"Fuck," I whispered, raking my fingers through my hair. Still, I pulled the cabinet open and grabbed the bottle of eyedrops, applying them liberally to each eye and blinking rapidly. A couple of tissues cleaned up the residue, and a moment later I was good as new. Why the fuck hadn't I thought to hunt his drawers? Blame it on being tipsy.

When I emerged from the bathroom, John was nowhere to be seen, but as promised there were two hot and delicious pizzas waiting on the table. One cheese, one Hawaiian. Beside them, a big glass of orange juice.

"Trying to tell me something, huh?" I muttered, picking up the juice to take a sip. Then immediately choked on it.

"Oh yeah, that has tequila in it," John helpfully informed me, stepping back inside with his phone in his hand. "Just figured maybe you wanted something to drink instead of a shot."

I took another sip, this time prepared for what I was

tasting. "You mean it has juice in the tequila, not the other way around."

He flashed a grin. "Semantics." He tossed his phone on the table and sat down beside me once more, close enough that his knee touched mine but not close enough that I felt crowded. "Eat some pizza, Tris. I don't want you vomiting."

I was a little drunk, sure, but not *that* bad. "I'll have you know, I very rarely vomit while drunk." But I was hungry and it was a crime to let fresh pizza go cold, so I grabbed a slice.

"Rarely," John repeated in a dry tone, "is not never. I'd rather take precautions and make sure you eat." He leaned forward to retrieve a piece for himself then settled back into the couch, his leg casually touching mine once more.

For a moment, neither of us spoke, our mouths were too full of pizza. The question he wanted to ask was hanging thick in the air though, so when I finished my first slice I gave him a pointed look.

"You want to talk about it, yet?" he asked casually, his gaze sharp and calculating.

I shook my head. "Not a chance in hell. Can we just…not talk?"

John shrugged, then nodded. "Sure, we can do that. Movie?"

He'd officially stunned me speechless, so I just nodded with my mouth open like a damn fish while he grabbed the remote and flicked the screen on. When I'd suggested *not* talking, I hadn't been totally serious. Or, I had wanted to not talk but fully expected him to push the issue with all that arrogant stubborn manly bullshit. John struck me as the kind of guy who couldn't handle not *knowing all the things*...so I just didn't totally know how to react.

"Pick one," he told me, nodding to the screen. He'd pulled up a streaming platform with all the new releases on option. I chose at random, selecting an action comedy thing with The Rock in a lead role. Surely that was a safe option?

John made no commentary of my choice, just started the movie and grabbed another slice of pizza. "Get comfy," he told me, settling back into the couch. "We've got nowhere to be."

I only hesitated a moment longer, then did exactly as he suggested. A whole pizza and a shitload of tequila later, I found myself snuggling into his warmth as my eyelids drooped. Full stomach, fuzzy head, and John's safe embrace was a dangerous combination.

My head thumped like a jackhammer when I woke, and my mouth tasted like something had died inside. And then decayed. Ugh, hangover breath was lethal. Where the fuck was I? This wasn't my apartment…or my bed. It smelled like…

Crap.

Flashes of memory started up in my mind, and I buried my head in John's pillow. There were shots, then pizza and a movie and…I fell asleep, didn't I? No…shit. I woke up again when John was carrying me to bed, and I thought he wanted…

Oh my God, I can never look him in the eye again.

I would have sunk right there into the mattress and through the floor if I could, but my bladder was screaming at me to at least get up and pee before I died of embarrassment. Chanting a litany of curses inside my head, I forced myself to sit up—then nearly fell over again when my head swam. Tequila was never my friend, no matter how fancy the bottle was.

Giving myself a mental pep talk—mostly consisting of insults—I swung my legs out of the bed and stood up. The room dipped and swayed again, but I managed not to fall over. My bladder was in no mood to be patient, so I gritted my fuzzy teeth and headed in the direction of the bathroom. I didn't make it far before tripping over a whole ass human sleeping on the floor, though.

"Ow, shit, fuck!" I hissed, catching my balance on the dresser but not before cracking my elbow on the wall. Goddamn that hurt! There was nothing funny about the funny bone.

"Tris?" John mumbled, raising his head from the pillow on the floor. "What are you—"

"Shh, nothing!" I hissed, climbing over him. "Go back to sleep."

I all but ran the rest of the way into the bathroom and collapsed onto the toilet with a heavy sigh. *Fucking hell*. Talk about drunken regrets.

When I was done peeing, I rifled through John's bathroom cabinet for a spare toothbrush to clean my mouth. Then decided that wasn't enough, so I turned on the shower. In fairness, I was in *zero* hurry to get back out there and face John in the harsh, sober light of day.

The hot water did wonders to clear my head, but that only made space for the cringeworthy memories of last night to brighten in intensity. Why did I need to drink *that* much? Good decisions were never made after that much tequila! My God.

I was so lost in my self-flagellation that I nearly jumped out of my skin when the bathroom door opened and John casually wandered in. There was no way he didn't know I was in there, he was just...being *John*.

"Uh, do you mind?" I called out sarcastically,

wrapping my arms around myself despite the fact that the glass screen was totally fogged up between us. I could only make out his vague shape, so the same must apply for him seeing me.

"Not in the least," he replied, giving a small chuckle. "Do *you?*"

The challenge in his tone made me swipe a hand over the fogged glass, clearing just enough that I could see out and glare daggers. "Yeah, I do. Unless you do things differently in Finland, I'm *naked* in here. A little privacy would go a long way."

He met my eyes in the mirror, then smirked. "Not what you said last night."

My jaw dropped and I choked on a gasp. "Wow. What a gentleman, bringing that up again like it wasn't harsh enough when you flat out rejected me. In case it wasn't obvious, I was pretty drunk. Don't let it go to your head. I probably would have fucked a pillow."

His smirk turned mischievous. "I think you did, in your sleep." He spun around, leaning his ass against the vanity as he held my gaze. Dammit, he was shirtless and only wore a loose pair of gray sweatpants. What a slut. "The fact that you were drunk *was* why I turned you down, Tris. I don't prey on vulnerable women who may live to regret their choices the next day."

I rolled my eyes, something I seemed to do a whole

lot while dealing with John. "Uh huh, well that's where you miscalculated. I don't regret *shit*." Oh man, I was such a liar. I was so deep in regret right now I could feel it crawling all over my skin. But it wasn't making a move on him that I regretted. It was how drunk I'd been. Of course he turned me down; I'd have thought significantly less of him if he hadn't. That didn't lessen the burn of embarrassment, though.

John tipped his head to the side, like he was weighing the sincerity of my bullshit statement. Then he gave a nod. "Alright."

I raised a brow. "Alright?"

He shrugged, then stripped off his sweatpants and opened the shower door, stepping right into the suddenly *tiny* shower stall with me. Naked. So very naked and hot and hard and—

"John, what are you doing?" I squeaked, turning my back on him and covering my tits with my hands...like that was what mattered when my bottom half was *also* naked. Where was my damn brain?

His huge hand gripped the back of my neck under the spray of water, firm but not painful as he forced me to turn back around. "Calling your bluff, Tris. You sure you don't regret anything? Because like I tried to tell you before you passed out...I *badly* want to fuck you. Sober. So you can remember every little detail and know exactly why your cunt aches for the rest of the day."

My breathing hitched. I tried really fucking hard to come up with an incredibly witty response, but all that came out was a weak "Oh."

That was all the response he needed, though. His hand still on the back of my neck, he lowered his face to mine and kissed me under the shower spray. His lips teased mine apart, and his tongue demanded entry, something which I was all too happy to oblige.

I gasped as he pulled me closer, his hot hardness pressing against my stomach. Holy hell, my imagination had *not* failed me in size estimation. The demanding way he pulled me up to my toes as he kissed me had my whole body throbbing with need, but when his other hand skated up my ribs to cup my breast I hissed in pain.

He immediately released me, taking a deliberate step back even as his sharp gaze locked on my bruises. "Tris..." My name on his lips was a curse and a plea.

I shook my head, refusing to let Dexter ruin a moment that was about to go down in history as one of the hottest showers of my life. "You wanna help?" He nodded, his expression earnest. "Good. Then make me forget. Erase his touch from my skin and make it so I can only remember *yours.*"

He hesitated, his concerned gaze scanning over my skin, searching for more marks.

"John," I said, my voice cracking. "Please. Either make me forget, or get out. I don't need your pity."

That got through to him, his eyes snapping back up to meet mine. A split second later he had me pinned against the shower wall, both my wrists trapped above my head with just one of his hands.

"You make me feel a great many things, Tristian," he told me in a darkly sexy voice, his lips ghosting over my lips and making my pulse race. "Pity is not one of them. Want me to elaborate on that further?"

His lips met mine again, but when I tried to kiss him back he withdrew, grinning.

Oh. We were back to games? Thank fuck for that.

"Please, *professor*, educate me."

He gave a low chuckle, looking down at me with heated desire in his eyes drowning out any hint of pity or concern. "Anything for you, Venus."

A strange flicker of emotion passed over his face when he said that, but I had no time to analyze it further. His mouth crushed into mine in a kiss so all-consuming I nearly forgot where we were. He released my wrists, his hands exploring my body as he shifted to grip my waist. I didn't even flinch when he passed over my bruises this time, barely registering the pain. Fuck that noise, I had better things on my mind.

John lifted me, and I instinctively wrapped my legs around him before remembering we were both totally naked and soaking wet. He groaned, rocking against me, and I tilted my hips to get him right where I wanted.

"Dammit, Tris," he gasped as I kissed his neck, making sure to leave a nice deep mark just below his ear where there would be no hiding it. Take that, Professor Casanova. "This isn't what—" His pelvis rocked again and this time I moved with him so the thick tip of his cock notched just perfectly in my entry. "Shit," he breathed, the muscles of his neck and shoulders rock hard as he tried to hold back. "Tris, I wasn't thinking—"

"John," I whispered in his ear, nipping his lobe with my teeth. "Shut up and fuck me."

The speed that he pushed into me made me cry out in shock. Holy *hell.* My nails sank into his biceps as I dropped my head back against the tiles, gasping. "Yes," I moaned, "just like that."

He whispered something under his breath in another language, but his cock had already taken control of his movements, sliding out just enough to slam back in and make me gasp. When he'd taunted me about my pussy aching for the rest of the day, he hadn't been exaggerating. I'd bet I could feel the stretch of John's thick cock for *days,* and I wasn't even slightly mad about it.

Waves of intense pleasure curled through me, and I wrapped my legs tighter, pulling him deeper as his mouth found mine. For several minutes he kissed me just like he fucked me. Deep, hard, possessive, and totally intoxicating. The shower steam only added to how hot my entire body was, and the small space filled with the sounds of our wet flesh slapping together and the harsh gasps of breath between kisses.

Sure, we'd skipped the whole long drawn-out foreplay part that I'd fantasized about with John…but *this* was what I needed. I was tired, hungover, bruised, and embarrassed. I didn't need to be laid out and worshiped for hours. I needed a steamy shower fuck with a man I had no business screwing around with. Shit, this was *perfect.*

His mouth moved to my throat, sucking and biting as I moaned with pleasure. He shifted his stance wider, causing his next thrust to hit me deeper and making me cry out. I gasped for breath, licking my lips and clinging onto his wet, muscular flesh for dear life. Then my gaze snagged on something that instantly jerked me out of the moment.

"Um, John?" I panted. His motions slowed and he pulled back just far enough to meet my gaze.

"Not good? I can—"

"No! No, it's fucking great. I just...are your toe-nails painted?" I looked down again at his massive flipper-like feet. "Why do you have sparkly purple nail polish on your feet?"

He leaned away a little more, not withdrawing his dick from inside me but just pausing momentarily. "Oh, that. I ran out of acetone to remove it, then forgot."

Laughter rippled through my chest. "Okay but..." I pursed my lips, thinking. Then gave a small shrug. "You know what? You do you, Casanova." Pulling him back toward me, I crushed my mouth to his and kissed him until he restarted the engine.

I'd been building up to a climax when I'd stupidly decided to ask about his nail polish, though, so I was back at square one. He must have sensed it, because a moment later he gave a grunt and dropped to his knees.

A squeak of panic spilled out of me as I thought I was going to fall, but he caught me with my legs over his shoulders and his mouth on my cunt. He went straight to work as my hands scrambled for purchase on the slick shower walls. Eventually I just resorted to holding the back of his head against my pussy and probably drawing blood with my nails because *holy fuuuuck*.

John kissed my cunt like he was eating a damn papaya, then when he pushed two thick fingers inside, I exploded. I'd go ahead and blame the acoustics of the shower for the unseemly screams and curses I released while I came so hard that I swear I astral projected. So much so, I couldn't fathom *how* I'd managed not to slip and crash ass over tits into the base of the shower and crack my head open.

When I returned to myself, gasping for air and buzzing all over, I realized how firmly John held me. He'd never drop me. Not for anything.

"Dick," I exclaimed, my mouth dry and my tongue heavy. "John, I need your dick."

"Yes, ma'am," he growled, rising back to his feet and letting my slippery body fall back into place where he could easily reconnect us. Holy *hell,* that thick as fuck cock in my still tensed up pussy was the best goddamn feeling in the world.

Moaning, I gripped him with my legs, my hips rocking as I urged him to move. I was going to come again already. I could sense it with startling confidence.

"Fuck, Tris," he groaned as he rocked into me. "This exceeds even my wildest dreams...and there were *a lot* of dreams. At night, when I woke up with my dick in my hand...during class when I had to hide my erection from the class..."

Oh shit, I could never look at that lectern the same way again. "Professor Smith," I chuckled, my hard nipples rubbing against his chest as he fucked me harder. "So inappropriate."

"I'll fucking show you inappropriate, Miss Ives," he shot back, his breathing already shuddering and his motions losing rhythm. "Scream my name when you come." His hand slipped between us, finding my clit and rubbing it like the best rabbit ears around.

I did as I was told, crying out *Professor Smith* as I came, and a split second later he joined me. He didn't even try to pull out before his cock thickened and jerked, his hot cum filling the tight walls of my cunt while he whispered something in another language. Quiet enough I couldn't even make out what language it was.

Or shit, maybe that was just because my ears were ringing and my head floated lighter than helium.

For a few moments we just stayed as we were, both struggling to get our breathing under control and regain function of all our limbs.

"How's your hangover?" he eventually said, brushing a light kiss over my lips.

I gave a groaning laugh. "This helped clear my head. In more ways than one."

The mood between us shifted serious as he understood what I meant. Ever so softly, he brushed his fingertips over my bruised breast, and I shuddered.

"Thank you," I whispered, emotions thickening in my chest and making it hard to swallow. "You saved me."

A small frown touched his brow. "I didn't do anything. He was already gone when I got there."

I smiled, shaking my head. "You saved me from sinking into a pit of despair so deep I'd lose the will to fight back. Now...that slimy prick means nothing to me. I've got you at my back."

John gave a soft smile then dipped his head to kiss the bend of my neck. I sighed at the gentle touch, my whole body more relaxed than I'd ever thought possible. But then it was like a switch flicked and John withdrew into himself. He eased my feet back to the ground then quickly turned away to rinse under the still-running shower.

Unease rippled through me. It wasn't like he'd *said* anything to indicate the mood shift, but it was just something in the air.

"Uh...what just happened?" I asked, preferring to *know* rather than let my imagination run wild. "Why do I feel like you just went cold toward me?"

He glanced over his shoulder, his expression totally unreadable. "I don't know what you mean," he lied, his voice totally devoid of emotion. He finished washing with lightning speed, then stepped out of the shower cubicle, letting the glass door close again, leaving me alone.

Outrage and disbelief flooded me as I grabbed for the soap…because all of a sudden I was feeling way too damn vulnerable and really wanted my clothes.

"John…" *What the hell was going on right now?*

"We should hurry up if we want to make it to class on time," he said, still using that cold, detached voice. "Maybe it's not a good idea to turn up together. I'm sure you don't want anyone questioning your exemplary grades." He didn't even wait for a response before leaving the bathroom with a towel looped around his hips.

My jaw dropped. Did he just say what I think he said? I gave a bitter laugh, rinsing the soap off my body along with whatever tender feelings he'd conjured up just moments ago. Was I seriously that naïve? Apparently I was.

"Wow," I said sarcastically, loud enough for him to hear as I yanked open the shower door and snatched a towel from the rack. "You're really something else, John."

"Thanks," he called back from the bedroom.

I seethed, yanking my dirty clothes back on without even fully drying myself off. "That wasn't a compliment, asshole."

He reappeared in the doorway to the bathroom, somehow *magically* fully dressed and looking as perfectly handsome as ever. "Sure it was, Tris. Don't worry, you're not the first student at Boles to tell me as much." Shock froze my tongue and I just stared back at him as he gave me a quick, unimpressed once-over with his eyes. "You should probably run home to change, though. People might notice those are yesterday's clothes. I don't mind if you're a few minutes late to class; just close the front door behind yourself when you leave."

And just like that, I was alone again.

This time, though, I was filled with so much *rage* I nearly set fire to his fucking bed. What an insufferable *bastard.*

twenty-nine

JOHN

Panic. That was the only viable explanation for what I'd just done. I'd fucking *panicked* just like I had last week after telling Tris about Christophe. I'd let her in, bared my soul, then when I realized that her feelings were becoming *real* I'd straight up panicked. Last week was bad enough, when I up and left with the weakest of excuses. But this? Oh man. I'd fucked it all up this time.

"You stupid, moronic, damaged asshole," I muttered to myself as I stalked across campus grounds toward my classroom. Tris was still back there in my cottage, her jeans unbuttoned and her bra barely concealing the purple bruises all over her breast, and I'd just walked away. Like a stupid fuck.

What was *wrong* with me?

Stupid question. I knew perfectly well where that'd all gone bad. Right when I realized I wasn't fucking a sexy woman as a means to an end...I'd been utterly lost in her the moment I stepped into that shower, and it spiraled out of control from there. I hadn't fucked her. There was too much emotion involved in what we'd just shared to call it *fucking,* and that terrified me. I was losing pieces of myself every time I kissed her, and now I was genuinely worried I wouldn't be able to walk away after the Grimaldi party.

So I did the only thing my useless pea-sized brain could think of. I sabotaged it.

Now I was sweating bullets as I made my way to class, knowing she was probably mad enough to shred my mattress with a butcher's knife. As soon as I suggested she go home and change, I regretted it. I didn't *want* to give her space, even if I knew it was the best possible thing to do. She was too involved, and if I was perfectly honest, so was I.

I needed to gain her trust and steal her access. Nothing more. I *definitely* didn't need her falling in love, and that seemed dangerously close to what was happening. I'd hurt her with my callous, calculated comments. Hopefully that made her realize that this thing between us was purely physical and allow her to safeguard her heart a little better.

Either that, or she'd hit me with her shitty Corolla. Right now, that was feeling like a more likely outcome after the way I'd just treated her.

"Idiot," I muttered again as I let myself into the empty classroom to set up. The lecture didn't start for twenty minutes yet; Tris had enough time to go home and get back without being too late. I just had to…do what? I had no idea. I'd *done* what I needed to do…I'd made it clear that I wasn't interested in anything more than sex. Now I just had to keep my hands to myself, steal the fucking painting, and leave town. Three more days and we were done.

As I set up for the lecture, all I could think about was how incredible Tris felt. How sweet her kisses tasted, and how she turned to putty in my hands. More than that, I couldn't stop remembering those *bruises*.

Dexter. He was a dead man. It was the only thing that kept me going, knowing I could end his life with a quick call to an acquaintance in the Mercenary Guild.

Ten minutes after the lecture started, Tris still hadn't turned up. A trickle of unease filled me, but I *had* told her to go home and change. It was a ten-minute drive each way, so even if she'd left right after me that only left her ten minutes to change…Maybe she was taking her time. Understandable. I probably would if I were in her shoes, too. I'd bet she would turn up any second, looking like the jaw-dropping goddess she was just to make me regret my choices.

Another ten minutes passed, and I convinced myself she would walk through the door *any second now.* Tris was too stubborn to just not show up. She was a fighter, and it'd take more than a few dickhead comments from me to make her quit. Especially after how good the sex was. She was probably just making me sweat.

Fifteen minutes after that I was second guessing everything. *Had* the sex been good? Or only good for me? Did she fake it? No…no, no way had she faked that orgasm. I could *feel* how her body reacted to mine. Couldn't I? Was it possible I'd totally imagined that reaction to fuel my own ego? Maybe I'd inflated this whole tension between us to a totally unrealistic level inside my head and she wasn't feeling *any* of it.

No. The tension and attraction between us was real. I was sure of it.

But what if it wasn't?

When an hour of the lecture had passed with no sign of Tris, I was officially stressing out. I couldn't concentrate on the course material and my eyes were drilling holes in the door while waiting for it to open.

At an hour and a half, I snapped and assigned my students an independent study assignment for the rest of the lecture period. I didn't even wait for their questions or confusion, just packed up my things and bailed the fuck out. Screw it, Dean Lawrence could extort me later if he really felt the need, but right now I needed to find Tristian and make sure she was okay.

What if Dexter had found her again?

I was *such* an idiot.

First thing I did was return to my cottage. Maybe she was still there? I don't know why she would be, but it just felt like I needed to return to the last place I'd seen her.

Unsurprisingly, the cottage was empty. My next step was to check if her car was gone from the staff parking lot—it was—so I jumped in my own and headed across town to her apartment building. She was probably just at home, maybe lost track of time in her painting studio if she had to work through her anger toward me? That abstract piece she'd been working on definitely conveyed a whole lot of rage, so it was possible she'd chosen to skip class to paint. Except that this was Tristian, and she *never* skipped class…

One of the other building residents was leaving as I arrived, and I turned up the charm to gain entry into the foyer and elevators. Then I stood at Tris's door, knocking for way too long.

Eventually, I accepted the fact that she wasn't home. So I glanced down the hall to ensure the door to Nelson and Hank's place was closed and the elevator showed it was back on ground level. Then I picked Tris's lock and let myself in. Again.

As expected, her home was silent and empty, but that didn't stop me snooping around and looking for clues on where she might be. My *biggest* worry was that Dexter had got his hands on her again, but that didn't explain why I was in her apartment. I guess I hoped she was just chilling here, making me sweat. The fact that she wasn't definitely had my insides twisted up in knots.

I browsed around, taking note of the smell in the air. She'd been painting recently, and if the smudges in her studio sink were any indication she must be working on something new. Unless she'd decided to introduce yellow into her predominantly red and gray piece?

Curious, I hunted down the abstract therapy painting I'd seen last time I was here. Nope, it hadn't been touched. In fact, it was stacked with some other finished pieces like she'd decided it was done.

Anxious dread swirled through me. Did that also mean she was done with me?

I shook that sickening thought away, abandoning the studio and heading for her bedroom. There was nothing here to clue me into her whereabouts, but I couldn't leave without checking her bedside drawer. It was more than a casual game now; it was an addiction. It hadn't even occurred to me that I'd quit stealing random items to quell my urges or that all I'd thieved in *weeks* were Tristian's vibrators.

"What the fuck?" I whispered aloud, staring at the *three* new toys lurking in her drawer. "Does she buy in bulk? Or is there a subscription crate for vibrators?"

Either way, they were mine now. I took all three, then searched her rumpled sheets for any I might have missed, since that was where I'd found them before.

The two smaller toys went into my coat pockets, but the larger one, identical to the hot pink weapon I'd snatched last week, had to be tucked into my pants again in order to be hidden. It was worth it.

My next plan was to check in with Nelson and Hank, if they were home. Maybe she'd gone over there to vent about what a prick I was to her? She definitely seemed to have that bond with them, like they were more friends than paternal figures. Though, they were definitely protective like she was their child.

I closed up Tris's apartment and went back down to the street so I could stash my stolen toys in my car and avoid having one fall out when I bent over. Then I buzzed Tristian's neighbor from the ground level, like I'd just arrived.

Hank buzzed me up straight away, and my toe tapped the floor of the elevator impatiently as I rode it back up to Tris's floor. This time I bypassed her door, though, heading straight down to the only other apartment on the top floor.

"John, how lovely to see you," Hank said with warmth as he let me inside. "After that rather colorful dinner with Ivy, I wasn't sure we'd cross paths again. What can we do for you?"

I winced, running a hand over the back of my neck. "Ah, actually Ivy is the reason I'm here. Have you seen her today? She didn't show up for class and that's not like her..." I barely needed to exaggerate my concern because I *was* concerned.

Hank's brows rose, then he seemed almost uncomfortable. "Oh, hmm. Yes I see...that's not like her at all." He didn't sound nearly as worried as I was, though.

I narrowed my eyes. "So you've seen her?"

He shook his head. "Seen her? No. But I'm sure she's fine. She probably just needed a mental health day. Don't we all, every now and then?"

I frowned, then glanced around like I expected to find Tris chilling on the couch and watching Netflix. She wasn't, though. Nelson wasn't home, either. It was just Hank.

"But you haven't seen her?" I rephrased my question.

Hank shook his head. "No...why do I get the feeling

there's more going on here than just Ivy missing class?" He tipped his head to the side, his gaze questioning. "Did something happen between the two of you?"

My mouth went dry. *Something* seemed such a meaningless understatement of the explosive chemistry between Tris and me. But that *something* was like playing with fire, and both of us were dangerously close to catching third degree burns. So I just gave a tight smile and shook my head.

"Just worried, that's all. Do you have an idea where she might be? I tried her apartment, but she's not there and she hasn't answered her phone..." Okay yes, now I was starting to sound like a stalker. Or a jealous boyfriend. Neither of which I was, even if I walked the line a little.

Hank squinted at me a moment longer, then sighed. "Come take a seat, John. I'll pour you a drink and you can tell me what's going on between the two of you."

I shook my head. "Thank you, but there's nothing to tell." Liar. "And I should get going."

Hank gestured to the kitchen. "Go. Sit. I won't tell you where she is, but I can see you're genuinely worried so I'll tell you that she is perfectly fine and in no immediate danger. Now, would you like lemonade or something stronger?"

I glanced at my watch, then arched a brow at Hank. "It's not even midday."

He shrugged. "It's midday somewhere."

Grinning, I sat on one of the barstools in front of his island counter. "Well then, I'll have whatever you're having."

He chuckled, nodding. "Good choice, *John Smith*. You know that name sounds terribly fake, don't you?"

"That's surely how you know it's not," I countered with a smile, feeling the tension ease somewhat at his reassurance about Tristian's mysterious whereabouts. "Only an idiot would pick such an obvious fake name, right?"

Hank laughed. "Good point." He pushed a crystal glass of whisky across the counter then raised his own. "Cheers."

thirty

TRIS

Seven messages. That was it. Just seven messages from John since he'd left me half-dressed in his bathroom this morning, and when I previewed them—without opening—they were nothing special. Just him being irritated that I didn't show up for class, like he honestly believed I was *that* much of a masochist. Even *I* had my limit, and John had officially reached it.

"You gonna reply to those?" Nelson asked as we rode the elevator up to our floor.

I glanced up, guilty that I'd been caught staring at my unread messages *again*. "Nope."

Nelson quirked a brow. "Why not?"

Because there were still only *seven*. He hadn't sent anything more. If I needed any further confirmation that I'd totally fabricated the feelings between us, that was it.

I'd thought maybe he panicked. He was commitment phobic and I'd scared him, but given a bit of time and space, he'd quickly regret the way he acted this morning. But apparently I was wrong. Seven text messages, all just terse, impersonal reminders that I was supposed to be in class. And *nothing more*.

Fuck. Had I really been that stupid? I'd gotten so caught up in the chemistry that I *thought* we shared, I hadn't really stopped to ask if it was all one sided. Now when I looked back at our interactions, I was embarrassed. This morning wasn't some explosive culmination of our intense, crackling tension. It was just a convenient stress relief. A bit of fun.

Either way, when I'd left John's house I felt *used*...and I had no interest in ever feeling that way again. I'd spent the day with Nelson but hadn't breathed a word of what'd happened between John and me. It was too humiliating, and I was dealing with it privately.

"Because it's not worth my energy," I muttered, finally answering Nelson out loud. "Or my time."

He pursed his lips and gave a small sigh. "If you say so."

"I do," I snapped, stepping out of the elevator when

the doors opened. "I've got studying to do. Thanks for today, though."

Nelson grabbed my arm before I could disappear into my apartment. "If you think I'm leaving you to sulk alone, you're more hungover than you look. And, my girl, you look *rough*. Come on. Hank had the afternoon off work, and I bet he's cooked up a feast."

I sniffed the air and shook my head. "I bet he hasn't. He probably got distracted reading fairy porn again."

Nelson chuckled, steering me down the hall to his home. "It's always a possibility. I know he was waiting for some new release to come out. Either way, you're not going home to wallow in self-pity alone. I can at the very least make you some tea and let you insult my latest attempt on that ring."

I grinned. "It's not my fault your attention to detail is slipping in your old age. If you want perfect, you'll take the constructive feedback."

He shook his head. "Impertinent brat. I just got some new stones delivered, too. You can take a look and pick the best one."

"Oh, you know I love looking at sparkly stones." That idea distracted me enough as we entered his apartment that I didn't realize they had company until it was too late.

My stomach dropped to the floor and blood rushed

from my head, making me dizzy. He just fucking *stared* back at me, then folded his arms across his chest like he was mad at me.

"What the fuck is *he* doing here?" I snarled, directing my question to Hank. The traitor.

Hank's brows rose. "Um, should he not be?" I glared, and Hank winced. "Okay, that answers that. He was looking for you, Ivy. Apparently you didn't show up for class and he was worried."

I scoffed. "Is that the story he told you?" Curling my lip at John, I pointed at the front door. "Fuck off, John, you're not welcome here."

"Whoa, what's going on here?" Hank demanded, rising from his seat. "One of you two better explain, because I don't appreciate being lied to." He scowled at John, who looked anything *but* apologetic.

"I didn't lie, Hank," he replied in a cool voice. "I was concerned when Tris didn't show up for class, and she wasn't answering her phone. I thought something bad might have happened."

A bitter laugh bubbled out of me. "Oh, you mean something bad like being used for sex by someone in a position of authority, then implied that I'm just one in a long line of slutty students ready to spread her legs for the teacher? Like that? *Fuck you, John.* There's the damn door. Use it."

The silence that followed was intense enough to hurt. Then Nelson gave a pointed look between the two of us and shook his head.

"Sounds like you should be heading off, John." My old friend scowled in the direction of the sexiest man I'd ever let into my head.

John was too fucking stubborn to be pushed around like that, though. He ignored Nelson and glared at me like I was being a brat.

"My concern has nothing to do with all of that, Tristian. When you didn't show up for class, I worried that Dexter Grimaldi had gotten his hands on you and done worse than leave a few bruises this time. So, my apologies for the intrusion, Hank. I see now that Tris was simply throwing a temper tantrum over our disagreement."

My jaw hit the floor. "Our *disagreement?*" I shrieked. "We didn't *disagree,* John. You fucked me then immediately insulted me and walked out the door while I was still half naked. As for calling my non-attendance today a temper tantrum? Go right to fucking hell. I quit."

That finally seemed to rattle him, and his eyes widened. "You can't just—"

"Silence!" Nelson snapped, his hand making a cutting motion through the air. "You can finish this spat later. Tell me what happened with Dexter, Ives."

Panic rippled through me, realizing John had outed my work issues that I'd been carefully keeping to myself. "N-nothing," I lied, my mouth suddenly bone-dry. "John made an assumption. That's it."

John scoffed. Fuck, I wanted to punch him right in the pillowy lips. "Tris, I found you terrified and inconsolable on the ground of a parking lot. That's fact, not assumption. You're really going to stand there and tell me that has nothing to do with Dexter Grimaldi? Or that he isn't the one that left bruises all over your left breast?"

Hank and Nelson both exploded at that, but I wasn't listening to them. I was too busy glaring absolute venom at John *asshole of the year* Smith. "I think it's time for you to leave, Professor Smith. You've done enough damage for one day, don't you think?"

He stared back at me, also not paying attention to Hank and Nelson who were both barking questions at us. "I guess so," John finally said with an edge of disappointment. "I'll see you in class tomorrow, Miss Ives."

I shook my head, giving a cold smile. "No, you won't. I've applied for a transfer to SGU for the remainder of my study."

Hank's jaw dropped, but Nelson just scrubbed a hand over his face. John, though? He seemed almost *amused* by this information. He gave a small nod, then rose to his feet and crossed the gap between us. Instead of passing by to exit through the front door, he stopped right in front of me. His forefinger and thumb grasped my chin, tilting my face back so I was forced to meet his eyes.

"For what it's worth," he said in a low, quiet voice, "I'm sorry that you got hurt, Venus. But it could always be worse."

With that cryptic warning, he stalked out of the apartment and left me to clean up the atomic bomb that he just dropped on my personal life. What an *asshole*.

"Ivy..." Nelson growled, folding his arms and scowling at me. "Start talking."

I ground my teeth so hard my jaw hurt. "There's nothing to talk about."

Hank sighed, giving me a sad look. "Talk to us, Ivy. We thought you had this Dexter thing handled?"

I wet my lips, feeling defensive. "I do."

Nelson was one step away from blowing his lid. I could see it. I just didn't trust myself not to have a breakdown if he finally cracked, so I had to extract myself.

"I'm tired and honestly, I need some alone time. I'll talk to you both tomorrow, okay? Good night!" I was already out the door and halfway to my own apartment before they could even protest. When they did, I ignored it and let myself into my safe, cozy apartment then secured the door behind myself. No way in hell was I risking another early morning wake up from the biggest dick on earth.

Despite what I told Nelson, I wasn't sleepy at all. I kicked off my shoes and made my way through to my studio instead. Painting was always my best therapy, and a hell of a lot more comfortable than talking about my feelings with a stranger. So I pulled out a blank canvas and let my mind heal itself through art.

It wasn't until the next morning that I realized… someone had been in my home. And I had a sick feeling that I knew who it was.

Suddenly I was second guessing *everything.*

thirty-one

JOHN

Tris had been so close to slapping me, I was amazed she'd held herself back. To be fair, I'd deserved it, and more. The way tension had crackled through her when I touched her face, and whispered my apology, I was lucky to walk away with my dick and balls all still in one piece.

She'd let me leave, though. She hadn't even said a single word to stop me, and my heart sank faster than the elevator ride back to street level. In *no way* did I expect her to chase after me. Not after the way I'd treated her this morning. But did I *want* her to? Hell yes.

Tris had too much dignity to ever chase after a man who'd wronged her, though, so she said nothing and I left the building unhindered by anything more than my own crushing sense of guilt. I'd known perfectly well what I was doing, exposing her abuse from Dexter like that.

What I didn't understand was why she was keeping it a secret in the first place. Nelson and Hank cared about her like she was their own granddaughter; they'd have been nothing but supportive and comforting had she told them. Hell, they'd have likely marched over there personally to hand over her resignation. They'd keep her *safe*. And that was what I'd been hoping for.

I didn't need Tris to access the Grimaldi house anymore. I *had* what I needed from her already and could get the job done with the distraction of the party. She never needed to return there, and it was better for everyone if she didn't.

Somehow, though, I knew I was dreaming. She'd manage to explain it all away, or simply dig her heels in just to be a stubborn bitch. Maybe that was why I found myself walking through the entrance to The Slippery Lips a half hour later.

It was still early, so the bar was mostly empty, but a helpful bartender indicated that the man I wanted to see was in the management office. She implied he was *occupied,* but I gave less than zero fucks about interrupting him and told her as much before storming down the corridor she'd accidentally pointed me toward.

It wasn't hard to find the management office; the door was halfway open and unmistakable grunts and groans came from inside. I gritted my teeth, pushing the door open the rest of the way and striding in.

Dexter was leaning against the front of the desk, making no attempt at privacy as a petite woman with long inky black hair—just like Tris—choked on his cock. She wore nothing but a G-string, her little tits bouncing as Dexter fucked her throat, then she gagged and spluttered as he came while jerking her hair.

"Who the fuck are you?" the youngest Grimaldi son demanded, shoving the girl away and making her sprawl awkwardly on the dirty carpet.

I arched a brow down at her, and she glared back. "That hair doesn't suit you, Tink."

"Fuck you, Hermes," she snapped back, picking herself up with graceful ease.

"Hey!" Dexter barked. "I asked you a fucking question!"

Ignoring him, I tipped my head to the door, telling Tink to get the fuck out. Meanwhile, little-dick-Dexter was fumbling around his desk looking for a gun. He barely got it raised before I was in his face, knocking the pistol from his flimsy grip and grabbing him by the throat.

A strangled sound escaped him as I lifted him off the

floor, then slammed him down on the desk with absolutely no fucks given for his spinal health.

"Who I am," I growled, letting my fury and disgust radiate through my voice, "is none of your fucking business."

My fingers tightened around his neck, and in my mind I saw just how *easy* it would be to finish him off right here and now. Killing wasn't something I often entertained, and never up close and personal like this. In the past, the only time I'd taken a life was to give someone already on the brink of death a nudge over the edge. A little poison went a long way to the elderly and ill-health community.

But this was different. This was entirely personal. He'd touched Tristian, and now all I could focus on was making him *pay*.

"Hermes," someone snapped, yanking me out of my own head.

I blinked, looking over at Tink still standing in front of the door which was now closed and locked. "What?" I snarled back.

She shook her head, giving me a hard glare. "This isn't the time, or the place. Don't fuck up the Game over a girl. Put it on ice and deal with it later."

Fuck. She was right. Of course she was. Tristian was

so deeply inside my head, I'd almost forgotten why I got involved with her in the first place.

Swallowing hard, I relaxed my grip on Dexter's throat, allowing him to suck noisy, wheezing gasps of air. It wasn't satisfying. Leaning down, I let him see the cold violence in my eyes.

"You put your filthy hands on Tris again, I'll cut your dick off and make you eat it. Am I clear?"

Dexter glared back, but there was something unfocused about his eyes. When I stepped back, allowing him to get up, he wobbled and fell to his ass on the floor. Jesus, I hadn't even hit him...

"He's been doing coke all afternoon," Tink told me with a shrug, "among other things. Chances are, he won't even remember this. Or certainly not the finer points."

I blew out a long breath, scrubbing my hands over my face and head. No wonder she'd so casually mentioned the Game in front of her target. He was so fucked up that none of those secrets would stick.

"Shit," I breathed. "I should..." *Do what?* I wasn't just sabotaging my relationship with Tris, I was quickly sabotaging my chance of winning the Game, too. Dexter was her target and I'd just directly interfered in her strategy, which was against the rules. If Dexter hadn't been drugged up, then I could be staring down a disqualification. "Tink...I didn't mean—"

"I know," she cut me off with a predatory smile, "but you did. No one else needs to know, for the right price."

I groaned, glancing back over at Dexter, who was wobbling his way over to the gun I'd knocked out of his hand.

"It's not loaded," Tink assured me. "I took care of that earlier when he thought he was being a big tough guy and sticking it in my mouth."

Dexter heard that and gave her a confused frown. "Wh-what did you fucking call me?"

She just rolled her eyes and ignored him, returning her gaze to me and folding her arms like she wasn't practically naked. "So? What have you got for me? Because this is going fucking *nowhere.*" She tipped her chin at Dexter.

"Fair point," I agreed, grimacing. I had to give her something of value, or she could turn me into the Game committee for review, which could take weeks. "There's a party on Friday night."

She grinned. "Perfect."

"I thought so, too." Casting another look at Dexter, I turned back to Tink and her long black wig. He'd clearly wanted her to look like Tris, the sick fuck. "Keep him away from Tris, or I'll kill him myself."

She wet her lips, then nodded. "Understood." I moved past her, unlocking the door and yanking it open before she spoke again. "Watch out for Igor, Hermes. He's been too damn quiet lately."

I frowned, glancing at her over my shoulder. "You think he's up to no good?"

"Always," she agreed. "But this feels different. Watch your back. He doesn't respect the rules like we do."

With that ominous warning, I stalked back out of The Slippery Lips. If Igor was up to no good, there was a good chance he was letting the personal nature of *this* Game cloud his judgment. But was I really any better? Every minute I spent with Tris had me losing focus, which was why it'd been *so* important to push her away.

I wished I could say I regretted caving to desire and fucking her in the shower, but I didn't. Not even a little bit. Hell, I was already thinking about how I could make it up to her, just so I could experience one more moment of bliss between her thighs before I disappeared for good.

It made me even more of an asshole than she already thought I was, but it was the truth. Before I left Whispering Willows, I'd get her to fall apart on my dick again.

thirty-two

TRIS

Nelson was not letting the subject of Dexter drop easily. He got so pig-headed about the whole subject that I nearly went to class on the Friday afternoon just to get a break from his never-ending litany of reasons why I needed to quit my job with the Grimaldis. Then I remembered John would be in class, and I decided I'd rather put up with Nelson *caring*—regardless of how annoying—over John's smug arrogance.

"This whole conversation is pointless!" I shouted to Nelson while putting on my makeup for the Grimaldi party on Friday night. "Dexter wasn't even at the house today, and it's all irrelevant once my transfer gets approved." I'd gone back to work this morning, after getting a call from Mr. Grimaldi. I had to admit, I missed my work. It was both exhilarating and calming to work on those priceless paintings.

"*If* it gets approved," Nelson corrected, bringing me a mini cheese platter to eat while I did my makeup. I loved him so much. "And that could take weeks. Call me crazy, Ivy, but I'm not comfortable leaving you in a vulnerable position for that long."

I shrugged. "Good thing it's not up to you, then." I ignored his glower as I blended my contour. "Last I checked, I am an adult..." *and you aren't my guardian, old man.*

I loved him too much to say that last part out loud, but the fact still remained.

"Ives, it's my fault you're in this position in the first place. I don't want you going to this party tonight." Nelson rested his shoulder against the door frame and folded his arms like his decision was final.

I arched a brow at him in the mirror. "Okay. Noted."

He glared. "I'm serious. This job isn't worth the risk to your safety, Ivy. There will be *other* jobs. Safer ones. I've already made some calls to get something lined up with—"

"Nelson," I snapped, cutting him off. "While I appreciate your concern, I'm not a little girl anymore. I can handle myself, and I'm going to this party. Mr. Grimaldi expects to see me there."

"That's not a good reason," Nelson muttered, his brow furrowed.

I shrugged, smoothing on my lipstick and rubbing my lips together. "I'm not going in circles with you about this, old man. I'm going to the party, and I will be *just fine.* I'll stay in crowded rooms and avoid Dexter at all costs. Besides, Naomi told me this morning that Dexter's wife is attending tonight, so he will be more than occupied."

Brushing past Nelson, I crossed over to the dress I'd left out on my bed. It was a glittery sapphire blue with corset-style top and tea-length ballerina skirt. So pretty. I slipped into it and turned my back for Nelson to zip me up.

"How do I look?" I asked him with a smile as I stepped into my classic black Manolo Blahnik heels.

Nelson was still scowling, the old grump, but he sighed and shrugged. "Like $50 million, and you damn well know it. I should have made you buy a potato sack or something...How you think you'll escape Dexter's greedy eyes in *that* I have no clue."

I rolled my eyes, tossing my curled hair over my back and heading to my kitchen for a glass of champagne. Despite my casual confidence in defending my decision to keep my job, I was panicking inside. All I could hear in my mind was the hungry, determined way

Dexter had promised to assault me at his father's party. Tonight.

That part, I hadn't told Nelson. If I had, there was no way in hell he would be letting me go, even if it meant tying me up and sitting on top of me.

"Since when have I ever given you reason to worry, Nels? I can take care of myself." I gulped my champagne then sneezed when the bubbles got to my nose.

"Is that meant to be a joke? I worry about you every damn day, Ives. Particularly now." Nelson sighed heavily and scrubbed a hand over his face. "I'm getting too old for this shit."

I smiled and patted his arm. "Nonsense, the stress keeps you young. Now, shouldn't you be getting back to work yourself? My car will be here in a few minutes anyway."

He grunted but didn't reply. He glanced at my front door ever so quickly, raising my suspicions. Then he checked his watch and sighed again. What the fuck was he up to?

A moment later, someone knocked on my door and I narrowed my eyes at Nelson. "What have you done, old man?"

He winced and gave an unapologetic shrug. "I figured you probably wouldn't be talked out of going to the party tonight, so I arranged a back up plan."

A chill of dread ran down my spine as the person at the door knocked again. It was a heavy knock. Masculine. Like that was a large hand doing the knocking.

"Tell me you didn't..." My horrified whisper faded out as Nelson crossed the apartment and opened my front door, revealing a six-foot-five *fuckstain* in a tuxedo.

"Tris," John greeted me with a tight smile as he stepped inside. "You look stunning."

My anger turned ice cold. "Go to hell, John. Nelson? We officially have problems."

The old goat just checked his watch again and gave a dramatic gasp. "Oh dear, is that the time? I'm late for my appointment. Must run. Have fun tonight, kids. Stay safe." He gave John a firm slap on the shoulder then ran away like a little bitch.

"Don't be mad at Nelson," John said, accurately reading my mood. "He's just trying to keep you safe."

I barked a sharp laugh. "And this is how he goes about it? Calling in *you* to act as my bodyguard? Maybe he really is getting old. Apparently his judgment is becoming severely impaired."

John gave an easy shrug, unaffected by my seething fury. "Maybe. But I'm here now and willing to do whatever it takes to ensure you don't go to this party alone. So…what's it gonna be, Venus? Easy way or the hard one?"

"Don't fucking call me that," I spat, snatching my coat and bag off the back of the couch and storming out ahead of him. Logically, I was smart enough to understand I couldn't *stop* him from attending the party whether it was as my date or on his own. I didn't doubt for a second his ability to charm his way in without an invitation, so I was only wasting my own energy by fighting it.

I'd called a car service to drive me over to the Grimaldis'—knowing perfectly well that I'd be drinking —and with impeccable timing, the driver pulled up in front of my building as I stepped out of the foyer.

I slid into the back seat and just barely bit my tongue against the urge to leave John behind.

He was a douche bucket of the lowest order, but he'd already made it clear that he *had* what he wanted from me. He'd nailed me once, ticked my name off his list or made a notch on his bedpost or whatever sleazy professors did to mark their conquests…and we were done. So that offered me some level of reassurance that *John*—at least—wasn't planning on assaulting or raping me tonight.

As unpleasant as I now found his company, I couldn't deny that I felt safer for having him escort me.

That silent admission only pissed me off even more, and I ignored him for the entire drive over to RBD's. Not that he tried to engage me in any conversation himself. He seemed just as uncomfortable and reluctant to be there as I was, which made me wonder what Nelson had offered to make him turn up tonight.

The car dropped us off at the main entrance, and my pulse skipped as John extended a hand to help me out of the back seat. My palms were sweating, but there was nothing I could do about it.

"Any time you want to leave, just say the word." His offer was quiet and murmured right into my ear as I climbed out, making me shiver.

I licked my lips. "I'm fine. Just feels weird to come through the front door at RBD's, that's all." Such a liar. "I usually use the staff entrance around the side."

John quirked a brow as we ascended the stairs to the door. There were several couples ahead of us, getting their names checked off the guest list and being patted down for weapons, so we weren't moving quick.

"RBD's?" he asked. "What does that stand for? I thought this place was owned by Luther Grimaldi."

A small smile tugged my lips. "It is. RBD's is just a nickname that I use with Nelson and Hank. It's turned into a habit."

John's gaze was so intense I could feel it even as I

tried to ignore him and focus on the people ahead of us. "Do I get to know what it means?"

I was tempted to just say no and leave it at that. But the whole evening was already awkward enough without adding to the tension unnecessarily. Besides, maybe it would help him to understand who he was messing around with here.

"*Really Bad Dude*," I murmured, keeping my voice low. "Because that's what Mr. Grimaldi is. A *really* bad dude." I tilted my head up to lock eyes with John. "As are his sons."

John must have already heard rumors, or maybe he was just excellent at schooling his face into a neutral expression, because he showed no shock or surprise at that information. Weird.

Neither one of us spoke again as we proceeded through the front door security screening. My invitation had specified *plus one,* which admitted John in, but they still patted him down thoroughly for weapons. Not me, though. Me, they just waved through. It'd serve the Grimaldis right if a female assassin came for them one day, since they seemed to assume women were no threat to their safety.

The party was being held in the main ballroom of the Grimaldi house, and a cold chill swept over me as I hesitated in the doorway. My eyes went to the crystal chandelier in the center of the room, my mind recalling the sight of a bloody, beaten man hanging there from chains.

"Tris," John's deep voice pulled me back to present, his warm hand resting on the small of my back to ground me. "You okay?"

I swallowed hard, then licked my lips. My face must have been pale as a sheet, and my hands were sweating again, but I gave a faint nod. "Yeah. Fine. I just haven't eaten anything." Not entirely a lie.

John wasn't buying my shit, but he was either too polite or didn't care enough to call me on it. Instead, he just steered me across the room to where a waiter in a sharp white suit was handing out canapés.

Maybe having John escort me tonight wasn't such a bad idea after all. He was tall enough to see over people to spot the food. Silver linings.

thirty-three

JOHN

Tonight was the night. My plan was all set, I had everything I needed all lined up. I'd have *preferred* that Tris not be there, because she was pulling so much of my attention it was hard to focus on the objective, but at the same time I was glad she was. When Nelson called to ask me this *favor,* I couldn't say yes fast enough.

Anything to get another chance with her, even if I still planned to disappear tomorrow.

After she said she hadn't eaten, I made it my mission to steer her toward every canapé waiter I could find. Eventually she grumbled that she was so full she was going to split a seam on her dress, and I relaxed a little. Of course, her mentioning her dress only made me glance down at the enticing way her breasts were propped up and damn near spilling over.

It was becoming harder and harder not to drag her away into an empty room and fuck her senseless...but considering the venomous glares she kept shooting my way, I doubted that'd go down well.

Dexter—the slimy fuck—had spotted her a few minutes ago but was occupied on the arm of a gorgeous, heavily pregnant woman. His wife, I presumed. Still, that didn't stop him from watching my girl like a starving falcon that had just spotted a mouse.

Tris was no mouse, though. She was more of a scorpion in mouse clothing.

"So this is where you work when you're not at Boles?" I asked, shifting my position to block her from Dexter's view. He didn't seem to recognize me, leading me to believe Tink must have been right about how fucked up he'd been the other night.

Tris took a tiny sip of her champagne and offered me a tight smile. "This is the only place I work, now that I've quit my TA job at Boles."

Irritation rippled through me. I'd torn up her resignation and swapped it out for a sick leave medical form, but she didn't need to know that. I wasn't going to let her throw away her academic prospects just because I hurt her.

"Uh huh," I murmured. "I don't see any of these amazing paintings you mentioned, though. These all seem to be…replicas?" I eyed the closest one, noting the subtle signs of a forgery. It was supposed to be a Manet, but instead it was just a good copy. A very good copy, but not good enough to fool anyone who knew what they were looking for.

Tris tipped her head, giving me a curious look. "Yes…these are all replicas here. Mr. Grimaldi discovered some years ago that he can't trust people not to ruin his artwork, so he employed an artist to create forgeries that he could display while keeping the originals safe within his personal gallery."

That…was unexpected. I squinted at her in suspicion. "You?"

She scoffed a laugh. "No, this was long before I moved to Whispering Willows. I can't even imagine how hard it'd be to create a convincing forgery of one of the greats. The sheer talent that a painter would have needed…crazy. And why would anyone be wasting their time and skill on replicas instead of creating their own work, you know?"

I could think of a few reasons. Mostly monetary ones. A skilled forger could make *huge* money in my line of business. Instead of just stealing a painting, they could make a swap and it would be anyone's guess how long it'd take before the theft was discovered. It was something that I'd thought about a lot, but sadly I lacked the innate talent for recreating great art. I just stole it and escaped unnoticed, leaving the fallout in my dust.

"What happened to the painter?" I asked, curiosity burning inside me. Maybe there was a future business connection to be made there.

Tris wet her lips, looking ill. "I don't know for *sure*, but I heard whispers that he tried to steal from Mr. Grimaldi…and got caught."

I winced. "Ah, I see."

She screwed up her nose, looking up at me with interest. "Do you? He didn't go to jail, John. Mr. Grimaldi didn't report him to the cops and press charges. He had him killed. This isn't just a nice old rich man we're talking about, he's a—"

"Tristian!" A smiling man with white hair called out her name, making her eyes widen and her face pale before spinning around to greet, I assumed, Mr. Grimaldi himself. "You look gorgeous, Tristian. I'm so glad you came. Oh, but you brought a date?" The old man's smile slipped as he looked me over, his gaze turning cold.

"Thank you for inviting me, sir," Tris replied, sweet as sugar. "John is just a friend. He was concerned about me attending alone and offered to come as my escort."

That information seemed to ease the irritated expression on her boss's face. "Ah, I see. Not a date, hmm?"

Tristian shook her head, shooting me a glance. "Most definitely not. John is actually one of my professors at Boles."

Mr. Grimaldi's expression brightened. "Ah, how lovely. What do you teach, John?"

I rested my hand on Tristian's back, unable to help myself. "Art History," I replied, "I'm only here temporarily, covering while—"

"Sorry, so sorry," Mr. Grimaldi interrupted as a woman approached. "Just a second." He leaned in while the woman whispered in his ear, then gave us a polite smile. "My apologies, how rude of me. I need to go speak with someone, but I look forward to speaking with you later, John. Tristian, sweetheart, enjoy the party."

As he walked away, Tristian noticeably relaxed and a thread of concern tightened around my chest. Was that the level of tension she carried every damn day while working? Why on earth didn't she simply quit?

"It's kind of hot in here," I commented. "Is there somewhere we could get some air? Or maybe that isn't so crowded?"

She quickly nodded, clearly wanting to get out of the

ballroom herself. "Yeah, there's a courtyard. This way." Almost in a subconscious gesture, she slipped her hand into mine, our fingers interlacing.

I squeezed lightly, letting her lead me out of the room, and she gave a small frown at our hands. She didn't pull away, though, so I'd chalk that one up as a small win.

After we'd exited the ballroom, she pointed out a few things throughout the house. All the usual ostentatious mansion bullshit, like a library and wine cellar. The courtyard came into view, but she hesitated before leading me down a corridor away from it.

"Where are we going, Tris?" I asked, excitement already warming my insides. Did I hope she was pulling me into an empty bedroom to work out some of this suffocating tension between us? God yes.

She glanced at me over her shoulder but continued leading me down the hall until we reached a heavy glass door flanked by two windows. A quick glance told me that it was bulletproof glass, and the security locks were impressive. I already had the blueprints of the house memorized. I knew this was the gallery, but I was curious why *she* was showing me it.

"This is where I work," she told me, indicating the door. It was dark inside, all the lights turned off and no external windows to let in natural light. All I could make out were a few shadowed picture frames illuminated from the light of the hallway.

I peered through the glass like I was genuinely interested, then gave her a smile. "Can we go in?" It was worth a try.

She gave a quick laugh and shook her head. "Definitely not. Only two people have access to the gallery, after one of Mr. Grimaldi's prized pieces got shot six times during a, uh, business meeting."

"Only two?" I repeated. This was new information.

She nodded. "Mr. Grimaldi and me. He might change things at some stage, but right now he keeps saying how none of the other people hanging around his home have any true appreciation for art so why should he let them see it?"

Well that confirmed my initial gut feeling that she was my best possible access. Tink was officially not a threat to my win anymore, if Dexter didn't even have access to the gallery. Igor was another matter, since I hadn't worked out what his angle was.

"It means that once I'm in there, I'm totally safe," she said softly. "No one *else* can get inside."

That was reassuring, to know Dexter couldn't harass her while she worked. It clearly didn't stop him finding her at other times, though. So what would stop him when I was gone?

"Of course, it also means that if anyone steals from Mr. Grimaldi, I'm the prime suspect," she added with a laugh. "Thank fuck for all his security measures. Come on, I'll show you his koi pond. He's got a fish in there that's worth something insane like half a million dollars."

A *fish*. That was new.

"What happens if a cat gets in and eats it?" I asked, letting her lead me away from the gallery and back out to the courtyard. She was *talking* to me, and not with all the hurt and anger of earlier. Like the stress of being in the Grimaldi house, no doubt feeling Dexter's hungry gaze on her every movement, had made her forget why she was mad at me.

Tris snickered a laugh. "Surely that's the risk you'd run when you put a half-million-dollar overgrown goldfish in an outdoor pond."

The courtyard itself was like something out of a home and garden magazine, but she was right about the pond. It didn't even have any wire mesh over the water. For a few minutes, we stood there looking at the big fat orange fish swimming around in the water, and it was strangely mesmerizing.

"Tris..." I started with a sigh, the weight of my own guilt piling up on my mind. "About the other morning..."

She swallowed visibly, staring down at the fish. "I don't want to talk about it, John."

I frowned, placing my hand lightly on her waist to turn her more towards me. Still she kept her eyes downcast, like she was scared to meet my gaze for some reason.

"I need to apologize," I admitted, damn near choking on the words. I couldn't leave things the way they were, though. I had to make sure she knew it was nothing to do with *her* and everything to do with my own lies and deceptions. "That shit I said to you, it was all—"

She gave a small gasp, her eyes finding something behind me that scared her. I paused what I was saying, confused, but before I could turn to look she'd grabbed the back of my neck and pulled me down to kiss her.

It went without saying, Dexter was somewhere nearby. That was the only explanation for her sudden desire to kiss me, when earlier this evening she'd have happily fed me razorblades. But her reasons meant nothing once our lips met.

The tension between us crackled and flared right back to life, and she gasped against my mouth. Then her fingers were digging into the muscles of my neck as she pulled herself closer, kissing me hard enough to nearly make me forget where we even were.

My tongue found hers in a flurry of desperation, my

lips committing every part of her kiss to memory as I drank her down. Banding my arms around her slim waist, I lifted her clean off the ground so I could kiss her easier, and the moan she released made my knees weak.

"Tris," I groaned, holding her so tight against me she must be struggling to breathe. "I need to be inside you. Just one more time…"

She pushed out of my grip, her high heels meeting the tiled ground with a sharp click as I released her. A flash of panic ripped through me, convinced she'd just realized her mistake and was now running away.

But the heated look in her eyes when she looked up at me was anything but horrified. She tipped her head to the other side of the courtyard, then linked our fingers together and tugged me after her. Fuck the Game. This was better.

thirty-four

TRIS

As pissed as I was at John for the way he'd treated me this week, it didn't even slightly compare to the fear that rolled through me when I saw Dexter stalking down the corridor looking for me. Somehow I just *knew*, if he caught me, if I walked away from John's safety…

So I did the only thing I could think of. I kissed John. Because if all Dexter could see was John's broad, suited back and a woman's arms around his neck, he wouldn't look any closer. Right? Fuck, I didn't know. That was my reasoning and I was sticking to it.

Of course, nothing prepared me for the intense rush of emotion that slammed into me when our mouths met. Then he went and tossed gasoline on the fire by telling me he *needed* to be inside me, and I was a fucking goner.

I knew the layout of RBD's well enough to already have a plan formulating in my head. Tugging John along behind me, I keyed in my staff access code to a service door which led us into Mr. Grimaldi's private garage.

We didn't bother turning on any of the lights, and I was confident no one would be coming in there during the party, since the valet had already stacked cars all the way along the driveway. It was the perfect, private location.

Neither one of us spoke as I twisted around, looping my arms around John's neck to kiss him again. He eagerly returned the gesture, his huge hands skating down the sides of my corset, then boosted me up onto the hood of the nearest car. Thank fuck it didn't have an alarm, or that could have seriously killed the mood.

"Tris…" he groaned as I shoved his jacket off, then pulled his shirt free of his pants. "We should—"

"Shh," I quickly hushed him, unbuttoning his shirt with quick motions. "The kitchen is through that wall, and we don't want anyone coming to investigate."

I was so full of shit. I just didn't want him ruining the moment by trying to apologize for being such an *asshole* right now. Yes, I was still mad as hell, and no I hadn't forgiven him for treating me like a cheap whore. But I was also so turned on right now I couldn't think straight, so he needed to keep his pretty mouth *shut* or I'd have to give it something else to do.

"Yes, ma'am," he murmured in a husky voice, his hands smoothing up my legs to bunch my skirt up. His fingers hooked into the edges of my panties and gave them a tug. "These need to go."

I leaned back on the hood of the car, bracing my elbows and lifting my hips for him to slide my underwear down my legs. He didn't take my heels off, just my panties. Then he dropped to his knees and hooked my legs over his shoulders.

"Oh, fuck," I gasped as he buried his face between my legs. *That* was more like it. His full lips devoured my pussy in a way that sent me straight to cloud nine. My breathing spiked hard, and I gripped the back of his head, holding him against me as I rocked my hips, fucking his mouth without a single care in the world. When he paused for air, he pushed two thick fingers into my cunt and I exploded.

My quiet panting quickly morphed into moans and curses as his tongue found my clit, sucking and flicking that little point of ecstasy while his fingers stretched my pussy, fucking me hard as I climaxed. Intense shivers chased through me, but he didn't let up.

"John..." I moaned as he continued thrusting with those sinful fingers. "Holy shit..."

"You taste so fucking good, Tris," he whispered in the sexiest fucking voice on earth. "The way your sweet cunt grabbed my fingers as you came makes me want to throw you over my shoulder and carry you home right now. Then I can really take my time..."

Fuck that sounded tempting.

"Okay but first I need you to fuck me properly," I panted, writhing on his fingers, desperate for his cock. "Please, John...I need to feel you inside me." Then, because I was still pissed at him, I repeated what he'd said. "Just one last time."

He inhaled sharply, his eyes flashing with determination as he kissed my inner thigh, wiping his damp stubble on my flesh. "I said one *more* time, Tris. Not *last*."

I swallowed hard, choking back all the potent emotions that he seemed to conjure up in me. Those emotions were what sent him running last time, and I intended to get my fill before he panicked again.

"So? Same thing." I sat up just enough to grab his belt when he returned to his feet, pulling him in close as I freed his massive erection from his tux pants. "Is that a problem for you, Professor?" My hand circled his thick cock, stroking down the length as his tip leaked slippery fluid. "Are you asking for more?"

His lips parted, and a conflicted look pinched his eyes. Then he hitched my legs up and slammed his cock into me with one brutal thrust that made me see stars. A low moan rolled out of me as he pulled back and repeated the motion, making my bare ass squeak on the hood of the car. Fucking hell, he'd been holding back in the shower.

"Yes, God, John…" the way I whimpered his name sent him wild and he bent down to kiss my throat while his hips rammed that huge cock into me over and over.

My hips tilted, taking him deeper and making him curse. Then his hand was in my hair, pulling the strands as my back arched and my tits spilled out of my dress.

"Holy fuck, Tris," he breathed, dipping his head to tongue my breast. His lips closed around my nipple and he sucked, making me buck beneath him with intoxicating shivers of arousal. One of his hands snaked down between us, finding my clit with ease as he slowed his thrusts ever so slightly. "You're so close, aren't you?" he asked, his gaze dark and heavy. "The way your pussy is grabbing my cock is *insane*."

Ugh, who knew dirty talk could be so hot? When Chad had done it, I just wanted to gag him. When John did it, I wanted him to gag *me*...with his cock. But that would mean taking it away from my cunt, and it felt *so damn good* where it was.

"Uh huh," I agreed, bucking my hips to meet each stroke from his enormous dick. It was like he was trying to split me in half, but I loved that he wasn't treating me like I was breakable. I could take it, and he damn well knew it. His fingers rubbed at my clit, getting the pressure and speed just right until my orgasm was looming like a tidal wave.

A gasping litany of curses fell from my lips as he smirked, sensing I was about to detonate, and he fucked me faster. *Harder.* When I came, my balance went haywire and I nearly fell off the hood of the car. Thankfully John was there to catch me, hoisting me up into his arms as my whole body quaked and I looped my wet noodle arms around his neck to hold on.

He chuckled into my sweaty neck, his arms full of my sparkly tulle skirt as my legs wrapped around his body. His cock was still buried deep inside me, but he seemed totally content to wait me out before continuing.

"Still with me, Venus?" he asked, his own breathing heavy as he sat himself down on the hood with me still in his lap.

I nodded, gasping for air and licking my lips to try and make them stop tingling. "Um, yeah. Barely, but yeah."

He chuckled again, and God help me - another little wave of orgasm made my pussy clench and spasm around his thickness. "That feels so good," he breathed, moaning lightly as he kissed my throat. "Are you gonna come again for me, Tris?" He gripped my hips, lifting me and dropping me down again, creating enough friction for my nerve endings to all spark back to life.

I gasped, then whimpered at how damn good it felt. "I dunno," I teased, bracing my knees on the car so I could bounce on his dick. "Am I? You tell me…"

He laughed louder this time, his fingertips biting into the flesh of my ass cheeks as he guided me to ride him. "Like you have any doubts, Venus. This pussy was made for my cock. Look at how good you take me." He lifted me up further this time, peering down at his slick cock sliding out of me. Then grunted a curse as he slammed me back down, his tip hitting so deep inside I could swear it made me hiccup.

"See?" he groaned, his chest slick with sweat as he wet his own lips. "*Made* for me." His fingers twisted into my hair, jerking my head back as he kissed me breathless. He fucked me from below, one arm holding my waist and the other yanking my hair, and only moments later I found myself cresting another climax. He swallowed my moans, his teeth sinking into my lower lip and giving a sharp sting of pain while I convulsed in his arms.

His arms flexed around me as I trembled with aftershocks, but he was holding out…

"John…" I gasped, my inner walls clenching sporadically as endorphins drowned my system. "Are you gonna come inside me?"

He gave a pained sound. "You want me to?"

I swallowed. I usually *hated* the uncomfortable feeling of jizz-drip after the fact. Hated walking around with damp panties, knowing it was cum sliding back out of me. But I was quickly coming to realize it had very little to do with the feeling and more about *whose* cum it was. So it was an easy answer.

"Fuck yes," I whispered.

That seemed to snap his control. "Shit," he breathed. "How can any man deny a request like that?" He smirked a wicked smile, then lifted me off his lap. Before I could protest, though, I was face down on the hood of the car with my skirt flipped over my head. His big hands gripped my hips and with one push he'd fully sheathed his monster cock within my cunt.

"This is what I was telling you, Tris," he growled, our flesh slapping together as he fucked me fast. "You. Were.

Made. For. My. Dick." He grunted those last words, thrusting so hard my nipples were getting friction burn against the car, but then he was coming with a gasping moan, hot jets of his release filling me up inside and sending me into another mini-climax myself.

When he was done, we just stayed locked like that for a moment with our entwined panting breaths filling the otherwise quiet garage. Then he pulled out so damn slow there was no way he wasn't simply enjoying the view.

"I had been planning on blowing my load on the side of Dexter's car," he admitted with a husky laugh while helping me to stand up once more. "But this was better. So much better. Now you're going to have my cum leaking out of you for the rest of the party..."

Fuck, why was that so hot?

Then an idea hit me and I grinned taking his hand as I crossed to Dexter's car. It was hard to miss, with a license plate reading LGOPNR. Gross.

"What are we doing?" John asked with a lopsided grin.

I smiled back at him, leaning my back against the car and lifting my skirt once more. "Best of both worlds, Professor." Then dipped my fingers between my legs and coated them with our combined juices before smearing that hand on Dexter's windscreen.

John's mouth dropped like he was in shock, then he tossed his head back laughing. "Holy shit, Tris. You're unbelievable...in the best fucking way."

Then he kissed me, and I *knew*...I'd fucked up. I was already falling for him.

thirty-five

JOHN

Laughter and conversation trickled down the hallway as Tris and I returned to the party some minutes later. I needed to leave her. This was the best opportunity I'd ever get to steal *Poppy Flowers* and win the Game. But I couldn't make myself do it. I'd hesitated when she said she would be the prime suspect in a theft, then quickly reassured myself that she'd easily be cleared of suspicion when they realized she did *not* have the stolen art.

No, I was struggling to do what I needed to because I couldn't keep my hands off Tris. She'd given me that second chance, and now I was hooked. The thought of never tasting her again was an idea so agonizing it didn't even bear thinking about. Add to that, the worry of

Dexter getting his paws on her if I left her alone...The risk was too great.

So rather than find a convenient excuse to leave her side—then never return—I found myself hovering by her side as she made polite conversation with the Grimaldi party guests. Time was ticking away, my opportunity slipping past me, and I still couldn't make myself move.

I'd lived the Game for so damn long, and *this one* had literally put my grandfather's legacy on the line, so I was at war with myself inside my head. Something that must have been showing on my face, because Tris pulled me aside and frowned up at me.

"What's going on, Casanova?" she asked quietly. "You look like someone just kicked your dog. I'd have thought you'd be all smug and glowing and shit."

The corner of my lips tilted as amusement replaced my indecision. Tris was worth losing the Game for... wasn't she? "Glowing? We had great sex, Tris, I'm not pregnant."

She scoffed. "Yeah well you look like I just shut your nuts in a car door, so what gives? And for the record, that was more than just *great* sex, so don't even pretend you've had better."

Fuck, now I had that whole garage scene playing out in my mind again and my dick hardened. Curling my hand around her waist, I walked her backward a few steps until her back met the wall. Dipping my head down, I kissed her neck where she already wore a few red marks from my mouth.

"I'd probably need to fuck you again just to double check," I murmured, pinning her with my body and delighting in the way her breathing spiked. A small part of me worried she was just getting me out of her system, but she was definitely still hot for another round.

Her grin was pure sex as she tilted her head back to meet my eyes. "Right here? With all these people around? I didn't realize you were into exhibitionism, John..."

"For you, Tris? Anything." I fucking meant it, too.

She laughed like I was joking and slipped out from beneath me. "Somehow, I think we'd get a little too much attention from the wrong kind of people." She dragged her hand down the front of my shirt, then grasped my erection through my pants.

I groaned, leaning into her hand, and she gave a wicked chuckle before pulling her hand away.

"Cruel," I muttered, adjusting myself to hide the evidence of arousal before turning back to the room. A passing waiter held a tray of fresh champagne, so I snagged us one each. "Want to duck out early and fuck in the back of a limo?"

Tris had just taken a sip of champagne and choked on it when she laughed, pulling attention from several guests nearby. Her face went red with embarrassment, and she glared daggers at me like it was *my* fault she'd inhaled alcohol.

"Insanely tempting offer," she admitted, "and one that—" She broke off, as her attention paused on someone nearby. "Huh, I think I know her."

I turned to look at who she was talking about, but my little spitfire was already on her way over to the familiar blonde woman nearby.

"Hey, Katinka?" Tris touched my petite colleague on the arm, pulling her attention from the man she'd been flirting with. "Oh, it is you!"

Tink smiled at Tris, then flicked a worried glance at me. "Tris, I didn't expect to see you here," she said in a careful tone of voice.

My girl was none the wiser to the viper she was handling, giving Tink a warm smile. "I work here. Sorry, this is John. He's my, uh…"

"Boyfriend," I smoothly finished for her, enjoying how her brows nearly hit the roof. Tink looked equally as shocked, but covered it better. "Katinka, was it? How do you two know each other?"

She hummed an affirmative, shaking my hand

lightly. "That's right...*John*. Uh, we just ran into one another on the street."

Tris laughed. "Literally. I nearly knocked Katinka over outside the Royal Orchid last week."

I narrowed my eyes at Tink. "Oh how funny. That's the night you forgot your wallet?"

Tris nodded, wrinkling her nose. "Yep, that night."

Tink's expression froze and I smiled. I'd been at war with myself over leaving Tris alone, for fear of Dexter catching her somewhere...but now I had someone who could watch her. Someone I trusted, to some extent, not to let anything bad happen. Maybe, just maybe, I could have my cake and eat it too.

"I was just about to head to the bathroom but was reluctant to leave Tris alone here," I said, giving Tink a loaded stare.

Tris elbowed me. Hard. "Fucking hell, John, I'm not a child. I can take care of myself. Look how many people are around, for fuck's sake."

Tink glanced between us with a small frown. "Is there a reason to worry for her safety?" she asked cautiously.

"Yes," I snapped.

"No," Tris said on top of me. "Just a spoiled rich boy who can't take no for an answer, but he's certainly not dumb enough to try anything *here*." She indicated to the dozens of party guests standing around with drinks in hand.

Tink sighed, running her hand over her short hair. "I know the type." Then, resigned, she waved a hand at me. "Go. I'll keep your girl company until you get back."

I smiled, but it was with a curling sense of anxiety inside. "You'd better," I said in a faux-joking tone of voice, "I'd hate to put a hit out on you for lying."

She forced a laugh, but she knew full fucking well I wasn't messing around. Tris, though, was looking at me like I'd just spoken in tongues.

"What the fuck? Maybe lay off the champagne, Casanova. Go, we're fine." She gave me a push, but I grabbed the back of her neck and tilted her head back so I could kiss her. Thoroughly. So much that Tink cleared her throat awkwardly and I very reluctantly released Tris.

"Geez, you're only using the bathroom," Tris teased, wiping a smear of her lipstick from the corner of my mouth. "Probably don't need to kiss me like it's the last time we'll see each other."

Jesus Christ. That struck me hard, and Tink's hard, knowing stare only made it worse. I forced myself to smile, though, then clenched my jaw as I walked away.

In the handful of seconds it took to leave the ballroom, I nearly changed my mind at least a dozen times. Tink wouldn't let me down, though. She knew she'd been caught breaking the rules herself—by stealing Tristian's wallet—so she owed me. This just happened to be my price.

Tink, unlike my father, was just happy to compete. Yes, she'd love to win, but she wouldn't jeopardize her position in future Games by getting disqualified.

Clinging to the knowledge that Tink was protecting Tris, I focused on the task at hand. Casually strolling through the manor halls, I acted like a drunk guest looking for a bathroom until I came upon the gallery hall. I'd clocked two security cameras earlier, both of which needed to be disabled to erase my presence.

I'd known there would be security screening on arrival, and although I didn't often carry weapons I also couldn't risk my usual tools being discovered. So I'd gone with my expensive but *discrete* equipment. An electromagnetic laser in the side of my watch took care of the cameras with just a one-second blast each.

Of course, I was risking being *physically* seen entering the gallery. I had a passcode cracking device tucked in my wallet, but thanks to Tris opening the garage door earlier, I no longer needed it. When I was sure the hallway was empty, I keyed in her code and the door blinked green. It could never be so simple, knowing now that she and Mr. Grimaldi were the only ones with access. So it didn't shock me to see a little biometric panel slide open.

From my breast pocket, I pulled out the silicone strip that I'd 3D printed with Tris's fingerprint. I'd lifted such a clear impression of it from the power button of her little purple rabbit toy, it was too damn easy.

The silicone conformed to my own finger and the biometric scanner clicked the door unlocked without even a moment's hesitation.

Moving quickly, I slipped inside the dark gallery and closed the door behind me. The fact that the door itself was glass meant I needed to be a whole hell of a lot quicker than I'd planned. And not turn on any lights. Clenching my jaw against the mounting worry about how this would play out for Tris after the fact, I flicked on the tiny pin light in the side of my watch to search for my painting.

Fucking *Poppy Flowers*. It was worth more than $50 million and depicted a vase of yellow flowers with just three red poppies tucked into the side. Luckily for me, it was a small painting and could be easily smuggled out without any fancy bullshit distractions.

Maintaining the darkness, I needed to check each framed artwork one by one. I skipped past the larger ones, but Luther Grimaldi had a lot within that same size as *Poppy Flowers,* so it took me a minute.

When I got back to where I started, a cold sense of dread filled me. It wasn't here.

Fuck.

Had my intel been bad? Yes, there were a whole lot of priceless, black-market traded artworks within the Grimaldi gallery, but to my utter dismay, *Poppy Flowers* wasn't one of them.

"Shit," I breathed aloud, panic rippling through me with dizzying waves. "Shit, shit, shit. Okay. Think, John. Think. He must have more…" Because Tris had a workshop somewhere, didn't she?

Yes! Maybe it was inside her workshop?

Moving quickly, I looked around the nearly pitch black room again. One of the larger paintings I'd skipped past wasn't a painting at all, it was a window. And beside the window was a door, seamlessly built into the wall with no door handle.

Having already poked around at the Grimaldi security somewhat, I had a vague idea what to look for, so I ran my hands down the smooth door front until a little light blinked and a keypad displayed.

"Bingo," I breathed. My fingertip hovered over the numbers, but before I typed in the same code from the door, I paused. This wasn't a six-digit code like all the other doors; it was a twelve-digit one. And, as I knelt down to take a closer look, the key panel itself had built-in biometrics which meant I needed more than just one fingerprint from Tris.

My heart sank. I could force it, but that'd activate a silent alarm. From my testing, I knew exactly how long I'd have to get in and out once the lock was broken, but that assumed I would even be able to locate *Poppy Flowers* in that time.

It was too risky. Voices outside the gallery sent me diving for the floor, flattening myself against the tiles and hiding in the shadows until the people passed by. It sent enough adrenaline running through me that my head cleared.

I knew what I needed to do, even if it was risking everything.

Fuck. She was going to murder me.

thirty-six

TRIS

Chatting with Katinka was enjoyable, even if she had been giving John weird looks before he left. For a moment there I thought maybe they already knew each other, but John—for all his many flaws—didn't strike me as the strip club kind of guy. And Katinka said she was new in town, so I chalked it up to my own paranoia.

After a while, though, I started to worry.

"Maybe I should go and find John," I finally said out loud, after watching the door like an obsessed creep for way too long. "He might have run into…someone." Like Dexter.

Katinka shrugged. "Honestly, he's probably just waiting in line for the bathroom. Everyone blocks them up at these parties, doing coke off the vanity like there isn't a whole freaking table for it in the gaming room." She rolled her eyes and gave me a smile. "I don't know the guy, but I get the feeling he won't let anything separate you for long. Have you guys been dating a while?"

I laughed slightly, shaking my head. "No, definitely not. We're…" I trailed off with a grimace. I liked her, but it was probably a bit too soon to go spilling my relationship drama at her feet. "It's complicated."

"Tristian, dear," Mr. Grimaldi called out, approaching with a gorgeous, somewhat familiar man at his side. "There you are, I was looking all over for you."

"Ah, I stepped out to the courtyard for some air," I admitted with a polite smile. "Crowds aren't my favorite."

"Hah, that's something you two have in common," Mr. Grimaldi commented, looking from the handsome, thirty-something man to me and back again. "Sorry, where are my manners? Tristian, this is my son, Sin. I thought you two should get to know each other." He beamed at both of us, then nodded like he was satisfied. He looped an arm around Katinka's waist and smoothly steered her away before she could even protest.

She glanced back at me with a helpless expression, but I just smiled and gave her a wave that said I was *fine*.

"So…" my new friend said, running a tattooed hand

over the back of his neck. "Sorry about that. My father thinks he's subtle, but in reality a tossed grenade would have been more tactful." I blinked up at him, slightly mesmerized by his Irish brogue. "He's trying to set us up," he explained, apparently thinking I'd missed that fact.

I nodded and gave a small laugh. "Uh yeah, I picked up on that. Now I'm starting to understand why he seemed so upset that I brought a date tonight."

Sin's eyes widened, then he gave a small sigh. "You brought a date? Thank fuck for that."

Surprise saw me blinking at him in confusion. "Um…should I be insulted by that?"

"Fuck, no. Sorry." He winced, realizing what he'd just said. "Let me try that again." He extended his hand. "Hi Tristian, I'm Sin. My father thinks we would hit it off, but that's largely because he doesn't know that I'm already in love with another woman."

I gave a short laugh, shaking his hand. "Got it. Why not just tell him about her?"

"Uh, long story," he admitted with a grimace. "Come get a drink with me, and I'll give you the CliffsNotes. Then we can pretend like we're flirting, and my father can stop harassing me about meeting a *nice, young woman* for a few days."

The bar was just at the other side of the room, so I

agreed and let him lead me over there with a respectful hand on the middle of my back. He ordered us a couple of cocktails and leaned an elbow on the bar top.

"So, I take it Mr. Grimaldi wouldn't *approve* of this girl you're in love with?" I was officially curious. "Also how come I never knew Dexter had a brother?"

Sin curled his lip. "I'm sorry you even have to know *he* exists." He paused as the bartender delivered our drinks. "And no, my father would probably kill her if he ever saw her again, so even if I knew how to find her, she couldn't exactly come over for Sunday dinner."

My brows hitched with the intrigue of it all. "Wait, you don't know where she is? How very Shakespeare."

Sin gave a sad smile. "Not even the slightest clue. And I've *looked*."

"How long has she been...missing?" Because I was getting a *bad* feeling. Having already seen what Mr. Grimaldi did to people who crossed him...was there any guarantee this woman was even alive?

He took a sip of his drink and cringed. "That's awful." Then he looked to the ceiling like he was doing the math before returning his gaze to mine. "One year and three months. She's not dead, though."

I sipped my own drink, not wanting to be the voice of negativity no matter how likely it was that his woman was lying in a shallow grave somewhere.

"My father mentioned you've had some unpleasant interactions with my little brother," Sin commented, changing the subject.

I shuddered, remembering Dexter's *promise* to rape me at this party. So far, John had done a good job of keeping me occupied, so I'd barely given him much thought. "Yeah, he really doesn't like the word *no*, does he?"

As soon as I said that, I regretted it. What if Sin was as bad as Dexter? Their family was far from saints, so why should this son be any different just because I'd never seen him around the house?

Sin just laughed, though, and there was no trace of malice in his smile. "He's a bully and a spoiled brat. So no, he doesn't hear *no* very often, and it's turned him into an ugly human. If he causes trouble, you can tell my father. He likes you, and if he thinks something is going on between *us*..."

I nodded my understanding. "He'll intervene. Good to know, thank you."

"Something worth thinking about," he murmured, taking another sip and squinting as he swallowed. It really was a bad cocktail. "You'd be doing me a favor."

If I was reading between the lines correctly, Sin was suggesting we fake date each other. It'd give me protection from Dexter—I'd bet anything Mr. Grimaldi would be furious if Dexter touched Sin's girlfriend—and it'd give Sin some space to…what? Hunt for a dead woman, I guessed.

But then there was this thing with John to consider. After how he'd been acting, I had every intention of using him to blow off some steam—since I hadn't located any of my missing toys—and then giving him a taste of his own rejection.

"I'm kind of seeing someone. Sort of. I don't know, he's very…hot and cold. Can I think about it?" Because I got a feeling that Sin was a good person to have owing favors to me. And if it also got Dexter off my back…?

"Of course," he agreed. "I promise, this was far from my intention. The idea just came to me, and you seem like the kind of girl who can keep a secret."

I smiled, giving a small laugh. "Oh, you're right about that. So, I'm assuming you also work for the family business?"

He nodded. "Small talk. Good idea. Let me order us another round of this crap…"

Before he could catch the bartender's attention, though, I spotted a familiar face scanning the ballroom looking for me. "Ah, there's my not-date-date," I said quietly. "I should…" I gestured to John, who'd just spotted us.

Sin gave him a once over, then smirked. "I see. Yes,

by all means. Here, take my number. Think things over. If *that* doesn't work out, maybe we can come to an arrangement." He handed me a business card, and I tucked it into my little purse as John reached us.

"Tris," he growled. "Where's Tink?"

I frowned up at my flustered date. "Uh, Katinka? She got pulled away by Mr. Grimaldi. I was talking with..." I glanced back to Sin, only to find him disappearing into the crowd. Apparently he had no interest in meeting John, which was actually fine by me. "Never mind. What took you so long anyway?"

His brow dipped. "There was a line, so I went to find another and got lost."

I wrinkled my nose. It was a big house, sure, but not *that* big. "Okay well I'm drunk and tired and my feet hurt so...I'm probably going to go home." The use of *I* was deliberate. Talking to Sin reminded me what an absolute prick John had been lately, and one excellent sex session didn't erase his crappy behavior. Yes, I liked to fuck, but I wasn't going to just forgive and forget because he made me come three times.

"I'll call a car to come get us," John said, pulling his phone out. "And no, it didn't escape my notice that you excluded me from that statement, but like it or not, I promised to see you safely home. That includes actually getting you home. So let's go."

His hand on my lower back as we exited the ballroom was a thousand times more possessive and sexually charged than Sin's hand had been earlier. I liked it a thousand times more, too, even if I didn't want to.

By the time we collected my coat and got outside, the car service was pulling up, ready to collect us. In strange symmetry to when we arrived, neither one of us spoke much on the way back to my apartment. Except this time instead of the friction of anger and annoyance between us, it was all sexual tension. Damn it. I loved that feeling, and it was going to be nearly impossible not to drag him inside with me.

I climbed out of the car when we arrived, not waiting for John to open my door for me. He got out as well, sending the driver away and leaving us standing on the sidewalk in the dark together.

"John..." I said in a warning tone. "You've seen me home safely. Consider your job done."

He shook his head, reaching for the lobby door. "Tris...I was tasked with keeping you *safe*. What do you think Nelson would do if I left you here and Dexter was waiting upstairs for you, hmm?"

I rolled my eyes, passing him to enter the lobby. "Okay, bit dramatic, John. You and I both know he's more than occupied with his pregnant wife at the party right now." We'd seen them briefly on our way out of the manor, but I hadn't hung around to chat.

John shrugged. "You never know. Better to be safe." He pressed the elevator call button, then quirked a brow at me. Like a fucking challenge.

Holding his gaze, I stepped into the elevator when the doors opened, and spread my arms wide. "Sure looks empty to me."

He got in with me, instantly sucking all the air from the little box. Fuck me, I already wanted to ride him like my own personal pony, and we were still in the common area where anyone—Hank or Nelson mainly—could see us and be scarred for life. I couldn't have that on my conscience. What if they had a heart attack?

"Who was the guy you were speaking to at the bar?" John asked as the elevator closed and started to rise. "You looked very friendly with him."

Amusement filled my chest. "You sound jealous."

His brows hitched. "Should I be?"

I smiled but didn't answer. His eye twitched with irritation when he realized what I was doing, and he stubbornly clenched his jaw. The doors opened a moment later, and I damn near gasped for fresh air as I exited.

John waited while I unlocked my door, but I stopped

him from coming inside with a hand on his chest. "That's far enough, Casanova."

Confusion crossed his handsome face, then resignation. "I see."

I smiled. "I'm so glad you do."

"Is Nelson home? I'd like to let him know you're back." He tilted his face to my neighbor's door down the hall, but I shook my head.

"He and Hank had a work thing tonight," I told him. "I'd be shocked if they were already back. Hank loves to party."

John hummed. "I could see that. You know when I was looking for the bathroom, I could have sworn I saw Nelson in the kitchen at Grimaldi's place."

Laughing, I took a step back into my apartment and gripped the door, ready to close it. "He'd be horrified to hear that. Good night, John."

"Wait." He reached out, snagging his hand around the back of my neck in a way that made my knees weak and my reservations turn to pixie dust. "I know you're punishing me for how I acted this week..."

My eyes widened with innocence. "Am I?"

"Funny," he replied. "It's well deserved. But can I take you out tomorrow night?"

Oh shit, I hadn't expected that. I figured he'd get

pissy when he realized I wasn't going to let him in, then act like a prime twat waffle again. Not *ask me out*.

"Umm..." I stalled, panicking. "I'm not sure."

His grip on my neck tightened, his fingers tilting my head back and his lips crashing into mine. I melted, my tongue finding his as he dominated the kiss and stole the air clean out of my lungs. Shit, if I'd had any panties on—which I didn't—they'd be drenched again.

"How about now?" he asked in a husky voice.

I swallowed hard, then licked my lips. What was the question? Oh. Date. "Okay," I agreed in a breathless whisper. "I guess even if I didn't agree, you'd just turn up like a stalker."

His laugh warmed me right through. "I'm so glad we understand each other, Tris."

He kissed me again, this time leaving me flushed with heat and wavering on dragging him inside with me. Fuck making a point, right? What even was my point?

"Good night, Miss Ives," he teased, backing away and pressing the elevator call button without taking his eyes off mine. The little mocking wave he gave me as he stepped backward into the elevator made me groan, and I extended my middle finger. Because he knew exactly what he'd just done to me. Dick.

thirty-seven

JOHN

Waiting a whole day to go back and see Tris was pure torture. Or, I was guessing it would have been, had I not broken into her apartment again before dawn to watch her sleep like the goddamn stalker she accused me of being. I was man enough to admit that it'd become a habit, and I was already fantasizing about what it'd be like to just wake up there with her. With her *knowing* I was there.

This time, I'd done a thorough search for any new toys and found none. Which was off putting because it meant that my need to steal shit wasn't satisfied, and I ended up taking one of her paintbrushes instead.

She'd been painting before bed, and I had to exert restraint in not stealing the still-wet picture of the night sky that she'd been working on. *That* she would notice.

Since we hadn't agreed on a time for our date, I turned up unannounced at five in the afternoon then just smiled at her grumbles about going for senior citizen's specials.

"You never did tell me how old you were," she pointed out as I drove us away from her building.

I glanced over at her in my passenger seat. She was as beautiful as ever, and a stupid naïve part of my brain daydreamt about what it'd be like to have a future together.

"Does it matter?" I asked instead. "You don't strike me as the kind of woman who puts much stock in numbers."

She rolled her eyes in that adorable way that she did *so* damn often around me. I liked getting under her skin. "I'm just curious, but no it doesn't really matter. Where are you taking me anyway?"

"To dinner, of course," I responded, being deliberately vague to annoy her. I glanced over and caught her glaring, which only made me smile. "I'm thirty-six. Almost thirty-seven."

She blew out a long breath and shook her head. "Shit, who knew I'd be into old dudes? How almost?"

I drummed my fingers against the steering wheel, hesitating with the truth. "Next week," I admitted.

Tris gave a small sound of surprise, but that was it.

That shouldn't shock me, though. She likely approached birthdays a lot like I did, since we had very similar childhoods with shitty absentee parents.

I pulled into the parking lot outside a little cottage a minute later, and Tris peered at the sign with curiosity. "Wagyu in Watercolors," she read aloud. "Oh, I've heard about this place. Good choice, Professor."

I smiled, getting out to open her door. My choice of dinner location was a new steak restaurant that also doubled as an art gallery. I figured it was the perfect place to make Tris feel comfortable and maybe let her guard down.

Inside, the hostess escorted us to our table but advised that we were welcome to wander the gallery while waiting for our meals to be cooked. Tris eagerly took the offer, barely even glancing at the menu before ordering, then impatiently tapping her fingers on the table while I took my time reading over the steak choices.

"Finally," she muttered when I placed my order.

"You're awfully eager to look through an art gallery when you work in one every day," I commented, letting my hand rest on her waist as we made our way into the next room.

She glanced up at me but didn't move out of my touch. Small wins. "I just like to see what kind of art these places consider *worthy* of showing. Professional curiosity."

"Uh huh," I murmured, giving her a sidelong glance. "Not professional jealousy?"

She quirked a brow. "I understand that our tastes run somewhat differently in regards to modern art, but the judges of the Cloudcroft Classics exhibition clearly disagreed with your assessment of my work. Perhaps my accolades escaped your attention?"

I chuckled, remembering our first encounter at Boles. "Point taken." We took our time looking through the paintings on display—all watercolors—then returned to our table when the waitress advised that our appetizers were ready.

"Those replicas on display at, uh, RBDs?" Her nickname for the Grimaldi manor had me amused as hell. She nodded. "They got me curious what you *are* working on, if not those."

She took a bite of her caprese salad and swallowed before answering. "I'm doing some restoration and cleaning work." She gave a shrug. "It's not very exciting, other than the painting itself."

I let curious surprise play over my face. "Oh? Is it one I'd know?"

Her smile turned secretive. "If you didn't, I'd be checking if your credentials are faked, John Smith."

Anticipation filled me up, and I reached for my water to hide my eagerness for answers. "Can you tell me? I'd of course take it to the grave." I mimed zipping and locking my lips, but she just chuckled and shook her head.

"I can't tell you. I signed an NDA, remember?"

Dammit. Of course Tris was the type of woman who took legal paperwork seriously. I bet she even read the fine print on terms and conditions while buying online.

"Ah yes, the NDA," I murmured, thinking of another angle. "You must have to remove the paintings from their frames to conduct cleaning and restoration work. Is there a secure place to keep the art you're working on? Or does he expect you to reframe and replace the painting every day that you work?"

She wrinkled her nose. "No, of course not. My workshop is basically the most secure location inside the house." Then she paused, thinking. "Actually, I don't know that for sure. If Mr. Grimaldi secured the gallery workshop as well as he did, I'd bet he has a vault somewhere that has ten times the security on it."

"Oh, almost guaranteed for a man like that," I agreed, playing the part of curious civilian. Normal people who don't steal shit for a living would be naturally curious about things like that. It'd be totally acceptable to theorize on a mafia boss's valuables.

"What kind of security are we even talking? Like swipe cards?"

Tris scoffed a laugh, her mouth full of food as she shook her head. "Oh, John…sweetie. No. We're talking fingerprint scanners, long ass passcodes, and one of those James Bond style things that literally scans your eyeball. Mr. Grimaldi doesn't fuck around with his black-market art, that's for sure. I can only imagine what he'd do to protect his late wife's jewelry."

Retina scan? Jesus, his security was better than most banks.

"That's intense," I commented, acting impressed. "But also kind of reassuring to know Dexter can't get to you inside your workshop." I paused, giving a small frown. "He can't, right? You mentioned he didn't have access?"

"That's right. Once I'm inside, I'm totally safe. It's just getting to and from the gallery that's the problem." As soon as she said that she winced. "Uh, so…have you heard any updates about Dr. Bailey at all?"

I allowed the change of subject, seeing that she was uncomfortable discussing Dexter—the fucking creep—and gave her a sly grin. "Why, are you trying to get rid of me already? Last I heard from Dean Lawrence, there was no improvement."

She sighed, placing her appetizer cutlery down. A

few more tables had filled up, so we were no longer alone in the restaurant. "I don't need to get rid of you, John. I already resigned as your TA and applied for a transfer, remember?"

As if I could forget. Maybe now was a good time to mention that her resignation never made it to the dean? Then again, I really wanted this date to last a little longer so maybe I'd keep that to myself for now.

Instead I just shifted our conversation to her dissertation, getting her talking about that while we waited for our main meals to arrive. Then, while we ate our wagyu steaks, I casually circled back to her work at RBDs. This time I asked about her shifts, as though I didn't already have her schedule memorized.

Talking with Tris was genuinely enjoyable, and it was easy to forget what my primary objective was. At some stage, though, I must have pried a little too hard or probed too deep, because there was a noticeable coldness between us as I drove her home after she declined dessert.

"Not to be *that* guy," I said carefully as I pulled into a space in front of her building, "but did I fuck up somewhere? It feels like you're suddenly pushing me away again."

Her brows lifted, and a flash of panic crossed her face as she shook her head. "Nope. No, I just...have a headache. I think I drank way too much last night and it's catching up to me now."

That excuse seemed...bullshit. Not that I had any intention of saying as much, but now anxiety was curling through me like barbed wire tentacles. I opened her door, like usual, and escorted her inside to the lobby.

"Um, I'm pretty wrecked," she told me awkwardly. "So..."

I could take a hint. She wasn't inviting me upstairs with her. That didn't mean I was willing to give up without a fight, so I slipped my hand around the back of her neck and tilted her head back.

"Call me tomorrow," I told her, my lips ghosting over hers without properly making contact. I wouldn't force myself on her when she was pushing me away, but I also wouldn't make things easy for her to do that. "When you're feeling better."

I didn't close the gap between us. She did. Her sharp inhale as she kissed me suggested she hadn't meant to, yet she also wasn't peeling herself away in a hurry. So I kissed her back, unhurried as I committed the shape of her lips to memory and relished every shiver and moan she gave back.

Somehow, without really meaning to, our kiss turned heated. A minute later I had her pressed against the elevator doors with my hand inside her shirt and hers making quick work of my belt buckle. Had we not been interrupted, I'd have happily fucked her right there in her apartment lobby.

Sadly, fate had other ideas, and Tris nearly fell backward when the elevator doors opened. I caught her around the waist, but when she locked eyes with Hank her whole face flushed red.

"I'll, um, I should..." She carefully extracted herself from my hold and stepped further into the elevator. "Thank you for dinner, though."

"Any time," I replied, swiping my thumb across my lower lip. "Call me tomorrow, Tris."

"Mm hmm," she nodded, still blushing as she stabbed at the door-close button.

Hank peered at me with a bemused expression, then at the now closed elevator doors. Then back at me. "So...I see you two mended some broken bridges?"

I smirked, thinking of the garage last night. "You could say that."

Hank walked with me out into the street but paused as I unlocked my car. "I'm glad," he commented, tucking his hands into his pockets. "She seems so much more *alive* these days. But let me be perfectly clear with you, John Smith. You hurt her again and you'll wish you never stepped foot into Whispering Willows. Am I understood?"

I jerked a nod, not doubting him for a second. "Understood."

"Excellent," Hank replied with a nod. "Then in that case, I wish you two happiness. Just make sure it's *responsible* happiness, though. I'm too young to become a grandfather." He said it with a laugh, then walked away, but it struck a lightning bolt of panic through me.

Responsible? There hadn't been a single responsible part of *either* time I'd had sex with Tris.

Fuck. How had this not even crossed my mind?

Palms sweating, I slid into my car and immediately pulled out my phone to call her. All I could do at this stage was *pray* she'd been more of an adult than I clearly had. I really was a selfish prick.

thirty-eight

TRIS

Raking my hand through my hair, I stared down at my phone sitting on the table in front of me. John was trying to call me, and I couldn't bring myself to answer. My emotions were all twisted up in knots, and I was starting to feel paranoid.

"Just answer the man's call," Nelson told me with a sigh. "He clearly wants to speak to you."

I tossed my hands in the air. "Of course he does. He's probing me for information on RBD's security system! Jesus, Nelson, he's probably been playing me all along, and I was too fucking dick drunk to even notice."

Nelson placed my chamomile tea down in front of me, then sat down across the table. "Okay let's say for argument's sake, he wanted to steal from RBD. For one thing, he'd have to be either totally idiotic or the best damn thief alive. But assuming he *is* casing the joint—"

"Stop making fun of me," I groaned, shaking my head. "I know how I sound right now."

Nelson chuckled. "Okay, okay, just...let's talk it through. Assuming he is *casing the joint,* then did you give away any sensitive information that could land the blame on you? You haven't given him your access codes or anything, right?"

I shook my head, frowning. "Of course not. I'm not that stupid. But he was asking whether..." I trailed off, hearing myself before the words came out my mouth and instantly feeling stupid. "He asked if I had a swipe card, and I said that there were fingerprint scanners and all that stuff..."

Nelson arched an eyebrow. "So...you told him information that any two-bit thief would have found out for themselves should they attempt to break in?"

I licked my lips. "Well...when you put it like that, I feel even more silly."

He smiled sympathetically. "You're a little jumpy, but that's okay. What else happened to make you all suspicious of John suddenly?"

I frowned, trying to remember what it was that set my alarm bells ringing. We'd been talking about the gallery and Mr. Grimaldi's collection… "Oh, he made some comment about how there must be so much pressure when I'm working on a painting worth more than fifty million dollars."

Nelson blinked at me. "So?"

My brow tugged lower. "So? So how'd he know what I was working on right now? That's an awfully specific figure for a guess, isn't it?"

"Is it?" Nelson shot back. "Kind of seems like a vague guess that just happens to be accurate. But I certainly wouldn't have seen anything suspicious in that alone. Something else must have happened, Ives. Spill the rest."

Exhaling heavily, I locked eyes with my tea. "At the party last night, he disappeared for a really long time."

Nelson chuckled. "The man probably needed to rub one out. Give him a break. What else?"

I gritted my teeth, feeling my cheeks flame. "I'm pretty sure he's been stealing my vibrators."

A moment of silence followed that admission, then Nelson laughed so hard I worried he was going to fall out of his chair.

"It's not funny," I muttered, my face still on fire. "I've replaced them like four times, and they keep mysteriously disappearing."

Nelson wiped tears from his eyes as he tried to

control his laughter. "So your best reasoning is that John...your Art History professor boyfriend—"

"Not my boyfriend."

"Okay, *sorry*. Your Art History professor *fuck buddy*, is breaking into your very secure top floor loft apartment and stealing your vibrator? Just...for fun? Like, do you mean while you're at work or...?"

I ran a hand over my eyes, instantly hearing how ridiculous this sounded. "Sometimes? Or...fuck, I don't know. They seem to disappear overnight. Like, while I'm asleep."

Nelson tightened his lips, holding back the laughter that still shook his shoulders. Fucker. Obviously now that I was saying it out loud, it sounded insane. I groaned and dropped my forehead to the table with frustration and embarrassment.

"Okay well if it's not John, then where the fuck are all my vibrators disappearing to?"

Nelson coughed another laugh, getting up from his seat. "That I don't know. But I also don't know where all my left socks end up, either. Some things in life just can't be explained."

I sat back up, perplexed. "How do you know they're your left socks? Socks don't have a left and right."

Nelson gave me a superior look as he returned

holding a manila folder. "Because, smartass, when I'm getting dressed I have no problem finding a sock for my right foot but then when I go to put on the left one… nowhere to be found."

I snorted a laugh. "That's…okay, beside the point, weirdo. Back to John."

"Back to John, indeed," he teased, smirking. "Here. I wasn't going to admit that I looked into your professor, but I did. This is what my guy discovered."

Curious, I took the envelope and opened it. It didn't take long to get the general vibe of what Nelson's research had uncovered, though. "Seriously?"

He shrugged. "Yep. John Smith is exactly who he says he is. Considering his paper trail and online presence, he's more real than either of us, Ives. The man pays his taxes on time, volunteers for a women's refuge shelter, and donates heavily to charities…" Nelson sighed, giving me a sympathetic look. "Crazier things have happened, but from what I've found? I don't think he's breaking in and stealing your dildos."

I wrinkled my nose. "Vibrators, not dildos. And…fair call. Now I feel like a massive dumbass for even thinking that."

"Go home, get some sleep," Nelson ordered, pointing to the door. "Call your professor back in the morning. It wouldn't hurt his ego to sit on ice overnight. But it's okay to have good things happen to you, Ivy. Just because most men have been trash, doesn't mean this one is. He seems to genuinely care, so maybe let yourself be open to that? Who knows, maybe John Smith will be your Hank."

Uncomfortable with the raw emotions that advice stirred up, I just hugged him good night and went home. He was right, though. John could sweat it for the rest of the night, and I'd call back tomorrow.

Come morning, my phone was dead because I'd forgotten to plug it in overnight. Then I got sucked into my painting studio, working on a new muse project and just forgot all about John's missed calls. I didn't forget *him*—far from it when I spent the entire day recreating the curves of his muscular arms on my canvas—but my phone? Yeah, I forgot.

I was so engrossed in my art that I lost track of time and skipped lunch entirely. Then I ate leftovers for dinner and crashed right out. Monday morning saw me waking to someone buzzing my doorbell repeatedly.

Sleepy and annoyed, I stumbled across my apartment to snap at whoever was interrupting my beauty rest.

"What do you want, and why should I care?" I snarled into the intercom without bothering to wait for the video image to appear.

"I want to know why you're ghosting me, Tristian," John barked back. "Let me up."

My eyes widened, the memory of his Saturday night calls resurfacing in my head. Guilt filled my stomach. "Um, yeah, just a sec," I mumbled, then pressed the button to allow him access to the lobby and elevators. Then I ran through to my bathroom to check my appearance.

Fuck. I was in a paint-stained t-shirt and my hair looked like birds had nested sometime overnight. So sexy. Groaning curses, I raked my fingers through my tangles and tied it all up in a loose bun. Then I yanked off my shirt and tossed on a silk robe instead.

"Crap," I whispered aloud to my reflection, "now you look like you're waiting on a booty call."

A heavy knock on the door said I had no time for another outfit change. With a sigh, I went to let John in, making sure the belt of my robe was tied well. Not because *he* might get ideas, but because I would. Damn overactive sex drive.

"Oh, so you *are* alive," he commented with sarcasm when I stepped back to allow him inside.

I tried not to smirk. "Geez, John. I never picked you for the codependent relationship kind of guy."

He was unamused, slamming my door shut and grabbing me around the waist. My feet left the floor and my back met the wall as his mouth met mine. Unable to help myself, I moaned and parted my lips, letting him kiss me breathless.

"I was *worried*, Tris," he admitted, his voice a low, husky growl. "I never worry…about anyone or anything. And yet here I've been losing my damn mind wondering why you weren't calling me back."

He still held me up, his hips pinning me against the wall and his arm banded around my waist like a safety belt. I licked my lips, trying to remember why I'd been so freaked out on Saturday night.

"I got distracted," I whispered. "And my phone was dead."

His brow dipped in a frustrated frown, so I leaned in and kissed him again. Fuck it, Nelson was right. I *deserved* something good, and John was it.

Our kiss turned heated, his dick hardening between us and a pained groan rolling from his chest. My cotton panties were already wet, and my robe spilled open with the tie being no match for the way he held me, but when I reached for his belt he backed away.

"Shit, Tris…I need to know before we do this again. I

can't believe we didn't discuss it the first time." He set me down on my feet and stalked away a few paces, running a hand over his face.

I wrinkled my nose, confused as hell. "Know what?"

He whirled around to face me. "You didn't listen to my message?"

Shrugging, I moved past him and headed for where I'd left my phone plugged into its charger beside my bed. It took a hot second for the device to turn on, then I listened to the slightly panicked voicemail from John... and busted out laughing.

"You know, for a *nearly* thirty-seven-year-old man, I'd have thought you might be a little more responsible with unprotected sex, Professor." I propped my hands on my hips, still grinning as I tried to chastise him. "Maybe if you hadn't run off like your balls were on fire last week, I could have reassured you that I'm on the injection."

The sigh of relief that ran through him was visible, even at a distance. It compelled me to drop my phone, then drop my robe and panties. Smirking, I closed the distance between us once more, wrapping my arms around his neck.

"John," I murmured, hoisting myself up and hugging his waist with my legs. "You're in the clear, so long as you don't have any nasty germs to pass on." He grimaced and shook his head, making me smile wider. "Good, then take your damn pants off and fuck me till I can't walk."

His eyes widened briefly, and then his lush lips tugged in a smile. "Yes, ma'am."

thirty-nine

JOHN

Tris was regretting her request a few hours later when she needed to go to work. Since it was largely my fault, I insisted on driving her myself. For one thing, it meant I had more time with her —despite having skipped my own lecture to stay in bed with her this morning—but for another, it gave me more access to the Grimaldi manor.

I'd called in plenty of favors over the weekend to confirm that Luther was still the current owner of *Poppy Flowers,* so I was determined it had to be what Tris was working on. Which meant it was locked up securely within her workshop, and *that* was where I needed to get access.

The uncomfortable way she shifted in her seat on the

drive over to Grimaldi's had me all kinds of smug. I'd genuinely panicked when she went cold on me the other night, and of course I'd broken in to check that she was okay. I justified it to myself that I was still worried Dexter would get his creepy little paws on her—the man really did have strangely small hands—but really, I was just addicted to breaking into her home and taking shit. I had a whole fucking collection of her things at my place now.

"You'll need to drop me off at the gate," she told me as we approached the manor. "Security will have a shit fit about an unregistered vehicle..."

I glanced over at her, then shrugged. "Can't hurt to try. You don't look like you'd enjoy that much walking right now."

Tris winced. "Good point." Her cheeks heated, and I could guess what she was thinking about. *Me too, beautiful.*

As I suspected, the guards at the gate barely put up an argument once they recognized Tris in my passenger seat. She made up a story about her car breaking down, and I just went along with it. For whatever reason, she didn't want Luther knowing we were involved *romantically,* but that was actually a relief. Maybe this way she'd escape the blame when they realized *I'd* stolen from them.

They waved us through, and Tris directed me to park around the side of the house where there was apparently a staff entrance much closer to the gallery. She tried to jump out quickly, but I played the chivalrous gentleman card by getting out and walking her right to the door.

"You can go now," she told me with a reluctant smile, typing her access code absentmindedly. She wasn't even looking at the keypad; it was just muscle memory. "I get off work at four."

I glanced around, ensuring we were alone, then kissed her hard. "I'll be here," I promised. "Get into your workshop fast, Venus."

She nodded, her expression sober as she understood my warning. Rising up on her toes, she kissed me again then disappeared inside the house. I watched her go, counting how long it took for the door to swing shut, then headed back to my car.

Logically, I *knew* I needed to make my move soon. It was already becoming too easy to make excuses for why I was still hanging around Whispering Willows. Pre-Tristian, I'd have already taken the fucking painting by now and been long gone. But I kept coming up with *reasons* to delay, not the least of which being concern for her being blamed.

Since when had the notorious *Hermes* ever given a fuck about collateral damage? I didn't even give a second thought to who I was stealing from, let alone who might get caught up in the fallout. Yet here I was risking *everything* while I thought about how I could keep Tristian safe from the Grimaldi wrath.

I spent my afternoon making some calls, and by the time I returned to collect Tris at the end of her shift, all my ducks were in a row. Favors had been traded, and protection for my little artist would be arriving within twenty-four hours. Once I could confirm they were in place, ready to take a bullet for her, I had nothing to keep me from ending the Game.

Deliberately, I arrived to collect my girl far earlier than necessary. The guards at the gate had changed, and this time they made more of a fuss about my unauthorized vehicle entering the compound. Eventually, they called their superiors up at the manor itself and after some discussion, I was allowed in.

I parked around the side of the manor where I'd dropped Tris off, but it was Luther Grimaldi himself who strolled out to greet me.

"Mr. Grimaldi, sir," I greeted him with an expression of surprise. "I am so sorry about that confusion with your gatehouse. Tris needed me to collect her..."

Luther waved a hand, dismissing my apology. "I pay them to be cautious. It's not a bother. Is there something wrong with Tristian's vehicle, though? Or…is there another reason you're escorting her?" His eyes narrowed in suspicion, and I remembered how cagey Tris had been about the nature of our relationship.

I gave an easy smile, more than adept at lying my ass off. "Yes, she has some mechanical failure so I offered to drive her while it gets fixed. Since she works as my teaching assistant, it's the least I could do."

Relief and understanding dawned on the old man's face, and I made a mental note to break something in Tristian's car when we got back to her place. Luther was the kind of man who'd check.

"Ah, well that makes sense," he murmured, nodding. "That's kind of you. John, wasn't it? Art History professor?"

I inclined my head. "That's right. Visiting." Which he already knew, I could tell. Luther had researched me. I'd put money on it.

"I'm sure you saw plenty of recognizable paintings in my ballroom the other night," he commented, watching me carefully. "I trust you wouldn't feel the need to report the whereabouts of any of them?"

Ah, I see. He was worried that as an art academic, I might feel compelled to make a report to Art Crimes and get his house raided.

"What paintings?" I asked with a conspiratorial smile. "I'd had a lot to drink, and I'm entirely sure I only saw lovely prints and no originals. Certainly none that have been missing for decades."

Not untrue, since all the paintings on display had been impeccable replicas.

Luther squinted at me for a moment then chuckled and wagged his finger. "I like you, Professor John Smith. You're a funny man."

I gave a tight smile, glancing past him as the staff door opened and a goddess stepped out. "Thank you, sir. Looks like my lovely assistant is here. I'd better get her home so she can work on her dissertation."

Luther glanced over his shoulder and gave Tris a genuine smile. He definitely had a soft spot for her, but I didn't get the impression it was anything inappropriate…unlike his youngest son.

"Tristian, my dear, you look lovely as ever. How did you find the party?" His question was just a touch too eager, and I gave Tris a curious look.

She darted a glance my way, wetting her lips then offering Luther a tight smile. "It was lovely," she answered. "Very, um, memorable." Another glance my way, and this time her cheeks pinked. Oh yeah, it was certainly *memorable*…

"Good!" Luther enthused. "Excellent. You and Sin seemed to be hitting it off, hmm?"

A flash of panic flashed over Tris's face, and this time she carefully *didn't* look my way as she nodded her agreement. "Yes, he seems nice. Uh, I should get home. I'm abusing John's good nature by making him my chauffeur today."

"I told Luther about your car trouble," I reassured her, opening the passenger door. "I'd think I might be driving Tris to work for a few more days, yet. If that's okay, sir?" I looked to Luther who flapped a hand at us.

"Yes, yes, of course. I'll tell the gate to add your car to our authorized access list. It was nice to see you again, John. Maybe we can chat more another day."

I smiled warmly. "I'd very much enjoy that, Luther."

All the pieces were falling together flawlessly. My victory was so close I could taste it. I only hoped my grandfather would be proud of how I achieved it.

Driving away from the Grimaldi house, I glanced over at Tris. "I'm guessing *Sin* was the man you were flirting with at the bar during the party?"

Her lips parted with outrage and she shifted in her seat to face me more directly. "I was not *flirting* with anyone, caveman. Sin is Mr. Grimaldi's oldest son, and he was trying to set us up. I thought it was probably smart to play along for the time being." She huffed and folded her arms, sinking back into her seat. "In case you didn't notice, he's not a man to piss off casually."

Oh, I was well aware. Despite how jealous it made me, she'd absolutely done the right thing.

"I'm starting to work it out," I murmured, tapping my fingertips on the steering wheel.

For the rest of the drive back to Tristian's place, I was lost in my own head. I *had* to let go of my claim on her, or I was going to fuck myself up when I left. The idea of her with another man made me see red, though. What kind of fucking name was *Sin* anyway? Who'd he think he was? Certainly not the kind of man who could take care of Tris, if he was letting his pushy father try to set him up with women that he employed.

I bet he has a tiny dick.

"What?" Tris asked, and I froze. Had I said that out loud?

"Uh, I thought I saw a tiny duck," I replied, pointing out the window. "Over there. But it was just trash. Maybe. I dunno."

Tris squinted at me, then shrugged. "Okay, weirdo." She unclicked her seat belt when I pulled in across the road from her apartment. "Are you coming up?"

I shot her a sly smile, climbing out of the car and

locking up. "I'll come wherever the fuck you want, Venus. Just say the word, I'm all yours."

The laugh she gave in response cut straight to my heart, and I stubbornly pushed aside the dread pooling in my gut. I wasn't going anywhere *tonight,* so why deny us both the fun?

forty

TRIS

My car was officially broken. Obviously I'd gone along with John's story to explain why he was driving me to work on Monday, but when I went to drive myself the next day I was confronted with a broken car. What was wrong with it, exactly? I had no clue. But since I was already running late—thanks to John joining me in the shower—I called him to come back and get me.

He'd only left a minute before I'd tried to leave for work, so he happily turned around to collect me. He didn't complain once about driving me *again,* and I was appreciative enough that we ended up late. I made him pull over before we got to RBD's, so I could get him properly out of my system before starting work for the day. It backfired, of course, because then I spent the day thinking about how freaking good he was at eating pussy.

The mechanic called while I was at work and advised that they'd need to keep my car for *at least* a week, which I didn't even mind. So long as John was happy to be my driver, I was all too content with the perks.

Half an hour before my day ended, the front door to the gallery clicked open and Mr. Grimaldi came inside with my sexy professor right behind him. My jaw dropped as I stared through the one-way glass of my workshop window. Mr. Grimaldi was talking animatedly, gesturing to one of his Degas ballerina paintings while John looked impressed and awe-struck.

I didn't rush out, quietly enjoying watching from my hidden workshop. For nearly twenty minutes, Mr. Grimaldi showed John through all his private artwork and told wild stories about how he came into possession of a few. Eventually, he approached my workshop and keyed in his own code to open the door.

A moment later—once all the biometric locks had been cleared—the door opened and I glanced over with a curious smile. "Professor Smith, this is unexpected."

"It's been so long since I've had anyone new who could appreciate my collection, Tristian," Mr. Grimaldi explained, "I couldn't resist showing John what I've been hiding away in here. Show him what you've been working on."

I inhaled deeply, watching John from under my lashes as I stepped back from my workstation. "Actually, I was almost finished on this," I told Mr. Grimaldi. "I'd just been giving it a final check over then planned to get it back in its frame tomorrow."

My boss clapped his hands. "Excellent! I've been so looking forward to getting this on my gallery wall, but the previous owner was a *heavy* smoker and the discoloration was disgusting. Ah, Tristian, you're a goddess. This looks flawless."

My attention was all on John, though. His expression was perfectly neutral as he circled my work bench and peered at the painting I'd spent months cleaning.

"Is that—?"

"The missing Van Gogh *Poppy Flowers*?" Mr. Grimaldi finished for him, practically bouncing with his glee. "Indeed it is. You wouldn't believe what this cost me at auction last year. The bastard who was selling it decided to create a bidding war, but I won. I always do. Isn't she lovely?"

John's eyes flicked up from the painting to lock with mine. "Utterly breathtaking."

Mr. Grimaldi checked his watch then gave a grunt. "I'm late for a meeting. Tristian, close this up and get on home. I'm sure John has things to do tonight also. Actually, come to think of it, why don't I ask Sin to pick you up tomorrow and save your professor from driving all over town?"

"It's no trouble, really," John quickly assured my boss while I returned *Poppy Flowers* to its secure drawer in my work bench and locked it using my code. "It gives us plenty of time to go over Tristian's research notes."

Mr. Grimaldi shook his head, his mind already made up. "You're too polite, John, but I know you must be busy with university work. I'm sure Sin would be more than happy to help out, since he's on a break between jobs right now. I'll call him tonight, Tristian, and give him your address for tomorrow."

I looked to John, trying to think of another reason why I needed my professor to drive me to work—aside from the orgasms—and coming up blank. John was frowning at something on my workbench, though, and just murmured a vague agreement as Mr. Grimaldi exited my workshop.

"Two seconds," I said, packing up the rest of my supplies and slipping my shoes back on. By the time John and I exited the gallery, flicking off lights and locking up behind ourselves, Mr. Grimaldi was nowhere to be seen.

Still, I didn't say anything until we were inside the car and driving away from the manor.

"I kind of like having you drive me to work, John," I admitted, giving him a long look.

He glanced over at me, then gave a small sigh. "The feeling is mutual...but your boss seemed pretty determined to make this thing with his son play out. If I'd pushed the issue it might have proven we were more than *professional.* Besides, he wasn't wrong about my workload." John grimaced and a wave of guilt ran through me. Of course he was swamped, his TA had recently quit.

We were both quiet for the drive home, but it wasn't an awkward silence. Just a thoughtful one. So I was surprised that he didn't turn the car off as I unbelted myself.

"Are you coming up?" I asked with a frown of confusion.

John shook his head. "I need to sort out some things for class tomorrow," he said with a strangely distant expression. "But if I get it done quick, would you mind a late-night visitor?"

Surprise had me reeling, and I just muttered something about staying up late to paint anyway.

It wasn't until I pressed the elevator button in my lobby that I realized he hadn't kissed me good night.

Hadn't even *tried* to. Like he was trying to put distance between us, and kissing would ruin it.

Lost in my own thoughts—and fears of rejection—I didn't realize someone else was waiting for the elevator with me until the doors opened and he stepped in behind me.

"Shit, sorry," I said after giving a stupidly dramatic gasp. "I was lost in my own head. What floor?"

He was carrying a moving box with a leafy plant sticking out the top, his hands clearly full. His answering smile was stunning, as he named his floor, one below mine. Then I remembered Nelson mentioning there had been a vacant apartment below me last week.

"You must be the new tenant," I said, like an idiot. Clearly he was moving in. "I'm Tristian."

"Nice to meet you, Tristian," the guy replied, glancing at the elevator panel. "You must be my upstairs neighbor? I'm Bram. I'd shake your hand, but…" He gave a small shrug and I smiled.

"Could be tricky," I agreed. The elevator stopped on his floor, and I offered a polite goodbye as he stepped out.

He paused, arching a flirtatious grin back at me. "I think I might like this move."

The elevator doors slid shut before I could formulate

a response, but my face flamed as I ran that entire—albeit brief—interaction through my head. Had I accidentally flirted with my new neighbor? I didn't think so…Maybe I'd misread that smile. Yeah, that was probably it. Unless I was suddenly oozing pheromones thanks to all the excellent sex with John.

Pushing it from my mind, I sorted myself out some dinner, poured a glass of wine, and headed into my studio. I'd been itching to keep working on my painting of…a model who suspiciously resembled a man who'd been frequenting my bed lately.

A WARM, STRONG ARM BANDED AROUND MY BODY, pulling me into a familiar embrace. I snuggled deeper, recognizing John's touch, and sighed with sleepy bliss as his hand cupped my breast. I'd crashed out some time after midnight, paint still dried on my wrists, but this was a more than welcome way to wake up.

"Hi," I mumbled, still mostly asleep.

John's fingers tugged my nipple, making my hips rock against his hardness. "Shhh, Venus," he breathed, his voice barely louder than the rustle of sheets as his hand danced down my body. Dipping between my legs, he found my clit and rubbed it with teasing circles as my breathing quickened.

I moaned, warmth spreading through my lower body as John reached lower, grasping his erection and lining himself up with my cunt. A shuddering gasp filled my lungs as he pushed inside, stretching me slowly as he progressed.

"That's it, Tris," he whispered, his fingers flexing on my hip as he held me tight. "Good girl, stay relaxed. You're taking me so fucking good."

A whimper escaped my chest as he thrust deeper inside without any kind of warm up, but the bite of pain was a good kind of sting. The kind I'd smile about in the morning.

"So fucking good," he moaned, bottoming out with a slap of his hips against my ass. His breathing was rough, and he held me tight against his chest, and I just gasped a sleepy plea for more. John whispered a curse, then started moving his hips. His huge cock rocked in and out of me, my wetness increasing with each stroke as he increased pace.

He gripped my breast, his fingers pinching and twisting my nipple as he fucked me harder, and I cried out. It hurt, but I also didn't want him to stop, and thank fuck he understood that because my noises only made him moan and do it again.

"Fuck," I groaned as he bit the side of my neck a touch rougher than he ever had before, "John, holy shit…"

His response was to roll me onto my stomach, momentarily flattening me before hauling my ass up into the air and plunging his cock back between my soaking folds. I cried out again, his length striking me so damn deep, and he grunted his agreement.

The combined sounds of our heavy breathing filled the space, mixed with the wet slap of skin on skin, and pleasure curled through my insides with dizzying intensity.

"John, *fuuuck,*" I moaned into the sheets as he gripped my ass cheeks like they were made of play-doh. "Oh my God, I'm going to come."

"Good," he grunted, fucking me so hard I could see stars. "I can't fucking control myself with you, Tris. You just feel too damn perfect."

A split second later and I really did see stars when his hand snaked underneath me to tweak my clit in *just* the right way to send me spiraling. I gasped and moaned, my whole body tensing up and my fingers twisting the sheet. His motions stuttered and he thrust so deep I nearly collapsed into my pillows as he climaxed, filling my cunt up with his cum.

When he finished, he picked me up and rearranged

us into a spooning position with his cock still buried inside me. It was weirdly intimate, but I liked it.

"John?" I mumbled, then yawned.

"Shhh," he breathed, his lips brushing kisses over my cheek. "Go back to sleep, Venus. I'm sorry I woke you up."

My lids were already falling shut once more. "I'm not," I replied, my lips barely forming the words properly as the endorphin crash mixed with my existing sleepiness hit me hard. "I like you being here..."

I couldn't make out his response, he whispered it so softly, and sleep was already claiming me once more. I just knew that it was said with utter reverence as he brushed featherlight kisses over my sweaty skin, and that was how I wanted to fall asleep every night.

forty-one

JOHN

Visiting Tristian one last time had nearly broken my resolve. I shouldn't have gone there…but I couldn't help myself. Tonight was the night, I had to take *Poppy Flowers* before she reframed it tomorrow. I'd dropped her off after work, leaving her with a cold shoulder to go and pack up my cottage. I had plenty of experience with walking away from cover identities, so it only took me a few hours to tie up all the loose ends.

With my belongings all packed into my car—including the whole box of things I'd stolen from Tris—I'd tried to drive past her building. Tried, and failed. Instead, I'd found myself sitting there in my car for *hours* as I stared up to her window. When the lights switched off some time after midnight, I attempted to make myself leave.

And yet. An hour later, I was breaking back into her apartment. One last time. I needed to say goodbye, even if she never knew I'd been there. That was my plan, and the moment I laid eyes on her splayed out across her royal purple sheets I'd lost control.

As she drifted back to sleep, sweaty, beautiful, and full of my cum, the guilt of our entire relationship nearly choked me.

"I'm so sorry," I whispered against her skin as I kissed her shoulder. "If I don't go now, I never will." Because as hard as it was to admit, my feelings for Tris had become real. I'd bet my skin that hers were, too, which made me an even worse kind of asshole.

I knew all along that I was using her. She had no idea, and the dread of that realization was what had held me back.

It *had* to happen tonight. Maybe when it was all over and the Game had been won, I might be able to reconnect with Tris. One day. But if I let her get between me and my grandfather's legacy, I'd always resent her for it. She deserved better than that. She deserved better than *me*.

I lay there with her as long as I possibly could, then

slipped away into the night to fulfill my destiny in becoming the most accomplished thief alive.

This time, unlike *every* other time I'd broken into Tristian's home, I didn't take anything with me. This time, I left something behind.

A small piece of my heart.

Hardening myself against the near crushing regret that swamped me, I drove away and didn't look back.

There was no joy in the heist tonight. My plan to enter the Grimaldi property was flawless, and my last-minute changes soothed a small measure of guilt while I entered the dark, silent gallery.

Once I made it inside Tris's studio, I needed to sit down in her seat for a minute. Everything smelled like her. My watch vibrated once, reminding me that I needed to haul ass, so I swallowed back the guilt and broke into her secure drawer.

Poppy Flowers was perfect, exactly where I'd seen her place it. My hands were already gloved, so I made quick work of securing it within the custom built, padded briefcase I'd brought along for the job.

I sighed heavily as I stared down at the empty drawer, but it was done now. I simply needed to *leave*.

It took a few scarce minutes to stage the scene as I wanted it to be found in the morning, then I was making my escape straight out the front door of the Grimaldi manor. I kept my pace brisk and professional, maintaining the illusion that I had every right to be there, and only hesitated once.

When I rounded the side of the house, heading for the broken fence where I'd made myself an escape route, I paused to hear a familiar woman's voice from one of the open windows.

"...come on, baby," she cajoled, her voice dripping sex, "just a little peek? I heard your father has a painting that has been missing for over fifteen years..."

I glanced through the window, catching an eyeful of Tink totally naked on her knees in front of Dexter. Her hand worked furiously as she batted her lashes up at him, and I felt fucking sorry for her. We'd both taken similar tactics to access *Poppy Flowers,* but mine had worked out a whole hell of a lot more enjoyable...and profitable.

Tink's gaze snapped to the window, and frustration morphed her pretty face as I shot her a sarcastic salute, holding up my case.

"Fuck!" she exclaimed, understanding instantly that she'd just lost the Game.

I didn't hang around to see how she'd extract herself. I had a getaway car to reach and a rendezvous point halfway across the damn country waiting. So I slipped into the shadows, making myself disappear entirely as I blended with the night and escaped the Grimaldi property.

Soon, their silent alarm would be tripped by one of my time-delayed traps. My break in and theft of *Poppy Flowers* would be discovered, but by then I would be long gone.

I just had to hope that the measures I'd taken would be enough to show Tris wasn't involved in any way. I had to hope that the security I'd placed in her life could keep her safe from Luther's wrath when he discovered his prized piece was gone.

As for me? The Game wasn't over until I reached the checkpoint and had the painting verified by the committee. Now, more than ever, I needed to keep my wits about me. Igor had been too quiet lately, and I suspected Tink was right. He was up to something, and if I knew my father at all, I'd bet he was planning to cheat.

This next step would be where he'd make his move. The Igor I knew would have been smart enough to know he was out-matched with myself and Tink vying for the painting…but he also knew that she and I followed the rules of the Game.

He would not, and thus it was now that I suspected he'd come for me. Now that I'd plucked *Poppy Flowers* from the ultra-secure vault drawer within Luther's manor. Now that its only protection was a padded briefcase and my own determination.

The only question was, how would he cheat? And who would get hurt along the way?

Sliding into my car, I felt calm in the knowledge that whatever danger was coming my way, it wouldn't impact Tris. The more space I put between us, the better.

If only that understanding could soothe the ache in my chest as I drove out of Whispering Willows one last time.

forty-two

TRIS

John was long gone when I woke up that next morning. For a few confused moments, I thought I'd dreamed about his sexy visit, but the slick evidence between my legs and the ache in my muscles confirmed it'd been real.

The range of emotions I went through as I woke up properly was like the steepest of rollercoasters. Disappointment that he wasn't there to wake up with me, skin tingling warm fuzzies about the late night sex session, then drunken butterflies as I remembered the way he'd brushed kisses over my skin while I drifted back to sleep. He'd been whispering to me in another language, but it'd been too soft to make out.

A sharp jolt of panic shot through me a second later, and I scrambled out of my bed. My legs tangled in my purple sheet, and I tripped but quickly recovered to hurry over to my front door. It was locked. From the *inside*.

"How the fuck did he get in?" I whispered aloud, staring at the internal lock that I'd started using after he pointed out my failures to lock my front door recently. "How the fuck did he get *out*?"

It wasn't possible. That bolt was manual and could only be activated from the inside. Maybe I had imagined the whole thing in some kind of intense sex dream?

That made more sense.

"You're obsessed," I muttered to myself, raking my fingers through my tangled hair and heading for my bathroom. Maybe a cold shower would wake my brain up a bit. I turned on the water, then dragged a detangler through my hair so I could wash it properly. As I turned to get into the shower, though, I spotted some bruises on my reflection. Fingerprint bruises on my hips and ass.

"Jesus, John..." I breathed, leaning closer to the mirror to take a better look. Then I smirked, remembering how good it'd been when he was gripping me that hard and—

Wait. So *how the fuck did he get in?*

There had to be a logical explanation. Right?

Convincing myself that I was just overlooking

something obvious, I got into the shower and went through the process of washing my hair and body. By the time I got out, I'd decided that I must have unlocked the door for him while half asleep and just forgotten I'd done it.

I blow-dried my hair, put on some makeup, then wandered out to my bedroom in a towel while thinking about what to wear today. I had work, so couldn't go too sexy and risk running into Dexter—shudder—but I was sure to see John at some stage. Crap, that reminded me, I had Sin picking me up for work instead.

A knock on my door interrupted my thought process, and I went to answer it, figuring it was probably Nelson or Hank if they were knocking rather than buzzing the intercom.

"Good morning," I said, opening my front door casually. Then I gasped when I saw my assumption had been rather incorrect. "Oh, hey, sorry." I wrapped my arm around myself, making sure my towel was still covering all the important parts.

"Expecting someone else?" my cute new neighbor asked with a half smile. "I get that a lot."

My brows hitched, sensing a big fat lie. But since he was basically a stranger, I bit my tongue. "Um, did you need something?"

"Yeah, uh, my key keeps sticking." He held up the key

in question. "I called the building manager and he said to ask you? For…some reason?"

Understanding dawned and I nodded. The *building manager* was Hank, and if he was sending Bram my way there was a good chance he was caught up with work. "Give me two minutes," I told the guy, taking the key from his hand. "I just need some clothes and I can fix this."

His answering smile was bright, and I just offered an awkward nod as I closed the door once more. I put Bram's key down on the counter as I headed for my closet, this time just grabbing the first outfit I could find to not be naked with the handsome stranger.

Once dressed, I took his key into my studio and grabbed a couple of fine metal files. Placing his key under a magnifying glass, I found the imperfection and made quick work of smoothing it out. When Hank had the locks on a few apartments changed recently, they'd done a shitty job on cutting the keys. Rather than sending them back and dealing with delays and complaints, I just fixed them.

Done, I took it back and opened my door to hand it back to Bram. "Should work now," I told him. "But let me know if not, and I can take another look."

His fingers brushed mine as he took the key, and his

gaze was just a touch more intense than polite. "Thank you, Tristian. I appreciate the help."

I waved a quick goodbye and closed my door once more. My phone was ringing somewhere, and the call ended before I found it underneath my bed where it'd disconnected from its charger.

With a sigh, I plugged it back in and flopped down on my bed to scroll through my messages and missed calls. There were a *lot* more than usual. The first one I saw was from Hank, sent about fifteen minutes ago to let me know the new tenant was coming up to get his key fixed.

Then I saw all the missed calls from Naomi, Mr. Grimaldi's assistant. Dread filled me up as I quickly pressed redial and waited for her to answer. It went to voicemail, making me nauseous with worry, then she immediately called me back.

"Tris," she said in a tense voice, "you need to get in here. *Now.*"

Panic made my palms sweat and my hands shake as I hunted for shoes. "Has something happened?"

"Yeah." She sighed and dropped her voice to a whisper. "Someone stole one of Mr. Grimaldi's paintings. He's on a rampage, Tris. I've never seen him so mad."

Blood rushed out of my head and black spots

crowded my vision. Sensing a panic attack creeping up, I sat back down and dropped my head between my knees. "Which painting?"

Naomi gave a frustrated sound. "I think you already know."

Fuck. *Fuck*. I needed to…run? I couldn't go in there. He'd kill me. I wasn't just going to go walking into my own execution.

"Sin is on his way to pick you up now," Naomi told me with a sigh. "He'll be there in ten. Good luck, Tris." She ended the call and I immediately ran to the bathroom to throw up.

When I was done heaving, I grabbed my phone with shaking fingers and dialed Nelson. The call went to voicemail, and I started crying before the beep even sounded.

"Nels," I sniffed. "Call me back. Mr. Grimaldi wants me to come in for…questioning, I guess? He's discovered someone stole *Poppy Flowers.*"

I didn't for a second think I'd be questioned for shit. Only two of us had access to that painting, and Mr. Grimaldi certainly didn't steal it himself. I was a dead woman. Should I run? Where could I even go that he wouldn't find me?

My door buzzed before I could even *start* to formulate a plan, and I drew a deep breath as I resigned myself to my fate. I'd known this was a possibility when I took on the job; it was part of the incredible hazard pay. But foolishly I'd thought it would never happen to *me*.

I answered the buzz and told Sin I would meet him downstairs. Then I sent out some text messages to the small handful of people I really cared about, telling them goodbye, and sucked up the consequences of my poor life choices.

The tall, tattooed man waiting for me beside his car seemed all too relaxed for someone driving me to my death, though. I hesitated halfway out of the lobby, frowning my confusion.

"Good morning, Tris," he called out, waving me over. "Sorry for the change of plans. I heard you're having car troubles?"

My nose wrinkled, I approached and waited for him to open the passenger side door of his Dodge Challenger for me. "Yeah…"

Sin closed my door, then strolled around to his side and climbed in.

"Um, you seem…" I couldn't find the right word for it. "Unconcerned?"

Her arched a dark brow in question, his tattooed hands gripping the steering wheel. "About what?" I just stared back at him for a moment and he gave a nod of understanding. "Ah the theft? My father is currently pitching a tantrum about it, but he'll get over it."

I blinked, trying to make sense of what he was saying. "Wait, Naomi said that I needed to come in early because—"

"Because she needs to reset all the security passcodes and recalibrate the biometric locks since the thief fried them entirely?" Sin squinted at me, curious. "What did you think you were...*ohhh*...you thought they suspected *you*?"

My mouth flapped a few times, but no words came out.

"Relax, Tris," Sin told me with a chuckle. "You're not in trouble. I'd avoid my father, for sure, but no one blames you for this. It was clearly a professional job. The security was all evaded, the alarms deactivated...I'm pretty impressed to be fair."

Words failed me. Again.

"If you'd been involved, they wouldn't have needed to go to such lengths to fuck the whole damn security system, that's for sure. You could have just walked out the door with it and no one would have been any the wiser, right?" He chuckled again, and I gave a weak laugh of my own.

Wetting my lips, I let his reassurance calm my racing heart. "This happened last night?" I asked, letting my brain catch up with the fact that I *wasn't* about to die.

Sin nodded. "Or early this morning, I guess. Just before dawn. Dex is in *huge* trouble today because he had brought one of the strippers into the manor without clearing her through security."

One of the strippers? Fuck I hoped that wasn't Katinka. I was sure they had *loads* of strippers on their employ though. "A stripper stole your father's Van Gogh?" I asked with a touch of disbelief.

"Nah, that was just a coincidence. The thief failed to deactivate one of the perimeter alarms, and when the security team responded they discovered Dex's friend and it just turned into a whole confusing thing about whether anyone *had* actually broken in. They did a full sweep of the house, and father discovered the gallery door was open." He glanced over, grimacing. "Someone definitely knew what they wanted."

I swallowed a lump of anxiety. "This could still be placed on my head," I admitted with dread. "I signed an NDA…but who else knew Mr. Grimaldi had that painting?"

Sin scoffed a laugh. "Only every person he drunkenly bragged to during the party last week. This isn't on you, Tris. I promise."

SIN HADN'T BEEN LYING. WHEN WE GOT TO RBD'S I JUST ended up spending the morning resetting my security codes and having my fingerprints and retinas scanned for new bio-secure locks. I didn't even *see* Mr. Grimaldi, though I definitely heard his raised voice from somewhere else in the house.

When Sin dropped me home later in the day, it was clear that I'd dodged a bullet. My palms were sweaty despite how cold I was all over--adrenaline crash, I guessed--but I was alive and that was all that fucking mattered.

I hadn't been allowed my phone at all while at the manor, so I waited until I got back into my apartment to check my messages. Most of them were panicked voicemails and messages from Hank and Nelson, which wasn't shocking considering the last they'd heard from me I had genuinely thought I was meeting my maker.

Only a minute after shooting them a message to say I was home, my front door burst open and the two old men came rushing inside to hug me.

For a while they just gushed over how worried they'd been, then it soon shifted to scolding me for leaving them in a state of panic all damn day. I apologized profusely and explained the whole story to them both.

The *whole* damn story, including the message I'd sent John...the one I wrote with my own mortality front and center in my mind. I'd said I loved him.

"And he hasn't replied?" Hank exclaimed with outrage. "Not even a thumbs up?"

Nelson scowled. "That'd be worse, in my opinion. Call him."

My brows shot up. "What?"

"You heard me, Ives. Call him. Right now. Call him and confront him over not having the balls or decency to at least respond with *something*." Nelson folded his arms, determined. "You nearly died. The least *he* can do is acknowledge your feelings."

I shook my head, my eyes wide. "I'd rather sit naked on a hot grill, Nels. I have every intention of simply erasing it from my memory and *hey!*" Hank had just snatched my phone from the table and was already scrolling for John's number.

Before I could grab it back, he'd hit *call* and turned it to speakerphone.

There was no ring tone. It went straight to a cold, mechanical message that the number was no longer in service.

Acid coated my tongue, the last piece of the puzzle clicking reluctantly into place.

"Holy shit," I whispered, the ice of regret hardening my spine. "He stole it."

Hank's brows shot up. "John?"

I nodded, feeling numb. "He stole it, I'm sure of it. That's why..." Truth bombs exploded in my brain. "He staged the scene." I groaned.

Nelson guided me over to the sofa and pushed me to sit—before I fell. "Out loud, Ivy. Make us understand."

I drew a deep breath through my nose, shuddering at the agony in my chest. He'd used me. The whole time... he was *using* me and I fucking fell in love like an idiot.

"He staged the scene," I said again, in utter shock at how stupid I'd been. "He didn't need to fry the security system or leave the gallery door open. Why would he? He had my codes, didn't he?" My gaze flicked between Hank and Nelson, crushing realization of my own incompetence making my skin prickle. "He had my codes. He probably had my fingerprints and...he had access."

In my mind, I vividly recalled how he'd charmed his way into my workshop and seen *Poppy Flowers* for himself. How I'd carelessly locked the drawer right in front of him, never suspecting that he was memorizing my code.

"So he staged the scene to make it seem like he *didn't*

use your codes?" Hank asked, clearly confused. Nelson was following, though, and sank to the couch beside me.

"To protect Ivy," he murmured. "He knew she would be killed if it seemed like she was involved, so he made it look more *mundane* and obvious."

Hank groaned and ran a hand over his face. "I see."

"Guys, you know I love you," I said in a weak voice, wrapping my arms around myself. "But I think I want to be alone right now."

Nelson clearly wanted to stay, but Hank got me. He ushered his partner out of my apartment and made me promise to come over if I needed anything. I agreed and closed the door behind them—locking it—then headed for my pajamas.

The betrayal was all consuming, and I just needed a minute to process. I needed to grieve a relationship that I had fallen head first into, thinking I'd finally found my *person*...only to discover he'd been playing me all along.

Fuck. He'd been breaking into my house and stealing my vibrators. I'd been right all along. That sick fuck.

For three days, I camped on my couch and wallowed in my own self-pity. I called in sick to work, and after all the chaos of upgrading their security, Mr. Grimaldi had no issue letting me take some time.

Toward the end of the third day of my pity party, my intercom buzzed. Groaning, I dragged my whole blanket over to the door with me to see who it was.

"Uh, hello?" I said into the speaker, trying to work out who was buzzing me. Maybe they'd pressed the wrong apartment? Then the person shifted into view, and Katinka smiled into the video feed.

"Hey girl! I brought you Kung Pao Chicken. Can I come up?"

Confused but hungry, I buzzed her up. When I let her into my apartment a minute later, I got a good idea of how shitty I must look.

"Damn," she breathed, running her eyes over me from head to toe. "You look *awful.* Sin mentioned you were sick, but this seems more...emotional."

I scowled, clutching my blanket tighter as I led the way to my kitchen for plates. I could smell Royal Orchid in her bag, and now I was starving. "Sin sent you over?"

Katinka nodded. "You came up in conversation, and I mentioned we'd met. He said you'd called into work sick all week and that he was worried. I offered to come check on you."

I just heaved a sigh, handing her a plate and fork. "That's nice of you."

Her perfect brow lifted. "Does this have anything to do with that guy from the party? John?" I grimaced, not ready to hear his name. Or even think it. Thankfully, Katinka was smart enough to figure that out. "Well, there are more fish in the sea, Tris. I ran into a stone cold *fox* coming into your lobby just now."

I wrinkled my nose in confusion, then remembered my new neighbor. "Oh, Bram. Yeah he's cute, I guess."

We dished up our plates then carried them over to the couch where I'd been living all week. Katinka didn't judge my mess, just cleared a spot for herself and got comfortable.

"What the fuck are you watching?" she asked, laughing as she peered at my TV. "Is that a vampire?"

"Don't knock it 'til you try it," I mumbled around a mouth full of Chinese. I flicked the channel over to the News, so we had a neutral background show to cut any awkward silences. "So…you and Sin are friends?"

She snickered. "Not like that. He's definitely holding a torch for someone else. We just got friendly while he was auditing the clubs. Dexter tried to pressure him into fucking dancers to *clear his head,* and I was more than happy to fake it and chat instead."

I nodded my understanding. That stacked up.

A news headline scrolling across the bottom of the

TV caught my attention as I chewed, and I nearly choked.

"Are you okay?" Katinka asked, patting me on the back. "What happened?"

"That," I croaked, pointing at the scrolling headline. "What the fuck?"

She arched her brow, then read aloud. "Alleged art thief released by authorities after priceless Van Gogh was found to be a forgery." She gasped. "Wait, is that the one stolen from the Grimaldi's?"

Suddenly, I'd lost my appetite.

"Um, Tris why do you look like you've seen a ghost?" she asked, worried.

I swallowed hard, my hands shaking as I placed my food down and reached for my phone. This was bad. This was *really* bad.

"Nelson," I exclaimed when my neighbor answered. "Turn on the news."

"What is it?" he barked, "I'm not near my TV right now."

"Shit," I breathed. "Shit. Nelson...he got arrested by FBI Art Crimes Division. They *arrested* him...and he was just released."

"*Fuck,*" Nelson exclaimed, understanding what I was telling him. "Don't move, Ivy. I'll be right there and we can come up with a plan. It'll be okay, kid. We have contingencies."

He ended the call and my phone dropped into my lap. Katinka was staring at me in confusion, but I couldn't explain it to her. I couldn't tell her that the thief just released was the man I'd fallen in love with.

I certainly couldn't tell her why I was currently panicking so hard. Because John had been released... which meant he knew he'd stolen a forgery of *Poppy Flowers*. And I'd bet that Mr. Grimaldi also knew. It didn't take a genius to put two and two together...that if the *thief* didn't take the original Van Gogh worth $50 million, who did?

Me. That's who. Me and my elderly con-man neighbor.

"Tris, what's going on?" Katinka asked.

I didn't answer her. Then my intercom doorbell buzzed.

I'm so screwed this time.

To be continued in
FORGERY
Valenshek Legacy #2

also by tate james

Madison Kate

#1 HATE

#2 LIAR

#3 FAKE

#4 KATE

#4.5 VAULT (to be read after Hades series)

Hades

#1 7th Circle

#2 Anarchy

#3 Club 22

#4 Timber

The Guild

#1 Honey Trap

#2 Dead Drop

#3 Kill Order

Valenshek Legacy

#1 Heist

#2 Forgery

#3 Restoration

Boys of Bellerose

#1 Poison Roses

#2 Dirty Truths

#3 Shattered Dreams

#4 Beautiful Thorns

The Royal Trials

#1 Imposter

#2 Seeker

#3 Heir

Kit Davenport

#1 The Vixen's Lead

#2 The Dragon's Wing

#3 The Tiger's Ambush

#4 The Viper's Nest

#5 The Crow's Murder

#6 The Alpha's Pack

Novella: The Hellhound's Legion

Box Set: Kit Davenport: The Complete Series

Dark Legacy

#1 Broken Wings

#2 Broken Trust

#3 Broken Legacy

#4 Dylan (standalone)

Royals of Arbon Academy

#1 Princess Ballot

#2 Playboy Princes

#3 Poison Throne

Hijinx Harem

#1 Elements of Mischief

#2 Elements of Ruin

#3 Elements of Desire

The Wild Hunt Motorcycle Club

#1 Dark Glitter

#2 Cruel Glamour (TBC)

#3 Torn Gossamer (TBC)

Foxfire Burning

#1 The Nine

#2 The Tail Game (TBC)

#3 TBC (TBC)

Undercover Sinners

#1 Altered By Fire

#2 Altered by Lead

#3 Altered by Pain (TBC)

Printed in the USA
CPSIA information can be obtained
at www.ICGtesting.com
LVHW030710300923
759787LV00049B/1623

9 781922 688309